Knight C

Nicky Singer has written four novels for adults, two books of non-fiction and five works for young people. Her first children's novel, *Feather Boy*, won the Blue Peter 'Book of the Year' Award and is published in 28 countries. It has also been adapted for TV (winning a BAFTA for Best Children's Drama) and commissioned by the National Theatre as a musical with lyrics by Don Black and music by Debbie Wiseman. Nicky's other novels for young people include *Doll, The Innocent's Story* and *GemX*.

In 2010 Glyndebourne will premiere a full-length operatic version of *Knight Crew* with a libretto by Nicky and music by Julian Philips. This is the first time Glyndebourne has commissioned an opera from a teen novel.

Nicky lives in Brighton with her husband and their three children. Her website is at www.nickysinger.com.

NiCKY SiNGER

⟨B *editions*

First published in 2009
by CB editions
146 Percy Road, London W12 9QL
www.cbeditions.com

The right of Nicky Singer to be identified
as author of this work has been asserted in accordance
with the Copyright, Designs and Patents Act 1988

Typeset by CB editions
Cover design by Shona Andrew
Printed in England by T. J. International Ltd,
Padstow, Cornwall

FSC
Mixed Sources
Product group from well-managed
forests and other controlled sources
Cert no. SGS-COC-2482
www.fsc.org
© 1996 Forest Stewardship Council

ISBN 978-0-9561073-2-9

2 4 5 3 1

Bumper Books
25|03|11

For Lee, who first showed me that a lost soul isn't.

1

Is every soul born good?

That's what Myrtle would have said. She'd have said we all tumble onto this earth brimful of possibilities. I think maybe we all arrive empty and life, oh so slowly, fills us up with love – or hate.

I've had plenty of time to think about this; the eternity of time, in fact, that I've sat here – beyond the mirrors. There are events which remain quite clear in my memory and other, darker things. But I need to tell this story and I have to start somewhere, so I will begin with the Mill.

The Mill was on a tidal island, just beyond the canal, and it had been derelict for years. It stood next to an equally derelict brewery which nevertheless still had two of those strange conical towers with the odd-angled chimney on top. Sometimes, when it was dusk and the mist was low, the frontage of the Mill and the brewery seemed to loom out of the water like some turreted castle from a bygone age. Or that's how it seemed to me. Maybe that was my mother in me, hoping, against all the odds, for the heroic. Perhaps it was Myrtle's influence. You can change things, Myrtle said, just by looking. And for a while I believed her. I still want to believe her, but it's not everyone that can live in a burnt-out car, or see a future in a discarded pot-noodle container.

This is a long story and a bitter one, but I will try to tell it as honestly as I can, because I've come to understand that what happened wasn't all my brother's fault. No, it wasn't Mordec's fault. Nor Lance's for that matter, nor Quin's. I was as much to blame as any of them. More so, probably, because, in the end, it was my hand on the knife.

I was one day short of thirteen when I came to the Mill. Sometimes I wonder how things would have been if I'd never gone? It wouldn't have stopped the killing, of course, but maybe fewer of the people I loved would have died. Still, what happened happened and nothing can change that now. Besides, if I hadn't gone to the Mill that day, I would never have met Quin, and there are times, even now, with the water closed over me, I think that I'd go through it all again, just to be near her.

It was Mordec, four years my senior, who gave me my instructions: I was to arrive in the afternoon; I was to meet OG. When I got to know OG, he told me that he'd got his name from a book about American gangsters, but I never saw OG with a book and I'm not at all sure he could read. But OG stood for Original Gangsta and in the Mill, that meant God. Even – at that time – to Mordec.

It was spring, I remember, the sort of time (Myrtle would have said) where you can feel life crouching just beneath the surface of things. Everything I ever learnt about nature, I learnt from Myrtle. Before I met her I'd never even seen a snowdrop. No, that cannot be true, because there were always snowdrops by the canal in February, shy blooms pushing through at the edge of the concrete. I just didn't see them because I wasn't looking. 'Just as there's a difference between listening and hearing,' Myrtle said, 'there is a difference between looking and seeing.'

I took the long route out of the estates, doubling back on myself before finally going through the graffitied underpass behind Tesco which leads to the track where the lights stop and the canal path begins. The air was chill and I should have been readying myself for whatever lay ahead. But I wasn't. Partly because I'd stopped being afraid – which is always a mistake – and partly because I was thinking about my mother. Not the crazy one who seemed to have exploded into our recent lives but the soft, quiet, long-ago one who used to read to me. Yes, my crazy mother used to read to me. Stories about castles and crescent moons, wise women talking in riddles and warriors battling bull-headed monsters. I remember the pictures, bright and frightening and magical. Fairy tales and myths that seemed too big for our apartment and that's what Keifer felt too. Keifer was my father – or the man I knew then as my father – that's part of this story too. Keifer didn't care for books; they reminded him, I think, that my mother's education had gone on longer than his and he wasn't to be humiliated by some *dum white woman* fallen on hard times. It wasn't long before my mother moved from reading me stories to whispering them to me in the dark, as though they were secret, dangerous things, which perhaps they were. At first she remembered well, and the pictures in my head were just as bold and colourful as the ones in the books.

'Hold these stories,' she'd whisper, as if giving me something precious, 'here in your heart.' But I couldn't hold them and nor, after a while, could she. Things became blurred, the moons clouded over, the bull-headed monster triumphed over the warrior, the wise woman's mouth was stopped with sand. No, it can't have been like that, that's just how I see it now, from beyond the mirrors. But there was a falling away, an increase of silence. If I'd thought about it at the time, which I didn't, I would have just supposed that I was growing up, growing away from her. Yet, at the edge of my knowing, something must still have remained. Because, deep

3

down, I still looked for the outline of a castle. Hoped for a hero. Perhaps that's why I went so meekly to the Mill that day, in case OG was that hero.

To get to the island you had to go over a metal bridge. It was a fixed structure, high enough not to have to lift for passing canal traffic, but I soon came to think of it as a draw-bridge – designed to keep strangers out and, perhaps, to keep us in. That day, I was the stranger. It was a mistless afternoon so I could see the buildings clearly, how they both seemed to rear straight out of the water itself, rising up five or six grey storeys towards the sky. On about level four of the Mill end, huge iron bars protruded from the building. I imagine they were to mount winches, to pull grain perhaps from the boats below. But by then, of course, they were rusted and wind-chafened and they looked like abandoned gallows. There were doors at the same level, right in the centre of the walls and, when he wasn't enthroned on the ground-floor mill wheel, OG sometimes positioned himself on the open door ledge, his feet hanging high over the river, staring at those gallows. And that's where I sat too, many years later. In fact I sat there the night I sent Quin to the slaughter.

As the Crew became both more organised and more afraid, we'd post lookouts, one on the bridge and one in the disused clock-tower of the brewery, but that day there was just Duane sitting on the river bank whittling a stick with a penknife. A penknife! Duane was about my brother Mordec's age, but leaner and darker with a kind of twitching quickness to him. He was also, as I was to learn that afternoon, very much stronger than he looked.

I was in no hurry, so I idled on the bank too, trying to guess from the spacing of the Mill windows what the layout inside the building might be. After a few minutes Duane made his way round the back and went through the kicked-in door.

I could hear the noise of voices, but only distantly, and followed him in. It was dark inside and smelt of damp wood and a kind of sweet muskiness. There was also the tang of cigarette smoke. I had been invited to come to the Mill, ordered even, so I should have stood up and announced myself. But I didn't. Perhaps I thought I'd just take a look and, if I didn't like what I saw, leave as quietly as I'd come. I was clearly nowhere near to understanding how much Mordec's life had spilled into mine and how, once you'd set foot in the Mill, nothing could ever be the same again.

I waited till my eyes got accustomed to the interior light and then picked my way across the dank floorboards, taking care to avoid the sudden soft-rot holes, the coils of rope and the empty beer cans. I made some noise of course, but there were noises in the building anyway: the slap-slap of water against the old mill machinery, the wind creak of the rusted gallows, the beating wings of some trapped bird, and the rich and dangerous sound of OG's laughter. I crept closer. The whole of the ground floor of the Mill seemed to be one giant room, divided by apparently random ladders, walls and machine wheels, so there were plenty of places of concealment.

It was not difficult to find the centre of operations. It was lit by candles, one or two of them stubbed into each tread of the giant Mill wheel where OG sat on high. The wheel must have had a span of twenty feet, but half of it was sunk beneath the level of the floor so OG's throne was the semi-circular top half. The zigzag treads where the candles burned were decades thick in bird shit. Using these as a sort of stairs, OG had lashed the seat and back of an office chair to the apex and there he sat, in flickering glory, looking down on the assembled company. He was big, OG, not tall, not fat, but hugely solid and even in winter he wore cut-off shirts (always baby blue) so you could see exactly how big the muscles in his arms were. And just as he was bigger than everyone else OG was also blacker. Many of us were mixed-race. Not OG. He was solidly, monumentally black, and he oiled his skin till it shone. I watched the cigarette smoke curl in and out of his very white teeth.

Everyone else sat at the foot of the wheel, either on up-turned beer crates or on pallets stolen from the yard that backed onto the canal. I don't know how many people were there that day, it was usually somewhere between fifteen and twenty and always more boys than girls. Quin was absent, so she never saw what happened next. If she had been in the Mill, I like to think she would not have joined in – but you never knew with Quin. Elayne was there and Tanisha, Duane of course, his twin brother Garvey, as well as Pels, Borz and Mordec.

They were talking about the Saxon Road Mob.

'Dey've got the soldjas,' Mordec was saying.

OG blew out a very slow, very deliberate smoke ring. 'But dey aint got no brains.'

Elayne broke off from drinking lager from a yogurt pot and giggled delightedly. Elayne was one of the yungas, a tiny spitfire kid, mixed-race with mad, triumphal hair plaited flat with myriads of girlie ribbons. That was the first day I ever set eyes on her and I remember thinking even then how strange the ribbons looked against her boyish face. 'The Knight Crew got brains,' she said. 'The Knight Crew got brains – and heart!'

Later I would find out just how much heart that girl had.

Despite the dark and the smoke, the word 'knight' didn't conjure the road I'd known from childhood, a decrepit, garbage-strewn place where every second building was boarded up; no, I suddenly saw (as if my long-ago mother had breathed through the window) a host of knights on horses,

lances in hand and, at the head of them, king of them all –
me. My vision was short-lived. As I shifted my weight from
my right to my left foot, the board beneath me creaked.

'Who's dat?' growled Mordec.

They were quick then, Duane, Garvey and Mordec. In one
fluid move, as if they were just different limbs of the same
animal, the three of them hauled me into the light.

'Oh,' said OG. 'A snake.'

I waited for Mordec to speak, for him to say something
like, 'Oh dat's no snake, dat's my lil brother, Art. I told him
to come.' Only he never said a word. And somehow, caught
in OG's gaze, I said nothing either.

'A snake in de grass,' said OG lightly.

Elayne giggled again, but it was nervous laughter now. I
could smell the fear in it – and the anticipation.

OG took a last, sharp suck on his cigarette and stubbed
it out in some bird shit. A float of ash extinguished against
the mill wheel.

'A Saxon boi,' OG added, making what I later understood
to be some sort of signal with his right hand, which is when
my brother kicked me in the back of the knees. Hard.

Taken unawares, I crumpled to the ground so I didn't see
whether it was Mordec or Duane who pulled me straight
to my feet again. But I know it was Garvey who threw the
first punch, a blow to the head that sent me spinning down
once more, only to be jerked up again by the collar. The next
punch was to my stomach, I doubled in on myself but still
managed to catch a side-blow to the chest as I fell. Hands
pulled me up again. And again. As many times as the blows
fell, and it wasn't just Garvey and Duane and Mordec, others had risen from the pallets and stood over me, waiting
their turns.

I was dizzy and disorientated and there was blood in my

mouth from the gape in my lower lip but I knew I mustn't go down another time, because then they would kick me properly. I don't know how I knew that, or why I suddenly found the strength to lash out myself. Maybe it was my brother's face, looming over me, grinning. Maybe it was just survival instinct, or plain anger or a straightforward sense of injustice, but I hit them, flailing about like a madman, grinding and gnashing and, mainly, missing.

At once their blows ceased. They all stood back, some resumed their seats, others just moved away. The breathing around me changed, I heard the click of cigarette lighters and another, more relaxed, laugh from Elayne. I stopped flailing.

OG looked down at me from his seat on the Mill wheel. My blurry vision made out two of him, his dual faces set in parallel expressions of total languor.

'You're alryt, Art,' he said.

He'd known who I was all along. That shocked me, but not as much as the tiny accompanying incline of his head which, I later discovered, meant that I was bound – life and death – to the Knight Crew.

2

Looking back, I can see patterns in everything that happened, but at the time events seemed to fall out as randomly as I fell over Myrtle's feet that evening. I was still bruised from my beating, but I didn't feel bruised. Perhaps the adrenalin had fired me to a place beyond pain, perhaps it was just the cider I drank that night. I didn't like the taste of the cider but I kept downing it because Mordec kept pouring it, pot-noodle container after pot-noodle container of it. After a time I could no longer smell the tang of curry which had initially clung to the plastic innards of the cup, or recall the number of refills.

So I wasn't exactly watching my footing as I slewed over the bridge from the island back along the mainland canal bank. Before the arrival of the burnt-out car (I'll tell that story later) Myrtle shifted her abode fairly frequently. That night she'd set up camp beneath a concrete arch notched into a brick wall. A flattened and extremely rusty oil-drum was all that lay between her and the damp February ground, and she was surrounded by other bits of neatly arranged urban swill: four polystyrene cups, a Lucozade bottle, a cement-encrusted industrial tape-dispenser, a single bright pink plastic glove, a hosepipe, half an office chair, a Value bacon packet (empty) and some rubble. Myrtle was a baglady without a bag. She never carried stuff about, it just seemed to move with her, as though she and the rubbish were umbilically connected.

I later learnt that Myrtle had been born in Jamaica but, if you looked at her face, you wouldn't have been able to tell if she'd been a black baby or a white one. She just looked weather-beaten, her face the colour and texture of those mud flats with cracks in that you see in news reports of parched continents where famine sets in. How fat or thin Myrtle was, was difficult to gauge. She wore voluminous, earth-coloured clothes which flowed rather than settled about her, so in movement she seemed to be a cloud of grey or green or brown. Her hair was knotted and wild and lay like ropes of ivy about her shoulders. I hear myself getting extravagant in describing her, as though she didn't really belong in this world, or she was a person from one of my mother's stories. But perhaps I'm really just talking about myself here, because Myrtle rekindled in me that feeling I'd had when I was a child that I didn't belong either, at least not in the place God seemed to have allotted me.

Sometimes Myrtle sat writing spidery notes with a pencil in a battered leather-bound book. There were so many notes in this book that she had to use the margins, or write between lines that already existed, or even write over what she had written before. If you saw inside the book (which was only ever for a moment, she didn't like you to look) it seemed like a place of spells. But now that I have read every word in that book, I shall name it for what it was: The Book of the Future. Sometimes the book was hidden and Myrtle just sat, apparently staring at nothing in particular for hours on end. Sometimes she lay, as she did that night, invisibly, as though she was just part of the landscape.

It was still not easy to trip over her because she was guarded by Shaman, her lean and muscular black mongrel dog. Shaman often lay outstretched, as though he was deeply, profoundly, impossibly asleep, but one tread near Myrtle and his head would lift and his eyes would be on you. Shaman's eyes were black and had the dense, reflective quality of polished marble. It was discomforting to be caught in his gaze for too long, you couldn't help but stare back into his eyes and yet, at the same time, you felt if you looked for a moment longer you might see things no human being should see. All this was clear to me long before what happened to Myrtle's soul – but I'm getting ahead of myself.

That night – as on all nights – Shaman must have raised his head and given his low, warning growl. But if he did, I never saw or heard him. The drink had obviously anaesthetised more than my bruises and I just blundered along the towpath until I tripped over Myrtle's extended left leg. I wasn't a moment in the dirt before Shaman was on me, the hot slather of his teeth bare against my face.

'Tch, Shaman, tch.'

They were such small, soft sounds, Myrtle rustling upright and whispering the dog's name, clicking her tongue against the roof of her mouth. At once Shaman withdrew, removing his jaw from mine and sitting down quietly as if nothing at all had happened. The click was an easy enough sound to make but no one but Myrtle could control the dog with it – except me. The minute Shaman became mine, I could do it too.

Mordec, who was close behind me that night, kicked neither the dog nor the old woman, which showed a respect which was clear to me even through the alcoholic haze. However, as I struggled to my feet, my brother did allow himself a shout:

'You best move out the way!'

Myrtle sat up, drew her cloths around her. 'What way?' she asked. 'Whose way?'

'My way!'

'It wasn't you who fell,' she said lightly.

'And wot!' Mordec snarled, more dog than the dog. 'Coulda been, baglady,' he continued, yet there was still something withheld in his challenge. I thought at the time it might be on account of Shaman because, as soon as Mordec began shouting, the dog had changed position, lifted his head, pricked his ears. Or maybe Mordec's restraint was about Myrtle being a woman, because even Mordec had codes about things like that. The idea that Mordec might actually be frightened of Myrtle never occurred to me.

'Good evening,' Myrtle said then, turning to face me. 'I've been waiting for you to come for such a long time.'

'Wot!' Mordec spat. 'You don't even know de boi!'

'I know who his father is.'

'Yeah. Right.'

'His father is a king,' said Myrtle.

Mordec laughed out loud. 'His pops is an alkie.'

'No,' said Myrtle, 'your father is a drunk, Mordec. Art's father is a king.'

That shut Mordec up. As for me, I thought I must have misheard. There was no way this bedraggled old woman could know my name, let alone anything about my parentage. I should have laughed out loud too, but I didn't. Every child, I imagine, has their moments of wondering. How did I get in this family? Do I belong? I'd been wondering about that since the moment I'd been born. It hadn't escaped my notice – or that of others – that Mordec and I did not look alike. His face was broad and dark with thick kiss-heart lips. My face was narrower, paler and my features finer. Keifer had commented on it more than once.

'I look very different from my sister, don't I?' was all our mother had said on the matter. But my mother's sister lived in Glasgow and none of us had ever seen her, not even Keifer.

But looks weren't it either. I simply didn't feel the way I imagined Mordec felt about things. I copied him of course, had even wanted to be him sometimes; I envied his control, I would have liked the latent danger that seemed to move about him to move about me. But I was also always looking for – *expecting* might be a better word – something else, something more. So, while I didn't believe for a moment that my father was a king, I didn't immediately discount the possibility either. It was something to hold close in my heart. Like my mother's stories. Like her long-ago whisper. *I named you for a king, Arthur.*

Mordec meanwhile had got to grips with the information. 'You calling our mum a slag?'

'Love has many forms,' said Myrtle.

'Dat come outta yur lil scrap book?' sneered Mordec.

'Everything that comes out of my book,' said Myrtle, 'I put in to it.'

'How did you know my name?' I asked. First OG. Now her.

'I know many things,' said Myrtle.

'You know nada,' said Mordec. 'You're jus some tramp living in some gutta.'

'Why do you always look down, Mordec,' she asked, 'and never up?'

I followed her finger heavenward. The black night sky was drilled with stars. 'That's where I live,' she said. She turned back to look at me, 'and that's where you belong, Art.'

It was weird, it was spooky and I was drunk. But my heart still fluttered. I'd never looked at a night sky before.

'You only go up dere when yur life is deaded,' said Mordec. 'Dat what you want for yur lil prince?'

'What will be will be,' said Myrtle and she took out her little notebook and began scribbling. I wanted more but the encounter seemed to be at an end.

'Move,' said Mordec to me, 'mans got plans an shit to do.'

'We all have a life and things to do,' said Myrtle without looking up from her book.

Mordec pushed me and we stumbled along the towpath and on into the outskirts of the city. I didn't look back but I wanted to. I knew Myrtle had more to say and I wanted to hear it.

By the time we arrived home my bruises had begun to hurt.

'Why did you do it?' I asked Mordec.

'You're a yunga. You need to learn.'

'You didn't have to smash me so hard.'

Mordec shrugged. 'If I hadn't banged you hard, someone else would of.' He went into his room and shut the door.

I began to feel not just bruised but ill and I realised I was going to be sick. I arrived in the bathroom in time to clutch at the toilet bowl where I lay for a while sweating and moaning.

'Pig,' yelled someone from the living room. It was Keifer.

I suddenly felt like a very small child. I wanted my mother, the old one, the quiet one, to come and tell me that everything was going to be all right. But nobody came, not then or later. I vomited. Most of it landed in the toilet.

The giddiness and the sweating stopped. I flushed the toilet, rinsed my mouth with cold water at the basin, dampened the flecks of sick on my T-shirt and washed my hands. Then I went through to the sitting room.

Keifer was lying outstretched on the sofa, watching the telly, beer in hand, empty cans on the floor about him. The programme was that game show where they unlock boxes with impossible amounts of money in them.

'Where's Mum?' I asked.

'Gone,' said Keifer, not taking his eyes from the screen. 'Taken away.'

'Where?' I asked

He turned to look at me and if he noticed my bruises he didn't mention it. 'Boi – you're a dirty animal, you know dat? You better of cleaned dat bathroom.'

'Where's she gone?' I persisted.

'I said *gone*, didn't I?' he yelled and I saw, with some astonishment, that his eyes suddenly seemed stung with tears. Seeing me stare, he immediately turned back towards the television screen and hit the volume button. The contestant had just opened the wrong box and lost all the money.

'Get outta here, boi,' he shouted.

I got outta there but the tears came with me. He loved my mother. I hadn't known that till then, and he didn't know that that love was to kill him. Which is pretty much the way it was with me and Quin.

3

Quin. I have to talk about her – need to talk about her. It excites me just to say her name aloud, taste it in my mouth again. There would be no story without her, and yet, so far, I've only given her the smallest of mentions.

Why?

Perhaps I'm still afraid, perhaps I believe she still has the power to reach beyond the mirrors and rip my heart from my breast. But then how can you rip from someone what they would give willingly, as I gave my heart to her, time and time again?

I wish I could say that I loved Quin from the moment I first laid eyes on her, because that would be a fitting beginning to the passion that consumed my life. But it wasn't like that. Quin revealed herself slowly, like a landscape at sunrise, only becoming visible as the darkness dispels.

Did Elayne introduce my queen to the Mill? Did Tanisha? She can't have been there from the beginning, but then there was never a moment of arrival, never a moment when it seemed she hadn't always been there. But I do remember when I first noticed her. Things were often edgy in the Mill, the boys – the young men – always on the brink of something, an argument, a spat, a play fight which could turn unexpectedly violent and then, just as suddenly, defuse. That day it was some beef between Duane and Garvey. The brothers were twins, but not identical, and there were always disputes between them about who was the strongest, or the quickest or the best-dressed. They were naturally competitive and other members of the Crew liked to weigh in on one side or another, increasing the stakes. That evening, the issue was hair, though I don't remember whether it was about whose head was braided more tightly or who had the funkiest beads or the sharpest style. Duane, who fancied himself as something of a poet, had gone into a rap about his hair.

'Allow yur spit, bruv,' said Garvey, ironically.

But Duane didn't stop, rapped on, and some of the others in the Mill began to pick up the beat. Borz and Pels, who were near one of the Mill's ancient and abandoned grinding stones, were banging their beer cans against the sandstone furrows. For some reason this enraged Garvey, who simply lashed out at his brother, and the rap stopped and a fight began. Pels and Borz laughed but the fight was genuine and soon other members of the Crew pitched in on one side or the other. Tanisha and Elayne got up from where the girls were sitting and came to cheer the boys on. That left one girl sitting by herself – Quin. And that's how I saw her first, sitting erect and still beyond the brawl.

How do you describe someone you've loved as long as I loved Quin? When I conjure her now, of course I can't help but see the fragile soul I held so often in my arms, but that night I only saw her outer side, her strong face, her rangy limbs, her compelling darkness. She had an elemental quality as though her creator had reached deep into midnight and fashioned her from whatever he'd found there. Yet if there was light in a room it was always on her. She never chose the light, but it chose her, and the candlelight that night brightened her forehead and reddened her lips. The light also picked out the small hollow between her collar-bones, a sweet place that I would come to kiss a thousand times. And he – I'm sure – kissed her there too. Yes, there and other places.

Then there was the way she held herself. People might have called it pride, as though she knew she was a queen before anyone crowned her so. And she could be haughty – shut you out, exclude you. But it wasn't only that, her poise also seemed to be a statement, a challenge: beat me as hard as you like, I will not submit.

A queen. There I go again, describing Quin as though she didn't belong where we found ourselves either. As though she could be part of the story I wanted to make up about ourselves, where I could be better, where life could be better, where the sun shone. Maybe this is what Myrtle recognised in me, the need to look up.

'Bubz – you both have good hair,' Quin said, 'because you both have the Proof.'

She wasn't speaking to me or indeed to Duane or Garvey, she was just speaking. I moved around the fight to be nearer her.

She pulled a jet-black strand of hair from her scalp. 'My grandmother always said that this was the crown, the proof, the single hair that marks out the black man, the African, as God's first son on earth.'

I'd never heard anyone talk like this before, so I said nothing. The fight stopped then, as swiftly as it had begun, Duane banged Garvey on the back and the moment was over.

But, after that, when I looked at Quin, I always thought of Africa. As though she should have been born under a wider sky or stood on a broader earth.

On the night itself, Quin turned away from me, resumed her conversation with Elayne, and I fell in with the boys again. But it wasn't long before OG mounted the bird-shit treads of the Mill wheel and the talk turned – as it always did – to the Saxon Mob. OG, who had a natural theatricality, stood on the lashed-up office chair to begin the war cry.

'Wah guan, boys – so Saxons tink dey can test mans?'

'We gonna rush em!' came the delighted response.

'We gonna jack em!'

'We gonna merk em!'

Merk meant kill, but it was only a figure of speech back then. It arose over time, like the chant itself, some outsized playground thing. But despite that, and the fact that we laughed a lot, it didn't mean that we weren't serious. We were deadly serious, the Saxons were our enemy and we hated them.

'Why?' That was Myrtle of course, rising from the mud to ask the unaskable. 'Why do you hate them?'

It was May, I remember, when she first asked the question, warm enough to sit outside, and that day OG had set up the chant by the canal bank.

No one answered Myrtle of course, not even with a laugh. The Saxons had always been the enemy. We lived south of Tintagel Road, they lived north of it. Our men came from the Cornwall Estate, theirs from Mount Bladon. What more did anyone need to know?

But later that question needled me – why. Why. Myrtle was always asking why.

'Three rules,' OG told us. 'Revenue, revenge, respect.' Revenue meant we were required to do work for the Crew; revenge meant we never let the Saxons get away with anything; respect meant we were entitled to jack anyone who looked at us sidelong, and also that OG was God, which, judging by Mordec's eyes, was always going to become a problem.

I knew my brother and the position of second-in-command didn't suit him. He would, I knew, be looking for openings.

As for me, I started with revenue. The first job I did was under Duane's direction, with Borz (who was built like an ox) as physical back-up. Nobody told me in advance what the job was, perhaps nobody knew, Duane lived by his wits and was quick to spot opportunities and there were always opportunities when you were around Duane. That day it was an expensive bike and a short post.

'*Rah*,' said Duane enthusiastically as he moved in on the red-and-black racing bike. 'That's bout one an a half Gs.' That was another thing about Duane, he knew the price – or at least the street value – of everything. To me it just looked like a bike, and one so heavily chained to a post that you'd need industrial bolt-cutters to get it free.

'Nah, man,' said Duane. 'Look.'

I looked. He was pointing at the post. I still didn't get it.

'Watch, son,' said Duane, 'an learn.'

The post was one of those parking ones, with a small sign at the top saying you could be towed between the hours of 9 a.m. and 7 p.m. A very small sign. Moving with undiscussed efficiency and speed, Duane and Borz simply took a wheel each and lifted the bike high over their heads – high enough just to loop it off the post.

I was impressed but there still seemed the problem of the chain which, as it remained threaded through one of the wheels, meant the bike still wasn't much use without the bolt-cutters.

'Exclusive to da man wid da key,' mentioned Duane.

I reckoned that meant we were going to rush the owner when he returned, lift the key and, finally, get to sell the bike.

The plan was actually far simpler.

Duane and I went with the bike to Tesco's car park. Borz waited by the post. When the owner arrived back Borz, the good Samaritan, said he knew who'd taken the bike and he could get it back – for a price. The price was ten per cent of the bike's value. I never saw the owner's face, but I can imagine it, because I saw plenty more such owners. First they looked shocked and then angry. Some of them began shouting, but it was a no-brainer. A hundred and fifty pounds to get the bike back, or no bike. They all paid in the end.

That day, making a hundred and fifty quid took thirty-five minutes. Often it was quicker. I never really knew how old Duane was, maybe sixteen then, but I could see why working in a conventional job didn't appeal.

And if you think we spent our takings on drink, you're wrong. Mainly we lifted that.

'Why?'

Same reason we lifted and raced the cars. Because we could, because we had good brains and using them was fun and because it was so easy.

Why?

Shut up, Myrtle.

It was often OG himself that took the cars. He got a silver Mercedes once. At some stage he must have had some mechanical training because he was good with wires. He got the car from a driveway, north of Tintagel, drove at a hundred miles an hour through Mount Bladon – which was certainly provocative – and then ended up in Cornwall, picking up me and Mordec and doing four handbrake turns outside our block before driving to the canal for the burn-out. And it wasn't the speed that excited me, or the danger, although we ploughed through the rubbish bins only missing the brick wall of the back garage by about half an inch. No, it wasn't that, or the mothers all shouting and screaming on the walkways, it was

21

the sirens that did it for me. Those great wailing moans from the Feds, arriving, as they always arrived, too late.

Shut up, Myrtle.

You never felt the rush, the buzz, the high. It was pure physicality. That tingle in your feet and then the whoosh of it up your whole body, electric current. Like anger. Like madness. All of you pumping. The boys and the petrol and the night sky lit not with stars but with the burning, the flames three or four foot tall and the metal just sizzling and the glass exploding (you had to be careful of that, a big screen would go like a gunshot and shower you with hot glass) and seats inside melting and stinking (if they were plastic) and if they were leather, taking longer to burn and you knowing just how much the owner must have paid and now he had nothing.

'Why should dey have everythin?' OG said. 'An we get de crumbs?' He was a regular philosopher, OG.

That car smouldered for about two days, as did my mother. She was back from wherever she'd been sent and was on medication. I knew this even before Mordec showed me the drug plan with the little plastic pot with different labelled compartments showing which pills had to be taken when. I knew because instead of wearing towering stiletto heels, a gold skirt no wider than a belt and her green fishnet tights, my mother was wearing her tired brown trousers and a perfectly ordinary blouse. The fridge had also calmed down and instead of being full to bursting with huge, lolling slabs of white stuff that looked and smelt like the insides of someone's stomach (and to which were pinned labels which read things like 'Dinner, Saddam Hussein' or 'The Last Supper'), there was just some cheese in a tube and a stray tin of baked beans. So – my mother was home and the best part of normal. Normal enough to be on my case anyway.

'It was you. Was it you? That car, Duane's mother said you and Mordecai were involved. Tell me, Arthur, was it you?'

'No,' I said. 'I weren't dere.' I wasn't really there, I was in some higher space.

'You promise me?'

'I told you, I weren't dere, Mum.' It seemed such an insignificant lie at the time. But small lies don't always stay small, sometimes they avalanche.

4

About a week later, I found Myrtle sitting inside the burnt-out Merc. OG had driven the car over the bridge right onto the island and set fire to it there, not a hundred yards from the front door of the Mill. Mordec had been too adrenalised on the night to care but now he was in critical mood.

'We shouldn't of brought it so close, man,' he said.

'*We?*' queried OG.

'Nah,' said Mordec dangerously, 'you. You blood.'

'You tryin to tell me wah blow?' OG asked, twisting the words out really slowly. With OG, sometimes the softer and slower his voice the more menacing he was.

Mordec chose to ignore the threat. 'If Feds find da whip,' he said, nodding at the car, 'they find da Mill, den us, den what?'

OG lit a cigarette. 'Boydem know where we are. Dey just can't touch us. Less you gonna help em, give em something they want, grass on us. You a snake?' Then OG, who was right-handed, took the cigarette from his mouth with his left hand and slid his right hand oh-so-slowly down to the long pocket of his trousers. I swear to God he wasn't carrying that day – there were no knives in the Mill then – but that was the first time I ever saw the movement that was to become so familiar to me. And sometimes I think it was at that moment, because of Mordec, and not because of the Saxon Mob, that the blades came into our lives.

'You havin a bubble?' Now Mordec lightened up, backed off.

'Good,' said OG. 'You're alryt.' He smiled on Mordec. 'Beside, we aint doin nuthin wrong, get me.' His knife hand re-emerged.

'You're stealing,' said Myrtle from inside the car, 'you're trespassing.'

OG knew perfectly well where Myrtle was but he swung his head this way and that as if unable to locate her. Then he said: 'Anyone spot dat ghost?'

Mordec, probably to ease the tension, laughed and so did Duane and Tanisha. Quin did not laugh. Anyone who was a ghost might be alive today but not tomorrow.

'Stealing is a crime,' Myrtle mentioned.

OG turned towards her then: 'Looks like you sittin in the proceeds of crime, den. Face down outlined in white chalk.' More laughter.

'What you doin in there, bubz?' Quin asked. She was quick, Quin, and knew instinctively that OG's anger with Mordec could deflect, without warning, on Myrtle, so I think she was trying to defuse things. So ironic, considering how she was later to inflame almost everyone.

But then Quin loved Myrtle. Love. I can say that now, but it wasn't so clear to me as events unfolded. I thought Quin just looked out for the old woman as you might do for some wounded bird that fell at your feet. Gave her food – and Quin did give her food, scraps from our erratic table. Quin also gathered bits of wood to add to the small pile Myrtle would light to shield herself from the night air. And they talked of course, heads bent together as if they were sharing secrets. But I never guessed there was anything really important being said. Perhaps I didn't know then that important things could be said. I lived in a place of action.

'I'm reminiscing,' said Myrtle in answer to Quin's question. 'Remembering.' She shut her eyes. 'The engine of a Merc is as soft as a whisper.'

'Not dat one,' said OG. 'I revved dat engine so loud, everyone in der manor heard it.'

'The Merc I had,' said Myrtle, 'that was soft as a whisper.' Her eyes opened. 'It's gone now, but I don't miss it. Not at all.'

'You never had no Merc,' said Mordec.

'Didn't I?'

'No, you never. People with Mercs don't end up livin like tramps.'

'Don't they?'

'Wot's dis, twenty-one questions?' asked Mordec.

'God gives,' said Myrtle, 'and God takes away.'

'Wrong,' said OG, 'God gives and I take away.' He guffawed, delighted at his wit. 'My man God likes da underdog, da sinner.' He flexed those powerful biceps. 'Besides it aint fair for the high rollers to have everything, I mean, de paper, de power and da buff gals. No way.' He dropped the butt of his cigarette and ground it into the earth with his heel. 'God and me, we're on de same side.'

'When you take, OG,' said Myrtle, 'you destroy. But when God takes He gives, He gives back a thousandfold.'

'Hold up, wot you chattin bout?' said OG. 'Wot did da Big Man give you back for yur Merc?'

'This,' said Myrtle, sweeping her hand around her. 'All this.'

'Not much for da dough, den,' remarked OG.

'And He gave me power.'

'Come again?' Mordec wasn't jeering, actually he sounded interested. Power always interested Mordec.

'If you have nothing to steal,' said Myrtle, 'no one can steal from you.'

'Oh dat,' said Mordec, disappointed.

'But once you have things,' Myrtle continued, 'you're vulnerable. Me – I'm invulnerable. There's nothing you can take from me.'

OG drummed his fingers against the bollard: 'Wot bout Shaman?'

Shaman, who was lying by the driver's-side wheel arch, not a foot from where Myrtle was sitting, raised his head at his name and growled.

'Shaman speaks for himself,' said Myrtle.

'Neways,' said Quin unexpectedly, 'why would we want to take anythin from you, bubz?'

Myrtle transferred her gaze from Shaman to Quin. 'You,' she said, as if she'd just been granted a revelation, 'will be queen. Yes' – her eyes were now locked on that elemental face – 'when Art is king , you will be queen.'

Which is probably the first time Quin ever really looked at me. The early summer light shone on her forehead, making her eyes seem darker than ever. She was still not laughing – not at Myrtle, not at me.

'No man,' said OG, 'gets to be Top Dog in da Mill, except me star.'

'True dat,' said Duane at once and then: 'OG respect!'

Elayne and Tanisha immediately jumped to their feet and gave the Crew salute – a clenched fist and then an open right hand, double-punched in the air.

OG waited, looking at me and also at Mordec. My eyes were still on Quin, but I was aware, at the edge of my vision, of Mordec's slowly raising arm.

'Safe OG,' Mordec said.

I too joined the salute, but I never once took my eyes

27

off Quin. Her arm rose at exactly the same time as mine, like a mirror reflection, so that inside that very public gesture there seemed something intimate, something teasing, as though there was already something between us. Which there wasn't. Later I thought that – by pairing us together – Myrtle created that moment herself. Lit the tiny spark which was to become such a conflagration. She would have denied it of course, just as she'd been denying me for months on the issue of my supposed kingship. I'd learnt that Myrtle would say what she said, make pronouncements, speak in riddles and then be silent. The most additional information I'd managed to get out of her was: 'There will be a time for your kingdom and you will know when that time comes.' But joining my name with Quin's was something new – as was speaking of the matter in public.

In ritual acknowledgement of the salutes, OG banged his right fist into his left palm. 'So wot next?' he asked Myrtle, then, lips drawn back from those big, white teeth, 'You gonna make a click?'

Myrtle shrugged: 'I don't need a gang. What will be, will be.'

How many times had she said that. *What will be, will be.* As if we were just pawns in someone else's game.

'I'll tell you wah guan,' said OG, and he leant back against a bollard from which a rusted chain hung. 'I'll tell you da future, cuzzie. Me an a big yard, dat's wot.' He rattled the chain, banged it against the metal of the post. 'Me an my swimming pool. Me an a hundred buff gyals.'

He made a small sign with his massive left fist and four or five of his current buff gyals, led by Tanisha and Elayne, went straight to his side. Quin did not join them.

'That's the future!' he continued. 'An tell you wot, cuzzie, if you're still about, I'll let you live dere too.'

The girls laughed.

'Living in a big house?' said Myrtle. 'That's nothing to me.'

'You hear me say *house*? I'd probably put you in da garage, next to da benz.'

'I'm content where I am.'

'You'd like the pool.'

'I had a big house. And a pool.'

'No, you never.'

'And I don't miss them one bit. Besides, I have the canal now.'

'You can't swim in the canal.'

'I don't want to swim, I only want to look at the water. To see how it changes, to watch the sky reflected.'

'You can do dat with my pool and it'll be cleaner.'

'Will your pool have ducks?' asked Myrtle. 'And, every year, ducklings?'

'Nat, it'll have gyals,' said OG. 'Gyals, gash – get me? Hundreds of buff tings.' Duane and Mordec roared a kind of approval and OG lobbed a stone into the canal, hitting a plastic bottle caught in some green weed along with some broken polystyrene packaging. 'Yeah, I'm leavin dis crap behind.'

'Ducks breed,' said Myrtle, 'they show you the circle of life.'

'Gyals breed,' said OG, delighted again. 'Trust. Mine'll all be breedin plenty, no worry bout dat.' Tanisha was still close to him and he slapped her bottom. She didn't mind, there were privileges to being one of his favourites. Quin would have minded, I realised then, which is why she probably kept herself apart. But then maybe OG wouldn't have joshed with her anyway, the exclusion zone she kept about herself was almost tangible, breach it – her body seemed to say – at your own risk.

But I wanted to breach it. It was perhaps then, that innocent summery afternoon by the canal, I first realised how much I wanted to touch Quin, and not just at arm's length either, not just with the tips of my fingers. No, I wanted to breach that space, big time.

OG lobbed a second stone in the canal, where it splashed beside a floating Red Bull can. 'Shit breeds an all. Where all dat shit comes from?' Then he pulled some plant from the bank beside him. 'Gyals breed. Shit breeds.' He waved the plant. 'Weeds breed. Everything breeds.'

'That's not a weed,' said Myrtle.

'You wot?'

'That's a wild flower.'

'Sez who?' said OG, who hadn't put in much of an appearance at school and hated people to be smarter than him.

'Silene dioica,' said Myrtle. 'Red campion.'

OG ripped the leaves from the plant stem, crushed its pink petals.

Myrtle watched impassively. 'Next year,' she said, 'that flower will grow back. Grow tall. But you' – she gave him the look she'd given Quin when she'd pronounced her queen elect – 'you will never grow tall.'

'Huh?'

'I see you,' said Myrtle. 'You're a little man.'

'Little?' OG stood up. He didn't look very little.

'Oh, you're all puffed up, all right, but you're swollen with other people's dreams.' She paused. 'Where are your own dreams, OG?'

Dreams. I had dreams once, dreams of getting out, getting away, outlines of castles, hopes of the heroic. Increasingly faint and ragged things.

OG moved from the bollard and came to stand over

Myrtle and the burnt-out car. The only thing between his fist and her weather-beaten face was Shaman.

'Tch, Shaman, tch,' said Myrtle. Shaman backed away, but not very far, his black eyes glowed.

'Get out of da whip,' OG said.

Myrtle got out of the car.

'Move from me, da whip an my island.'

Myrtle gathered her robes about her and set off over the bridge, Shaman trotting obediently behind her.

'Wot now superwoman?' shouted OG.

Myrtle turned to look over her shoulder. 'Your reign,' she said, 'is almost over.'

Behind a shielding hand, Mordec smiled.

We all watched where Myrtle went. She didn't go far, but OG had made his point and he didn't pursue her. So she resumed residence under the brick arch. Later that night, watching from the windows of the Mill, I saw Quin go to her, taking her food of course. OG might have seen that as an act of rebellion, as giving succour to the enemy, but then maybe he wasn't smart enough to see Myrtle as the enemy. Or maybe it was that Quin was too smart for him, making of her relationship with Myrtle something ordinary, something that was just part of the fabric of Mill life, nothing threatening.

It was May so they didn't light a fire that night, but they still sat in a tight ring as though around a fire, Quin, the old woman and the dog, their heads as usual bowed intently together. I remember wanting to join that little group, if only to sit as close as to Quin as Myrtle was sitting to her. I even wondered what it was that the old woman was telling my exclusion-zone queen. In time, I found that out – but only after the night of your murder, Myrtle.

5

It started innocently enough – a simple misunderstanding – but it was to end in full-scale war.

Up until that time the hostility between the Knight Crew and the Saxons had been confined to a kind of tribal territorialism. About two thousand people lived on the Cornwall estate and we knew who we were, just as the Mount Bladon people knew their own. Not that everyone on the estates were players in the game, of course. There were soldjas and civilians, people who'd joined up and people who hadn't, which is why the colour thing started probably, because we needed a uniform.

Baby blue – that was the Crew's choice. I always thought it a stupid colour but the girls liked it and so, of course, did OG. He wore it all the time to set off the silky chocolate of his limbs. When Elayne first threaded baby-blue ribbons into her braids, I think she did it as a joke, but OG took it as tribute, an obeisance, and he was quick to tell us that all the legendary gangs in America had their own colours, the Cripps, the Bloods, everyone. After a while, even those like Duane and Garvey, who took a great deal of care over their clothes, consented to wear small squares of blue cloth hanging from their trouser pockets. OG called them flags and said they were the mark of our belonging.

The Saxons' colour was red – bull-rag red. And it certainly

enraged us. As well as spray-painting their red-rag 'X' (as in SaXon) on the boundaries of all the roads they believed to be theirs, they occasionally made raids inside our territory and, if undetected, would leave a red handkerchief attached to some Cornwall landmark, like the refuse chute where we sometimes congregated if it was too late to get to the Mill, and even once (and once only) on the stairwell where OG lived.

Tintagel Road, which ran between the northern end of Cornwall and the southern point of Mount Bladon, was our frontline. It was there that boys from the Crew and Mob went flossing. We might flaunt bikes we'd nicked from their manor, or we might just parade with ludicrous numbers of gold chains about our necks to demonstrate our prowess at revenue raising. The flags helped us know who we needed to impress and who we could safely ignore. At a glance you could establish friend from foe.

And that was Lee's fatal mistake. I'd known Lee since school, or rather since bunking off, as we were more out of school than in. It was Lee who was with me the first time I knocked a posh kid off his bike for the dinner money. And it was Lee who, when we graduated to hotel raiding, was good at back stairs and long corridors and car park exits. Lee with the champagne up his jumper if we were just having a laugh, or the bread rolls down his trousers if we were hungry.

And Lee who, one hot July day, walked Tintagel Road wearing a baby-blue T-shirt.

Since I'd been at the Mill, I'd hardly seen Lee. We'd lost touch – and he'd lost touch with the streets. His gabby – and extremely large – mother was constantly on his case. He was to stay out of trouble, he wasn't to take part – did he hear her? He heard her, most of the block heard her. But that was the problem, the man had no one to look out for him any more. If he knew about the flags which hung from our pockets, he didn't know that OG's personal flag was his cool, cut-off, muscle-revealing top in baby-blue. A top almost identical to the one that Lee chose to wear that day. So there Lee was, an accident waiting to happen.

Lee had a cousin – Karl – who lived the other side of Mount Bladon. He could have skirted the estate, it would have only added about fifteen minutes to his journey. But he didn't. He chose to walk plumb through the middle of Bladon, he even cut onto Saxon Road itself. It was a miracle that he lasted the six minutes he did. Afterwards, with his eyes half closed up, he said he couldn't describe any of his attackers. Truth is, we only ever really knew the names and faces of the main players. Most distinctive among the enemy were the O'Dair brothers, Mack and Jimbo, with their pale skin and dark hair and their unmissably bright blue eyes. Also blue-eyed (most of Bladon had Celtic roots) was HellRazor, who, later, would more than live up to his street name. And then there was Big Shank himself, but Shankie, like OG, wasn't on the street much. He was the back-at-home Boss, running things from behind the scenes. Yes, we knew about Shankie, who was rumoured to be eight foot tall but turned out – when I finally met him – to be small and wormy, if utterly ruthless. The Saxon foot-soldiers were more anonymous. We only knew them because of their flags.

The three that jumped Lee were all wearing the correct uniform, they were displaying their colours and they thought – quite reasonably – Lee was displaying his. He tried to tell them – as they wielded a knife about his chest, slashing a large cross in that fateful shirt – that he was just a civilian. He wasn't involved, he didn't know who they were or what they wanted. I didn't see his face, but I can imagine it – I bet he looked just as he did when Mordec punched him that day for laughing at our mother in her green fishnet tights: hurt, shocked, disbelieving. But, because he wouldn't own up to being from the Knight Crew, they thought he was chicken, a pussy, so they also carved a cross in the skin of his right hand – where the scar would look at him for the rest of his life.

That was the first knife incident between the Saxons and the Crew, so if you wanted to attribute blame, you'd have to lay it at their door. And even now, I can still feel the anger rising in me as I remember the night Lee brought me his bleeding hand. His face was mournful and his flesh, beneath the split coffee-coloured skin, was sappy pink, as though he'd gone soft somehow. It made me mad looking at him, but it made me much madder to think the Saxons believed we were pussies. I took Lee straight to the Mill.

The place was packed that night, everyone had heard about the attack, the use of the knife. In fact, as news spread about the estate, Lee's hypothetical condition had worsened: he'd been stabbed in the stomach, his right hand had been cut off, he was in hospital, he'd bled to death. By the time we arrived OG, mounted on his throne wheel, was already presiding over a righteous fury.

'Was dat boy a soldja?' he was shouting.

'No!' came the ritual response. Often the Crew sat on the pallets during OG's rants, but that night they were all standing, even the girls.

'Did dey have beef wid him?'

'No!'

'Do dey have beef now?'

'Yes!'

Lee was walking a little behind me, hanging back, and, even though I hadn't told him what might happen to him if he came to the Mill (just as Mordec never told me), he smelt faintly sour, as though he was afraid.

OG spotted us at once and, with one movement of his massive right arm, commanded an immediate silence. The Crew all turned to watch the incomer. There must have been forty or fifty Crew members there that night and they parted like the Red Sea to let Lee and me through.

'Lee, cuz – show dem.' OG ordered from on high when we came to a stop in front of the wheel.

Lee stared up at OG as if he couldn't quite make him out, although it was high summer and there was plenty of light in the Mill that evening.

'Dat bandage, man,' said OG, 'take it off.'

Still Lee didn't respond, so I took his hand myself and began to unwrap the loosely wound white cloth. Lee hadn't been to the hospital, the bandage was just some makeshift attempt of his mother's. Eventually his hand came free, revealing two ugly, raised welts of red.

'Hold it up,' OG barked.

I held up Lee's hand.

When they saw the Saxon cross, the Crew went wild.

'What we gonna do, bloods?' OG sang above the melee.

'Rush em!'

'Jack em!'

'Merk em!'

I shouted it too.

'Merk, merk, merk!'

And it wasn't a playground chant any more. It was for real.

Which is when OG dug his hand into the deep right-hand pocket of his cargo pants and pulled out the knife. There was a generalised gasp of surprise and Elayne, who was standing close to the front of the crowd, shook so violently, her head was a blur of plaits and ribbons.

OG held the knife aloft and he smiled.

I will remember for ever my first sight of that blade. When

I came to be king and stand at the Stone, I got to know every inch and curve of that knife. It was a Buck 119 hunting knife, heavy in your hand, with a moulded black handle and a kicked aluminium butt. But that night I only saw the blade, the vicious purity of its steel point, the flash it made as it caught the light in the way that nothing else – except Quin's face perhaps – ever caught the light. That knife, I knew, was bound up with who I was, who I was meant to be.

'Move urself,' said OG, motioning Lee to approach the mill wheel.

Clearly OG had something more than a beating in mind for Lee that night and I was afraid for him.

Lee remained rooted to the spot.

'Dere,' OG said, pointing to the foot of the wheel, and when Lee still didn't move, OG simply leapt – big and soft as a cat – to land beside his victim.

'Hand.'

Lee had begun to tremble.

'Hand!'

Duane and Garvey moved in then, Duane holding Lee about the waist, pinioning his left hand behind him, while Garvey politely extended Lee's right arm, supporting it at the wrist.

Lee did find his voice then, a very little voice. 'No,' he gasped.

But the deed was already done. OG had carved a third line on Lee's hand, splitting the other two and making the Saxon X into two back-to-back Knight Crew Ks.

Garvey whipped Lee's hand aloft then and Lee's howl of pain was lost among the cheers of the Crew.

'Knight Crew, Knight Crew, Crew, Crew, Crew!'

Fists, closed and open, punched the air. Mine was with them, jerking with the adrenalin release of the moment.

Not Quin's hands though. As usual, she was apart, down on her knees by our newest Crew member. Beyond the punching air, I watched her bring him a bottle of vodka, pour a good deal of it down his throat (which stopped any further screaming) and then splash it liberally on his wounded hand. Alcohol, so she later told me, cleans. He made whimpering noises like an animal.

'You one of us now, cuz,' said OG, flicking his upper torso muscles one last time and then hunching – slowly – wiping the knife on his trousers, sliding it away.

But the boys weren't ready to let the knife go. They had scented blood.

'You gonna shank dem Saxons an all?' shouted Borz.

'Gimme da shank,' yelled Mordec then. 'I'm on it. I'll merk em all!'

And of course I hadn't looked at Mordec once while OG had been wielding the knife. I'd been looking at the blade, as had Mordec. I could see it in his maddened eyes. He wanted that knife as much as I did.

'Nah,' said OG and he re-mounted the wheel treads. 'Lee here, it's his beef. He's da one dey tinks a pussy. Lee here's gonna go see em right. Lee gonna leave here and not come back until he's gotta knife with dere blood on it. Aint that right, Lee?'

All eyes were on the boy.

'Lee?' OG repeated.

Lee shook for a moment, which might have been a nod, and then finally his legs or his brain refused to support him another moment and he simply passed out.

Quin was immediately down beside him again. 'He's new,' she said fiercely. 'He shouldn't go on his jays.'

And, before Mordec could open his mouth, I opened mine: 'Then I'll go with him.'

Why did I say it? Because I felt I owed Lee, or because I was putting down a marker, in front of my brother, in front of OG: *watch me, one day that knife will be mine.* Or perhaps is was a reaction to Quin. An alignment – her and me.

If she understood, she gave me no encouragement, just got up and moved away.

OG was watching intently, his eyes swivelling slowly from me to Mordec to Quin, but all he said was: 'Whatever, bruv.' He had sized us up and, for the time being at least, he obviously felt secure.

Later that night OG went to sit at the window by the gallows winch, his feet swinging high over the river. As the light died Myrtle emerged from the gloom on the canal bank opposite.

OG, in mellow mood, got out the knife and waved it at her. 'How doin, superwoman?'

'Those who live by the sword, die by the sword,' she replied.

'You know nada, sister.'

And about OG, she didn't.

6

L ee chose a steak knife.

    It had a cheap wooden handle and thin blade with a serrated edge. It felt light and insignificant in your hand, I know, because I took one too. We had four such knives in our kitchen drawer which, as we mainly ate baked beans in our house, hadn't had a great deal of use up till then. The reason the knives came from my kitchen and not Lee's was that for three days he played dead. He didn't answer his mobile, he didn't answer his doorbell, he affected not to hear if you threw stuff at his window or yelled through his letterbox.

His mother, however, did respond. She opened the door and stood like a mountain in the doorframe. She had a fearsome set of double chins and her eyes were blazing.

'Beat it!' she yelled at me. 'Get lost. Haven't you done enough already?'

When I asked, very politely, what I'd done enough of already, she screamed for her son. She had to shout four times before he came, and then he looked sheepish.

'This,' exploded the woman mountain and she held up Lee's still bandaged hand, much in the way that Duane and Garvey had.

'I never did that,' I said.

She dropped Lee's hand. 'Might as well have done. You're all the same. You're a bad lot.'

I thought about that.

'You keep away from my Lee, you hear me?'

I heard her, but I took the opportunity to give Lee a look and make a – very discreet – salute: clenched fist, open hand. We were in this together; if you weren't in the Knight Crew, you were against them. It was that simple. Lee looked down and his mother slammed the door.

Bad.

And good.

I can see now that Lee's mother was good, she looked out for her son, tried hard, did her best. But Lee still made it to my house the following day.

'Blood . . .' He wasn't looking at me, he was looking at a wall. 'I'm not on it,' he finished lamely.

'And wot, you think I am?' I said. 'But you're sworn. I'm sworn.' When we were younger, it was always Lee who took the lead. I didn't know whether he'd gone soft or my years in the Mill had made me harder.

'I can't,' he faltered.

'Jus jukk him in de leg,' I said, 'or de arm.' Just stab him. You see how the language had become mine, the habits of thought. 'No one's askin you to merk anyone.'

'No.' He refused me again.

'So you're goin to let dem get away wid it? The Saxons can come into Cornwall any time they like and jus slice you up?'

'No.'

I pressed my advantage. 'Revenge, brother. Respect.' If Lee didn't perform it would go badly for both of us. 'Come here.' I manoeuvred him into the kitchen, pulled open the cutlery drawer. 'Pick yur tool, man.'

Lee hesitated.

I began to hate him. 'Lee, if you don't do the job, the Crew

41

will do you.' I paused. He knew what I was talking about – loss of rep could put your life at risk. 'And me. They'll do me too.'

Lee's pale, uninjured left hand went into the drawer. He extracted the poor-quality steak knife.

I took a matching knife and then slammed the drawer shut. 'I'll organise the bikes an we'll link here tomorrow at seven.' One look at his face told me I'd also need to organise alcohol. I'd seen courage come out of a bottle before. 'Bruv,' I added grimly, 'you'd best be here, man.'

I asked Duane if he could provide me a couple of bikes for the job and I had them within two hours. Duane's only condition was that we had to bring the bikes back in good nick.

'You're looking at 2G there,' he said proudly. 'That's an investment.'

The vodka I got from an off-license where OG had a protection racket going – a certain amount of alcohol a week in return for no bricks through the windows. The vodka turned out to be a mistake. When Lee arrived – only three minutes late – the sight of the bottle made him shake.

'You'll need it,' I said. I knew I would too, so I poured two glasses. When I set Lee's in front of him, I swear he actually turned from his normal, weak-coffee colour to theatrical green. He'd probably thrown up the night Quin had ministered to him and this was his body's way of remembering. I realised then that I must have been in the Mill for a long time, because I couldn't recall when I'd last thrown up.

I got Lee some of Keifer's beer instead, hoping my father would be too gone when he came home to notice if any cans were missing from the fridge. I wanted to steady Lee's nerves but not make him take on so much liquid that he'd need to have a piss just when we were about to jump on our getaway bikes.

We were just about to leave the house when my mother arrived back from one of her cleaning jobs. She was wearing bright pink lipstick, very high-heeled blue satin shoes, a silver lamé skirt and her green fishnet tights.

'Where are you going?' she asked.

'Out,' I said.

Later I wondered whether, if my mum had been like Lee's mum, it would have made any difference? But then Lee's mum – who was good and who didn't, as far as I'm aware, have any health issues – she didn't end up making any difference to him.

'Do you want the Last Supper,' she said, 'before you go?'

There wasn't a flicker of a smile on Lee's face, I know because I checked. From the cupboard that also housed the tea and sugar, I took out my mother's compartmentalised plastic pill dispenser. It was full.

'You haven't been takin your meds,' I said.

'I don't need those,' she said. 'I'm well now.'

I flipped a lid, tipped four pills onto the table. 'Take them.'

'Well people don't need pills.'

'Yeah – which is why you need these.' I pushed the small purple pills towards her, but I didn't stay, I was in too much of a hurry to stop and watch her swallow them. For a long time afterwards I thought that it was this mistake – my mistake – which cost Keifer his life that night. You see, I didn't know then that you have to take the pills regularly, day after day after day, that they aren't instant wonder drugs. So I blamed myself. Ironic considering how I didn't blame myself for what happened in Bladon that night

Anyhow – I left. I had asked a boy, who we called Donkey at the Mill, to meet us just South of Tintagel Road. Donkey was our joey, he did what you told him when you told him to. That night his job was just looking after the bikes while we went into Bladon. If the Saxons gave chase, I didn't want to be on foot because some smart-arse had nicked our transport.

The main danger with Bladon were the number of dead ends. If you got cornered away from the main thoroughfares, there was no means of escape. Trouble was that Bladon only had two main thoroughfares, Saxon Road itself (which, as Lee had discovered, was potential suicide) and Essex Street. Essex Street was longer than Saxon and more curved, you never knew exactly what was around the corner.

'One of them's mans cud be on Tintagel,' I told Lee. 'We might not have to go into Bladon at all.'

We walked the length of Tintagel three times to no avail. Each time we passed Camraid Street, which is where we'd left Donkey, Lee looked back to check the bikes were still there. I half-expected him to make a getaway before we'd done the job.

'Well, it's gonna have to be Essex then,' I said.

I saw Lee fiddle with his flag, as though he wanted to push the square of blue back inside the pocket of his trousers. He was also making strange, wet little ticking noises with his mouth, as if he was having trouble swallowing.

'Move.'

He walked half a pace behind me, his head swivelling right and left, trying to keep his eyes on all the entrances and exits. That at least was useful. There were three blocks on Essex, each four storeys high with garages at ground level and walkways which, since the new security system had been put in place, you could only access with a fob key. We had this same system in Cornwall and while it supposedly meant strangers couldn't access the balconies, it also meant (as the doors were heavy steel) that it took that extra few seconds to get from the blocks to the street – which, that day, would prove crucial.

Up ahead was the first soldja we'd seen, a girl with red ribbons in her hair. Lee, who was wearing a glove over his bandaged right hand, twitched at his knife. The girl's hand went straight to her pocket.

'She's tooled up,' said Lee urgently. 'She's carryin!'

But the girl only extracted a phone.

'That probly gives us two minutes,' I said.

'What?'

'She'll be callin her bredrins.' I felt the first bang of my heart.

'What?' he said again. He was totally spooked. Just six months younger than me and you'd have thought he was a kid.

'Bredrins,' I repeated. Her reinforcements. 'We need to U-ee bruv, head back towards Tintagel.'

Lee turned immediately, looking relieved, as though I'd signalled the retreat.

'They'll follow us,' I said to his back. 'I'm on it, bruv.'

I scanned the block ahead of us and there they were, four of them, two emerging from the fourth floor, two from the ground floor.

'Jees,' said Lee, like he was still some little boy. 'Jees.'

He began to run. I did too, but only as far as the bottom of the steps which led to the walkways. I grabbed Lee then, holding him close and facing him towards the enemy.

'Cotch there,' I hissed in his ear. If we stopped at the bottom, they had to come to us – our advantage. And coming they were, pushing through the door, two white boys, one skinny and ginger-haired and the other pale with dark hair. The steel hushed shut behind them. I reckoned it would be under thirty seconds before the fourth-floor pair arrived and an extra ten for them to get through the door. Approximately forty-five seconds to do the job. How long did it take?

'Now, Lee. Now!'

They were coming down the stairs. I was glad to see a baseball bat. It meant they probably didn't have knives.

Lee took out his knife, held it in the air and then just looked at it. It was like one of those slow-motion moments in a movie, the white boys coming and the baseball bat coming and Lee frozen solid on the bottom step.

'Knight Crew,' I yelled, 'Knight Crew respect!'

Lee's hand released, he swung at them and missed.

They were on us now, but the skinny one was running too fast and lost his footing slightly. Above us the steel door began to hush open again.

What happened next was self-defence. The dark one had the bat swinging at my head, so I just struck out, steak knife in hand. I aimed at his arm, to stop the blow, but somehow the knife missed and caught him in the side. It went in easily and deeply. Pulling it out was more difficult, partly because its serrated edge snagged and partly because the boy was falling. When I finally got it free there was a surprising amount of blood both on the boy and on the blade.

The baseball bat clattered to the ground. Ginger, still unsteady, lunged for it but then, maybe because of his fallen friend, paused. The two Saxons coming through the door did not pause. They ran at us, but we were already two or three yards ahead of them and we weren't stopping for introductions. We could see the end of the street and the relative safety of Tintagel so, so long as we could keep on our feet and they couldn't put out any soldjas out ahead of us, we had a good chance. Behind us the noise was escalating, some of the mothers were screaming. You always knew when it was the mothers because there was a quality of anger and helplessness in their wails. In Bladon they sounded like that – and also in Cornwall, as though there were many different kids but only one set of mothers. Myrtle would have made something of that.

As we ran, Lee got out a plastic food bag.

'Give me the shank,' he said.

'You what?'

'The shank, the borer,' he urged, panting and waving the bag. 'To keep the blood fresh.'

I was impressed. He had done some thinking after all. I handed him the knife so he could bag it and bring it – still wet – to OG.

We had reached Tintagel. They were still behind us, but I didn't turn to look. I could see Donkey ahead, a bike in each hand; he'd come up Camraid and was waiting for us right at the junction with Tintagel. Not such a Donkey, then.

We jumped on those bikes faster than flash and Donkey just melted away. As I pedalled, I did allow myself one backward glance. The Saxons had stopped at the top of Camcaid. They were afraid to come into Cornwall.

I had a smile on my face when we arrived at the Mill.

We flung ourselves off the bikes.

'Watch it, man!' yelled Duane. 'Mash my interest an I'll mash yer face!'

It was hot and the Crew had dragged some pallets out into the sunshine and they were all sitting just outside the back entrance. Myrtle was also sitting there, but I didn't see her at first.

Lee extracted the knife from his pocket. The bag was smeared with red, but there was still blood on the knife too. Lee presented it to OG.

OG nodded. 'Safe, bruv.' He gave the Crew salute which Lee returned.

I hung back, waiting to see how Lee would play it. I was in no hurry. As Myrtle said, my time would come.

'It was down to Art,' Lee said then, perhaps feeling my eyes. 'Art led it.'

OG acknowledged me with a second salute. 'You're alryt, Art.' Then he got up and walked to the Mill entrance. The doorframe was wooden and had obviously once been black but was then a soft grey colour. He wiped the blade on the lintel above his head, back and forth, and we watched until the blood made a stain there. When there was no more blood to wipe, OG carved the number '1' beside it.

'Dey'll fall like dominoes,' he said.

'Did you look him in the eye?' That was Myrtle, arising, as she often did, out of nowhere, as if she'd been formed right that moment out of the earth under your feet.

'Who?' said Lee.

'The boy you killed.'

'I didn't merk no one,' said Lee.

How wrong we were.

'Did you look him in the eye?' This time the question was addressed to me, as though she knew it had been my hand on the knife.

'Who cares?' said Mordec. 'He jukked a Saxon. That's all you need to know.'

Myrtle ignored him, her gaze locked on me. She had the most astonishing eyes, they were almost as black as Shaman's. In their reflection, I tried to picture the Saxon boy. I tried to recall the shape of his face or the colour of his eyes. I tried to describe him in my mind. But he was a hole, a hollow, a blank.

'If you don't look,' said Myrtle, 'you don't see.'

'We saw him fall,' said Lee. 'We saw him smack on the concrete.' Lee, it appeared, was beginning to enjoy this.

'Knight Crew star,' said OG and handed the steak knife back to Lee.

Tanisha clapped and so did Elayne. 'Star,' they repeated.

Mordec grimaced. He didn't like the attention going Lee's way – or mine.

I was still thinking of that blank, blank face.

'Now your reign is over,' Myrtle said to OG. 'It's finished now.'

'You said dat,' OG said mildly. He got out the Buck and passed his thumb right and left across the blade, testing its sharpness. 'I told you, you know nada.'

'What happened today,' said Myrtle, 'it's the end for you.'

'Yeah?' OG began, very slowly, whetting the blade of the Buck on a concrete post. In the sun, the knife struck sparks in my eyes. 'Me, I tink dis is jus da beginning.'

'The end,' repeated Myrtle, 'the beginning of the end.'

Very slowly, OG began moving towards Myrtle. She remained sitting where she was on the ground, her hand on Shaman's collar.

He thrust the spine of the knife towards her face.

'You know wot dis is?' he asked. He was indicating the small furrow in the thicker, top part of the blade.

'It's the fuller,' said Myrtle lightly, 'a groove cut to lighten the blade but let it retain its strength.'

'Wrong, superwoman. It's da blood gutter. So you can leave da shank in a body and watch all da blood drain out by itself.' He twisted the blade so the edge came close to her face. 'An I tell you when da end will be – when dis knife is dashed deep into a body and comes out bloodless. Dat's when.'

He laughed and snapped the knife away. Myrtle delved beneath her ragged robes, brought out her book and untied its leather strings. Inside its soft pages was a pencil and she began to write. Normally when she wrote, she seemed to be writing on pages which already contained hundreds of previous scribblings. But this day she opened the book at what appeared to be a totally empty page. Which is probably why Quin said: 'What you writin, bubz?'

'The prophecy.' Myrtle replied. 'OG's prediction of the end.' Then she looked up at OG. 'And when the knife comes out bloodless, who will have the power then?'

OG just stared at her so it was finally Duane that spoke. 'It aint gonna happen, sister,' he said quite gently. 'Blades don't work like that. OG's having a bubble.'

'No,' said Myrtle. 'It will happen. Believe me. That knife will come bloodless from a body.'

'Then OG will have merked an alien,' said Mordec and the Crew laughed.

'And who will have the power then?' pressed Myrtle.

'The alien, I guess,' said Mordec. 'Or the ghost of the alien.'

'The ghost will have power,' said Myrtle thoughtfully. Her hands were at Shaman's neck, stroking him softly beneath the ears. 'Oh yes.'

'Tell you wah guan,' said OG, entering into the spirit of things, 'whoever draws out dat bloodless knife, he will be king.'

'Or she will be queen,' said Quin.

'No way,' said Mordec.

'What will be, will be,' said Myrtle. For a moment she wrote again in her book and then she thrust it towards OG. 'Now sign.'

'You wot?'

'Put your name to it. The succession.'

OG seemed afraid to take the book, or maybe he was afraid of the words because he really couldn't read.

Quin jumped up and stood beside him. 'I, OG,' she read, 'do solemnly swear that when my knife goes deep into a body and comes out bloodless, then my reign at the Mill shall be over and power will transfer to whomsoever draws the knife from that body. Signed . . . and then there's a space,' finished Quin.

All eyes were on OG.

'Safe,' he said with a flourish and a wide grin. 'Today we salaam de loonies.' He whipped out the knife, held it aloft a moment and then made a swift and small incision across the top of his left thumb. The sliced black skin bubbled red. He put the knife away and then rubbed his right thumb in the blood.

'Knight Crew, respect!' He made the salute with his bloody hand and then pressed his thumb to Myrtle's page.

Myrtle stood then and held the document as high above her head as OG had held the knife.

'Be it,' she said, 'as it is written.'

7

Another man might have spent that evening musing on the fate of the Saxon boy. Not me. The word on the streets – Myrtle notwithstanding – was that the boy was in hospital and that's where I parked him. He would come to occupy me, in fact he'd come to haunt me, but that night I had other things on my mind.

Like my mother.

I arrived home to find her sitting on the sofa with a man I'd never seen before. He had his legs wrapped around hers and he was lipsing her full on the mouth. My mother was so involved in the snog it took her a few moments to realise that someone else was in the room. Her reaction, when she did finally notice, was simply to wave to me around the back of the man's neck.

'Hi,' I said in reply.

The man, who was small and spotty and white, jumped up then, treading on my mother's feet in his hurry to disentangle himself.

'Hello, Arthur,' said my mother. And then, 'This is Arthur, my son.'

The man was tucking in his shirt and zipping his flies.

'And this,' she said, indicating the man, 'is . . .' She faltered. 'What was your name again?'

The man didn't seem inclined to give his name.

'Get out,' I said.

The man scrabbled for his phone and his keys. 'I was just going,' he said.

'You only just arrived,' said my mother.

'Move,' I yelled. I wanted to hit the man, I wanted to smack him in the face, I wanted to see blood running out of his spotty white nose. I could hear my breathing going harder and louder, and then I remembered the knife. I'd kept it in my pocket.

'Don't go,' said my mother. 'We could have fun.'

I stood in the doorway. 'You have three seconds.' My hand was on the weapon. The feel of the cold steel beneath my fingers changed things. It even changed the tone of my voice. 'Out.'

The man went.

'Oh,' said my mother. 'Bye.'

'And don't come back.' I banged the door shut behind him. I could, I thought, get used to carrying a knife.

My mother went through to the kitchen and began boiling the kettle like nothing had happened. She was still wearing the high-heeled blue satin shoes and her silver skirt, which barely covered her bottom anyway, was still hitched up.

'Pull it down,' I said, like I just turned into some priest.

'What?' she asked.

'The skirt. Pull it down!' And when she didn't do it immediately, I pulled it down for her. 'You turned into some kinda ho? Is our yard the new brothel?'

She poured boiling water into a cracked mug. Her pills were still on the table where I'd left them some hours earlier. 'You didn't take them, did you?'

She looked blank.

'The pills, you never took them.'

'I don't need pills . . .' she began.

'Ma, you're ill. You're seriously screwed, you know that?'

'You shouldn't have sent him away,' she offered then.

'You don't even know who he was.'

'He was nice.' She paused. 'He said I was beautiful.'

'I bet he did.' I felt that nameless coil of red again, how it pulled and twisted inside me. I had a sudden urge to put my hand to her too, smack that smile right off her face. 'What if Keifer had come home, what if Dad had found you together like that?'

'Keifer isn't your dad,' my mother said.

No, she didn't *say* it, she just let it slip, very casually, as if the information was a piece of nothing. And I had a very strange sensation then – felt my head inflate like some giant balloon and where my mind used to be there was only air.

'Keifer isn't your dad,' she repeated when I didn't reply. 'He's Mordecai's father, but not yours.'

I managed to sit down at the table. I put my hands either side of the balloon as if I could control it, stop it growing. I was faint, I was dizzy, my ears felt blocked.

'I meant to tell you,' said my mother. 'Only it never seemed the right moment.'

Bang. My head hit the table. Bang. Bang. Bang.

'Arthur,' she said, 'don't do that.'

Bang. Only a different bang. The balloon burst. 'And wot?' I finally yelled. 'That's all you have to say?'

She stirred her teabag-less water. 'What do you want to know?'

'Anything. Everything.' My voice is very loud. 'Without the lies.'

'Lies? What lies. It's all true,' she said and drank some of the hot water.

'So you don't even put the bag in the brew nemore,' I shouted.

'Lovely tea,' she said.

Bang, bang, bang. This time it's my fists on the table. I needed to see blood, feel something real.

'Arthur,' she said, quite tenderly, 'your father was a king.'

There's red on the table. 'What?'

Her eyes go dreamy. 'He was a beautiful man, an Egyptian . . .'

'An Egyptian!'

'Which is why you have such fine features, Arthur. His face was like yours and his hands.' She reaches for my raw fist. 'Long fingers and immaculately cut nails, artistic hands . . .'

I pull away. 'Which he pawed all over you –'

'Yes. He touched me. But only the once.'

'So I'm the product of a link for a night – yes?'

'It was a large night.'

I was still in that room, I was talking, having a conversation, making sense (was I making sense?) and at the same time I was standing right outside myself, right outside the exploded balloon, consumed by a madness, a fury. How dare she! She was taking my life apart, hanging me out to dry like I was some no-bit piece of washing. But there were things I needed to know, so I went right on talking.

'And does my new father have a name?'

'Penn.'

'Penn isn't an Egyptian name.'

'On the street they called him Dragon. He was a big man, Art. Is a big man.'

'Dragon as in chasing the dragon? So he's some top-dog scag dealer?'

'Heroin did come into it, yes.'

'Right – so he's a shotta, a Tony Montana. My father the king.' My anger is chopping me up. 'And does he even know about me, your top dog artistic shotta?'

'Yes. He knows about you.'

'Which is why he links me every week and slips me a score, right?' Then a cold thought occurs to me. 'Or you mean I know him already, I don't know who he is, but we've met?' My brain frantically scans the faces of all the other black men in my mother's life. I don't want any of them. I don't want a father plucked out of nowhere. Except my dream father, my king, my fantasy father into whom, into which, my real life always comes crashing.

'No,' she says, 'You don't know him.' She pauses. 'But he knows you.'

Then I'm really falling. 'And what does he think of me, this Pops the Top Dog?' I yell. As if I should care what this fraggle thinks of me. As if I should give a dee!

'He watches over you,' my mother says.

'Watches over me? Like he's some ghost?'

'Well, he has moved away now.'

'Away?'

'Colombia. Colombia's big business for him.'

Colombia. So in one minute I gain and lose a father. I feel like my whole life has balled up, speeded up, that I'm being asked to live ten lives all at once and all I want to do is rest. Just rest. Just, for once, lay my head down to sleep and wake up to a clear sky.

And we haven't even got to the basic questions yet.

'What about D–' I begin. 'Keifer. Does Keifer know?'

'Of course not. Keifer would die if he knew.'

How prophetic that remark was to be.

'And you kept it under wraps how exactly?'

She shrugs. 'One of his spells.'

Of course.

I try to imagine it, Wizard Keifer banged up for some petty (but repeat) offence, a small-time theft he was too stupid to cover up, a fraudulent dole claim that netted him an extra twenty quid a week. And in those few weeks (months?) my mother going mad one night with Penn.

'Wasn't Keifer suspicious of the dates? Didn't he suspect anything?'

'Maybe he didn't want to know. When a man's in jail, loyalty is everything. He has his pride, Keifer.' She pauses. 'Besides, I think it happened before he went in. Could have been his.'

Could have been his. Forget washing. I was left-luggage, I was a packet of fags. The red coil came again – wound about with shock.

And, if I'm honest, relief.

Keifer was not my father.

He was not my father!

I believed it not because that's what my psychotic mother told me so, but because, if he wasn't my father, a fragment, a tiny fragment, of my long-forgotten dream survived. I could still escape. Oh Myrtle, why did you leave it so long to tell me that escape can only come from inside?

I needed somewhere to go, someone to talk to. It was late, oh so late, but of course I knew where I needed to go, where I might find some sense. And maybe even some rest.

I pushed the four pills on the table towards my mother.

'Take them.'

'I had you at home,' said my mother. 'Here in this flat. I cut the umbilical cord myself, dusted it with talc and vinegar. Mordecai was almost three. He watched. You were a beautiful baby.'

'Take the pills.'

'I will,' said my mother. 'With my tea.'

What was I supposed to do – ram those pills down her throat myself?

'Where are you going?' She added to my retreating back.

'Out.'

'He'll be watching over you,' she called after me. 'He'll be watching.'

So he would have seen me go down past Tesco's and onto the canal path then. I didn't double back on myself, I didn't check if anyone was following me. I looked ahead and I also looked up. It was one of Myrtle's nights, dark with a forest of stars. I breathed more easily when I saw the stars, because they were bigger than me.

Myrtle was sitting in the Merc. The rain had washed away the charred smell of the wreck and she'd found some odd squares of foam to replace the burnt-out seats. She was sitting in the front passenger seat and Shaman in the driving seat, his head on her lap.

'Ah,' she said when she saw me approach, 'so you know.'

'Know what?'

'About your father.'

'Who are you?' I shouted then. 'You and your black hell-dog. Who the fuck are you?'

She shrugged. 'Just someone who has also lost things, lost people.'

There was no understanding her.

'And also,' she said, 'someone who looks.'

'What, like you went to Specsavers? Can X-ray right across the water and through the walls of my house!'

'I don't have to look through walls, your face tells me things, your presence. This is the first time you have come to me alone, that you have sought me out. Your face tells me you are distressed but also questing. Your being here suggests that something has changed, that something new has been said. Something, I imagine, as you have come here to talk, that is to do with what you and I have spoken of before.

You look at me as though I'm doing magic, but I'm not. Hear the whispers, Art. Let people speak to you with more than their mouths.'

Myrtle could always send shivers down your spine, re-arrange the world in front of your eyes. She talked the same way that river beyond the canal lapped at the island, as though she came from a place beyond any you would ever know.

But you wanted to know that place, in fact you'd kill to know that place.

I sat down on the canal bank and she got out of the car just, I think, to be beside me. Shaman moved with her, like a shadow.

'So tell me,' she said.

'Why?' I ask. 'You know already.'

'No,' she says. 'It's your story. And the words must be yours also, for the words tell the heart what it feels.'

But I didn't have any words right then. I didn't want Keifer to be my father but I didn't want him not to be my father either. He was, after all, the only father I'd ever known. The shadowy other man was just some new hole in my life. Some Colombian-sized emptiness.

'I can't do the words,' I said suddenly, hopelessly. 'But you can. You predicted this father thing, so you tell me what it means.'

'Do things have to have meaning?' she asked. 'Does the sky have meaning, does the river?'

'But those things' – I struggled – 'just *are*.'

'Exactly,' she said, as though I'd just solved the riddle of the universe.

'Exactly what?'

'Some things you can change,' she said, 'some you can't. Some things you can control. Some you can't.'

59

And I began to cry then, stupid tears just welling up. I didn't look at Myrtle and I hoped she wouldn't put a hand out to comfort me and she didn't. So I just cried until I was finished with it.

There were more stars out by then, I know because, when I wiped my eyes, I looked up. 'So wot next, Mystic Meg?'

'You have a choice,' she said.

'What choice? I've never had any choice. Never chose to be born, never chose some one-night-link shotta pops, or some drunk other pops, or a loony for a mother, never even chose Cornwall over Bladon. Nothing – ever – has ever been my choice!'

'You chose to knife that boy today.'

'What?'

'You chose to stick a knife in Danny MacMahon.'

'Who?'

'Danny MacMahon. The Bladon boy. Did you think he didn't have a name?'

I pulled my mind back to his blank face. He didn't have a face, how could he possibly have a name?

Danny MacMahon. Danny MacMahon. Danny MacMahon!

'And do you think,' Myrtle continues, 'he didn't – he doesn't – have a mother of his own and a father?'

A family. That was too much.

'Well, aint he blessed!' I say or rather I cry out, because she's needling me now. 'He's doing way better than me.'

'He's not doing much now,' said Myrtle. 'He's dead.'

'No,' I said. 'I jus jukked him in the side. I didn't merk no one. Neways, they rushed Lee, who gave dem dat right?'

'That's the choice you have, Art' said Myrtle. 'The future. The past – that's gone, but the future – it's all in your hands.'

60

I shouldn't have cried in front of her, I shouldn't have let down my guard.

'You're clever, Art. You're thoughtful. You have the capacity to love – and be loved. You could be a leader, Art.'

I thought of OG's knife, the big hunting Buck with the blood gutter. This is what Myrtle did to you, screwed with the inside of your head.

'And leaders can be good, Art,' she said, as if she could read my mind. 'Or they can be bad.'

I didn't have to reply to that because my mobile rang.

'Just as people can be good or bad,' she continued. 'You could be good, Art. The seed of it's still in you.'

The caller was Mordec.

'Get yur arse back here, *now*,' he said.

He was at home, our mother must have told him.

'I know,' I said, 'I know already.'

'You know jack shit,' he said.

8

My brother opened the door to me. Only he wasn't my brother any more, he was my half-brother. I checked his face to see if it had changed but there was the familiar, cruel mouth, the neatly braided hair. I was glad. Too much earth had moved under my feet already that day.

'She told you then,' I said.

'Wrong,' Mordec replied. 'She told Keifer.'

I felt a kind of buttoning panic in my stomach and couldn't stop myself scanning left and right as if, somewhere just ahead of me, I expected to spot our mother's dead body.

'Where is she now?'

'Hospital.'

I didn't know if that was the good news or the bad news.

Mordec went to the fridge, pulled a beer for me and started the story. He'd arrived home to find our mother in full flow. She'd been describing, in great detail, the beauty of her ex-lover's hands.

'Long fingers,' I commented, 'artistic.'

'What you telling me dis shit for, woman?' Keifer had asked.

'I thought you'd like to know a bit about Arthur's father,' our mother had apparently replied.

He hit her, of course, smacked her straight in the face, and she'd fallen to the floor where she'd sat, rubbing the blood off her chin and telling Keifer about drugs and Egyptians and the nature of kings. Keifer had moved in like an enraged bull, or would have done if Mordec hadn't intervened.

Mordec, I knew, would have acted quickly and instinctively. I could just see him standing between his maddened father and his mad mother, the only still thing in the room. At the same time as absorbing the revelation himself, he would have been thinking, calculating. I imagined the scene even as he described it:

'Leave her!' That was Mordec shouting. 'She's nuts, you know that. She's talking shit. She hasn't been taking her meds. Look at the pills, the pills on the table!'

Only the pills weren't on the table any more, they'd slid like our mother to the floor, they'd scattered about.

'I'll kill you,' Keifer yelled, 'you ho, you fucking white ho.'

'It isn't true, she doesn't know what she'd saying.'

'It is true,' said our mother, sucking her bruised lip.

'Dad –'

'Get outta my way, boi!'

'Dad – please.'

'I said move.'

But Mordec wouldn't have moved, Mordec never moved when he set his mind to something. No doubt he could have bested Keifer in a fight, but Mordec was cleverer than that.

'If it was true,' Mordec said, 'she wouldn't tell you, would she? That's how you know it's the illness talking. You're only listening to the illness.'

'You telling me wah guan, boi?'

'I'm telling you Mum needs help.'

'Right. Then I'm goin to get her help. I'll take her to the loony bin myself.'

Our mother stood up then. 'You are a good man, Keifer.

You are the best man I have ever known.' And she leant right over and kissed him.

Keifer put out a call to his mate Roy and the blue Ford Fiesta arrived.

'Thanks,' Keifer said.

'You alryt?' Roy asked.

'We're fine,' said my mother.

'And they left hand in hand?' I asked Mordec.

'Yeah right. But at least they left. Together.'

'How do you know they went to the hospital?'

'Followed them, of course. Well – kinda. Got Pels to do it on the motorbike. They went to A&E. Pels watched em right through the door.'

I sat down. I hadn't sat through all of the retelling, but my legs wouldn't hold me any more. Besides there was one thing I still needed to know.

'Do you believe her?' I asked. 'I mean about the father thing?'

'What's not to believe?' Mordec's lip curled. 'You've always been a bastard.'

I waited for the laugh but it didn't come.

It was five hours later that the doorbell rang.

'We expectin guests?' Mordec asked. That was a joke. Normally the doorbell only rang past midnight if Keifer was too drunk to find his keys.

Mordec opened up to two Feds, a woman and a man.

Behind him in the corridor, I didn't recognise either of them and there'd been plenty of Feds at our door over the years. The ones that had periodically come to take Keifer away, the ones that had come to ask our mother exactly what she thought Mordec was up to, the ones that had just knocked on the door hoping for information about this or that misdemeanor on the estate. They never left with any information.

'Good evening, sir,' said the man. He had watery eyes and a mouth like a pencil sharpener. The use of that 'sir' obviously intrigued Mordec because he didn't slam the door.

'Is your mum in?' asked the woman in a thin, nervous voice. Her hands were also twittering and I took an instant dislike to her.

'No,' said Mordec. 'Sorry.'

'Do you know when she'll be back?' persisted the woman.

'She's in hospital,' Mordec said and the man raised an eyebrow. 'She's a bit manic right now.' The man waited. 'She's bipolar.' It was the first time I heard my mother's condition named. I received the information like a punch. How long had Mordec known and kept the information from me? 'Probly just needs a change of meds.' He was making it sound small, normal. 'She'll be back soon.'

'And your father?'

'He's with her. Wot do ya want?'

'Does he drive a Ford Fiesta?'

'Sometimes,' said Mordec evasively. At least five men on the estate shared the car and it was often better not to know where the car had been or who had been driving it.

'Do you mind if we come in?' said the man and then he flashed a badge. 'I'm PC Holden and this is WPC Ramsbottom.'

I stood aside a little and they took this as an invitation.

'You must be . . .' said the woman, looking first at me and then at her notebook.

'Art,' Mordec said. 'My brother.' And I liked it that he didn't say *half-brother*, it made me feel safer.

'And you're Mordecai then,' she concluded.

'Mordec.'

'You're seventeen, is that right?'

Mordec didn't bother to answer that. Age had long since stopped mattering to us.

'Do you want to show me where the kitchen is, Mordec?' PC Holden asked. 'We could put a kettle on.'

I didn't like the way he steered Mordec away from me, leaving me in the front room with the woman.

'Do you mind if I sit?' she asked.

'Go on then.' I watched her arrange herself on the sofa where my mother had been with the man earlier in the evening.

'You might want to sit too.'

I said nothing, continued to stand. Having Feds in your house was bad enough but she was beginning to freak me.

'What is it?' I said. 'What have you come to say?'

'No!' That was Mordec in the kitchen, an ear-splitting shout through the wall. 'No!' Whatever Ramsbottom wasn't telling me, Holden was obviously telling Mordec. I was in there faster than light. I'd never seen Mordec looking shocked before, it was as though someone had ripped the skin off his face and left him just staring out of his skull.

'What?' I shouted. 'What! Is it Mum?'

'It's Dad,' he said. 'Keifer.'

'I'm very sorry,' said PC Holden. He hadn't even managed to fill his teacup. 'Road traffic accident.'

'Road traffic accident!' Mordec repeated, and he slammed his fist so hard down on the kitchen counter that the plates inside the cupboard below jangled and crashed. 'Only mashed himself round a tree and merked himself on the spot.'

'And Mum?' I heard myself asking in a tiny voice, a voice that suggested I didn't care at all about Keifer. But it wasn't that I didn't care, it was just that my brain wasn't working very well right then. The information couldn't penetrate. All this, I thought, is happening to someone else.

'Oh Mum's alryt,' said Mordec bitterly. 'Her number won't be up until Saddam Hussein comes for the Last Supper.'

PC Holden looked perplexed. 'Please don't worry about your mother. There was definitely only one victim at the scene. No one else in the car and no other car involved.'

'Just a tree,' said Mordec. 'A tree! Where did he find a tree in this blodclaut estate?'

'Do you have any relatives nearby, someone who could come and sit with you?' WPC Ramsbottom had rejoined the fray.

'No,' said Mordec. 'We don't do relations in this family.' He glared at me. 'We don't even do family in this family.'

'We can't leave you alone here,' said PC Holden.

'Why not?' asked Mordec. 'We're always alone. Even when they're here we're alone.' Then he turned his back and walked out of the room.

WPC Ramsbottom made to go after him.

'Don't,' I said. 'Leave him be.' If anyone was to follow him, it should have been me, but I didn't want to. Perhaps I was afraid that I might see the spike of tears in his eyes that I'd seen in Keifer's the night Mum first went 'away'. And that wouldn't have been good for me and it wouldn't have been good for Mordec.

'A neighbour?' asked PC Holden. 'Have you got a good neighbour perhaps?'

I thought of Lee's mum, how we might all go and sit in her place. But then I thought of her standing in the door-frame shouting.

WPC Ramsbottom looked at her watch. If they couldn't sort us out they wouldn't be able to leave, to get real tea. I very deliberately made tea. I re-boiled the kettle, I put three teabags in three cups and mashed them down with three separate teaspoons. I added milk and stirred. There are some things you can control, said Myrtle, and others you can't.

Keifer.

Dead.

I had the same reaction as I'd had all those years ago when one of those posh boys on bicycles didn't have any dinner money, so we stripped him to his underpants and he cried. And I thought I should feel for him, but I didn't. And here it was again. That feeling of nothing.

Eventually PC Holden and WPC Ramsbottom got to drink the tea. I don't drink tea so the third cup just sat on the counter by itself. Perhaps I'd made it for Mordec, hoping he'd reappear, which he didn't. Perhaps I'd made it Keifer, although he'd never drunk much tea. The person who actually drank it was my mother.

She walked through the door about ten minutes later, looked at me, looked at the Feds and looked at the cup of tea.

'Just what I need,' she said.

9

Mordec didn't want Aunty Gina to come and I didn't want her to come either, but come she did on the train from Glasgow. The Feds set it up after they'd informed our mother of the death of her husband and she'd replied: 'Serve him right for making me walk home.'

It turned out that Mum had never actually seen anyone at the hospital. Keifer had signed her in but, as it was past 8 p.m. by then, all the day-care psychiatric nursing staff had gone home and while A&E were waiting for an on-call member of the mental health team to arrive, Mum had simply walked out of the building. Keifer, by that time, was long gone himself, he'd driven to the pub – and who could blame him after the evening he'd had – and sunk a few. Quite a few, enough to be five times over the legal limit when he crashed the car.

The most curious detail was the tree. As Mordec had said, there were no trees on the estate and it turns out that Keifer had not been heading towards Cornwall but away from it. The tree was fully fifteen miles in the opposite direction from our house.

'Where was he goin?' I asked Mordec, because Keifer had operated an entire lifetime within a ten mile radius of the estate.

'Away,' said Mordec. 'Away!'

I thought about that, I even tried to imagine what Keifer would have been feeling that night. Keifer's feelings sometimes seemed more transparent to me than my own back then, as if there was a certain simplicity to his rage. Although now I think the simplicity was mine because I never noticed Keifer's frustration, his disappointment, never saw how trapped he was. Which is why the information that I wasn't his son probably pushed him over the edge that night. Keifer was an exception among the men on the estate in that he was still living with the woman who was mother to his sons and his – as he had supposed – alone. Most of the women on Cornwall had kids with two or three different fathers, none of whom stayed long enough to watch them grow. Keifer had never spoken about what that meant to him but then he had no words either. Oh Myrtle. *If you don't have the words, you don't know what the heart feels.* Wrong. Keifer knew in that twisting red way I knew things then. And the way he felt was hurt. I saw that the night he cried in front of the TV when Mum had her own 'away'. Those tears haunted me. They made me think that the only thing Keifer actually cared about – through all the shouting and the booze and the spells inside – was her. His woman. His *dum white psy*. And then she killed it dead – killed him dead – by telling him the one triumph of his life was a lie.

So he went away too.

That tree wasn't right by the verge, I know because I got Pels to take me on his bike to have a look. The tree was twenty foot from the edge of the road and I think it would have been very difficult to hit by accident no matter how drunk you were. I didn't share this information with Mordec. He and I weren't speaking. He blamed me for Keifer's death and I accepted that blame, not because it was my fault that Keifer wasn't my father, but because I wasn't sure that – had he lived – I could have looked Keifer in the eye and told him it didn't matter, that he was the only father that counted, that Colombian Penn meant nothing to me.

You see, right from that moment in the kitchen when I first heard his name, I'd begun to fantasise about him, my Big Shotta Pops. Had him down for the warrior who, despite being located on the other side of the world, might suddenly jet in, slay the bull-headed monster and lead me out of the labyrinth.

Yeah, right.

Need, you see, can rattle your brain.

Anyway, one thing I learnt that day is that there isn't really an away. Things come after you, they pursue you.

But I was talking about Aunty Gina. She was Mum's older sister and they had never been close, but she paid the money to come from Glasgow and, for a week, she sorted things out. She took our mother back to the hospital and stayed with her until she was actually given a bed in Hillview which – it turned out – was the place where she'd previously been admitted. Aunty Gina filled in the necessary bits of paper, made funeral arrangements and did the washing-up. No one in our house ever did the washing-up until we ran out of whatever it was that was still in the sink from last time. So finding forks or spoons or glasses (especially glasses) clean in cupboards or drawers was quite a novelty. I'm not saying I preferred it, just that it was different. As was the smell of cleaning fluid.

'My sister,' Aunty Gina exclaimed, as she worked granite-faced about the flat. 'My sister!'

Mordec and I went out and let her get on with it. Mordec went to the Mill, but I didn't, I just wandered about.

'You be back at six prompt,' Aunty Gina would say, but

we never were. Even if we wanted to be back at six (there was food on the table with Aunty Gina), we'd stay out later. We weren't, we realised, used to being told what to do.

'You're out of control,' Aunty Gina said. 'You need your father to come back and sort you out.'

And – surprising even myself – I wanted Keifer to come back and sort us out. Keifer was known territory, he was landscape, the backdrop against which, against whom, for good or ill, I'd lived the whole of my life. I had never loved Keifer and he had never loved me but he was a peg in my ground. Without him, my already shaky ties to the earth seemed to loosen a notch. If they loosened any more, I was afraid I might just float away.

As for Mordec he just said: 'Hush yur mouth bout my pops. Now.' I think it was the only time he ever replied directly to anything Aunty Gina said.

Aunty Gina muttered about ingratitude but there was nothing she could do. She was afraid of Mordec, even I could see that, and I liked the way he stood with his arms folded, just watching her. He was waiting for her to say that at least she'd come, whereas no one from Keifer's family had, but she was sensible enough to hold her tongue about that.

As for me, I might have wandered about indefinitely if it hadn't been for Quin. She just knocked at our flat one afternoon when Aunty Gina was out fixing some funeral detail or other. I opened the door and there she was, the queen of my life. It was summer and she was wearing something white and tight about her breasts and she had sunlight like a jewel on her forehead. She came inside and sat on the sofa where my mother had sat with the spotty man. I sat down beside her, but not close, not close enough to touch her. She looked at me with those deep-well eyes and said:

'You alryt, Art?'

I realised then that, although I'd been punched and kicked, hit all over in fact by many different people over the years, I'd never been struck like that before. Straight in the heart. I didn't answer because I couldn't, because, up until that moment no-one – not the police, not my mother, not Mordec, not Aunty Gina – not one of them had stopped to asked how I felt, and it choked me up. Quin could have pressed me, asked again, but she didn't, just moved a little closer and put her hands over mine. Yes, she reached across the distance and touched me. Her hands were slender and cool. But I felt like I just caught on fire. I was burning and burning. I had imagined this moment so many times and now it was as much as I could do to grit my teeth to stop the tears squeezing out of my hot eyes.

Eventually she let go of me.

'You should come back to the Mill. We miss you, bubz.'

I still didn't say anything but I didn't have to, because she spoke, she filled all the gaps. She told me the news, the Mill gossip. And it seemed incomprehensible to me that, since Keifer'd died, I had avoided the one place I had any real family. Why had I done that? I didn't know, except if it was to punish myself.

'So you'll come?' she asked.

'Yes.'

'Now?'

'Yes.'

It felt good to walk out of the block with Quin beside me. It felt like a new beginning, at least it did until Quin began speaking about the Bladon boy.

'His name's Danny,' I said, 'Danny MacMahon.'

'Yes – you been following it?'

'Following what?' I'd followed nothing, not seen a paper or

heard a rumour. In fact, since the accident, I hadn't thought about the boy once.

'He's on life support.'

'What?'

'The knife went close to his heart.'

And I really didn't know that, Myrtle. I mean, how can a heart be so close to the surface of things?

'He never regained consciousness,' Quin continued. 'They think he's goin to die.'

I tried to get my mind around what that meant. But I couldn't.

'OG's stressin,' Quin continued. 'He thinks there will be bare madness. Says we should smash them before they smash us. Smash em hard. That's another reason we need you back at the Mill.'

'Were you sent?'

Quin shrugged. 'My choice.'

And I wanted to believe her, so wanted to, but there was no time for any more questions because her mobile rang. It was Elayne.

'Wot?' said Quin. And then: 'Oh my god!' She broke into a run.

'Wot, wah guan, Quin?' I was running too.

'They've nabbed OG.'

'Who have?' I had visions of the ginger-haired one with the baseball bat.

'The Feds.'

'The Feds!'

'They've arrested him.'

We were running hard now, but not so hard we didn't hear Myrtle's voice as we passed the burnt-out car.

'If you kill a boy,' she said, 'it's murder.'

'Hush yur mouth, bubz,' yelled Quin.

'They've got OG,' I said, as if Myrtle wouldn't know. 'They've taken him away.'

'Ah well,' said Myrtle.

By the time we got to the Mill, Mordec was already mounted on OG's throne. He was standing on OG's wheel, in OG's chair, addressing the assembled throng.

'Did OG jack dat boi?' he was shouting.

'No!'

'Did he merk dat boi?'

'No!'

'So why dem Saxons grass im up?'

'Saxons mans are snakes! Pussyholes!'

There was only one person not shouting with the rest, Duane, but if Mordec noticed, he just pressed on.

'What we gonna do to dem snakes?'

'We gonna rush em!'

'We gonna jack em!'

'We gonna merk em!'

'Wait!' Duane had jumped on one of the flat sandstone grind wheels. He wasn't as high as Mordec, nowhere close, but he was higher than the mob. The Crew fell silent, looked from Duane to Mordec and back again. 'OG never made you Knight Crew Star.'

Mordec looked at him pityingly: 'Nah – but you heard OG say we should smash the Saxons before they smash us. You heard him say that. All of you heard that – right?'

'Righteous,' said Borz, as if that clarified everything.

'Safe den,' said Mordec and smiled.

But Duane wasn't finished. 'But he didn't say shit about leader – what makes you leader, Mordec?'

'Dis' – and, almost out of the air, Mordec produced OG's knife. The Crew gasped, just as they'd done the first time OG had shown it them. I didn't look at the blade this time,

I looked at Mordec's face. There was a maddened exhilaration in his eyes. Then I tried to look at that knife – and his face – through your eyes, Myrtle. But I could only see with my eyes. And I still wanted that knife.

In the quiet that followed, Quin spoke, 'Only when the blade comes bloodless from a body does the power transfer. That's what OG said, what he swore. We all heard that too.'

'Yeah,' said Mordec quickly, 'true dat, but till den I'm not going to cotch here arguin bout leader while dem Saxons mans breeze into Cornwall.'

'Mordec for leader,' shouted Garvey suddenly and then flashed a look at his twin. Duane's mouth twisted.

'Mordec,' shouted Borz and then Pels and then the girls and soon the whole Mill reverberated with the sound:

'Mordec, Mordec, Mordec!'

Only four people kept their mouths closed: Duane, Quin, Elayne and me.

Mordec waved the knife above our heads. I did look at it then, to see which was brighter, the blade or his smile.

It was the smile.

I left to get some air. Outside the day was ordinary, sunshiny. Myrtle was sitting on the canal bank a little way from the car, Shaman close beside her. She beckoned to me to come and sit by her and I wanted to sit there but I was too nervy.

'They call for him now, call him king,' said Myrtle, 'but it won't always be so.'

'I don't give a dee bout this king shit,' I shouted at her. 'Who says I want to be king neways? That's just more of yur madness.'

Shaman had put his head on her lap and she stroked him behind the ears. 'It's not madness,' she said. 'But you're not ready yet. Not by a long way.'

'He died,' I said, 'did you know that, Mystic Myrt?'

'Of course he died,' Myrtle replied. 'You stabbed him at the heart.'

'Not the Saxon boi! Why do you always drag him into everything? Anyway he isn't dead.'

'Not yet,' said Myrtle.

'Keifer's dead. Way dead. Crashed his car and killed himself.'

'Yes,' said Myrtle, 'Quin told me.'

'Dat's it? Dat's all you've got to say bout it?'

'What do you want me to say about it?'

'Like maybe you're sorry, like maybe you give a shit?'

'I'm as sorry about Keifer as I am about Danny MacMahon,' Myrtle said.

I'd never hit a woman, but I was near to hitting her then. She was doing my head in with the MacMahon stuff. Sometimes I'm so calm now, here beyond the mirrors, sometimes I think I have learnt all the words and got it all sorted, and sometimes, even now, it's like Myrtle still breathes – still screams – in my ear. And I feel just like I did then – all screwed inside. Myrtle made like it was easy, but it was never easy. Never. That day she got lucky, because when I was swelling up some of the Crew came by, Pels and Borz and Mordec, with Elayne and Tanisha trailing behind them.

'But OG,' Tanisha was saying, 'they can't hold him can they, I mean they'll let him go?' She was always OG's main girl, Tanisha.

'I told you,' said Mordec, without breaking stride, 'Saxons are in a maze, dey don't know wot to think. Dey haven't got anythin on him and the Feds aint either.'

'Mainly because OG didn't do it,' mentioned Myrtle, looking at me.

'Yeah,' said Borz, 'it was Art. Our Knight Crew Star. Bruv – he smashed it.'

'So if there's a rap,' I said, 'I'll take it.'

Elayne stopped in her tracks. 'What? You mean you'd admit it? Give yourself up for him, for OG?

'Ah,' said Myrtle.

'Now dat,' said Mordec, 'would be really dum.' And he laughed.

10

Turned out that Aunty Gina had been cleaning for God. She'd hoovered and dusted so as to be able to invite the vicar home for cakes after the funeral. I don't know where she found the cakes or the vicar. The cakes were pink and white in squares and wrapped in marzipan and the vicar was pink and white too but less square. He stood at the front of the sweatingly hot crematorium chapel and told the assembled company that Keifer was 'a child of God'. I don't know how he worked that out as he'd never met Keifer and Keifer had certainly not met God. In fact, in all of his life, I don't think Keifer had been within a hundred miles of a church or a churchman.

What would our mother have done for Keifer, I wondered?

That day she did nothing but arrive on the arm of some health professional, looking like she was a guest at the funeral rather than the chief mourner. She looked meek, not meek in the quiet, beautiful way I remembered from my earliest childhood, but mute and crushed, as though whatever medication she'd been given to calm her down had punched all the stuffing out of her. She waved at me and she waved at Mordec but only like you do at acquaintances. I was glad that she arrived slightly late, just as the piped music ceased and vicar walked up front where the coffin was, because it stopped me having to say anything to her.

Words, Myrtle, words.

Aunty Gina managed to steer her (and the attendant) down to the front and then the vicar began. He told us what a good man Keifer was, because he did what true children of God did, stayed with his family.

He didn't mention Keifer's 'spells', the times he went away.

And he didn't mention the tree twenty foot from the verge.

I wished Quin was by me, but she wasn't. Do you have to be invited to a funeral? But then if Quin had come and not held me, if I'd felt her separateness, I wouldn't have been able to bear that either. I looked behind me, half expecting Myrtle instead. But of course she wasn't there. I watched my hands twist about in my lap.

Some of Keifer's friends had come though, arriving even later than Mum. There was Roy, who'd brought the blue Ford Fiesta round that fateful night, Winston, Keifer's mate from the snooker hall, and James, who he'd met in jail I think. Winston was drunk; when he tried to sit on one of the benches at the back he slid to the floor.

Aunty Gina turned around and tutted, Mum didn't notice and I wished it was over. The vicar went on – and on – and then the music started again and the coffin went through some beige curtains all by itself, on some magical sort of trolley system.

Later, as we stood outside I saw a plume of black smoke come out of the crematorium chimney and wondered if it was Keifer making that smoke. Keifer liked a smoke.

Aunty Gina invited everyone back to the flat. I say everyone, but it was just me and Mordec, Mum and the attendant, the vicar, Roy, Winston, James and a couple of neighbours.

Not much of a turn-out for a whole life. The neighbours were both women, who'd come, so they said, 'to pay their respects' . But I think they came out of curiosity, or boredom maybe, so they could gossip about what my mother wore and whether she cried.

She wore an ill-fitting but long black skirt and her perfectly ordinary white blouse. She didn't cry. But then nor did I and nor did Mordec.

And she didn't speak to anyone until she got home. 'What have you done?' she asked Aunty Gina.

'Just pushed the table against the wall for the food,' said Aunty Gina.

I'm not sure this was the answer to the question Mum was asking, but Mum did follow it up by walking around our front room as if she was negotiating someone else's house and didn't know quite where to sit or was waiting to be invited. Eventually she chose a hard chair that had been brought in from the kitchen. The attendant finally left her side to get her some tea and cake and I went to stand in the space. My mother didn't even look up at me.

Roy passed on his way to the fridge to help himself to a couple of beers. 'Guess Keifer won't be needing these where he's gone,' he said.

The men laughed.

Mordec joined them, cracked a beer himself.

'Beer, vicar?' asked Winston from his crashed-out position on the couch.

The vicar declined.

While they were cracking cans I took my mother's hand. It wasn't cool like Quin's but small and dry. I wanted to talk, I wanted to fill the gaps as Quin had done for me, but it was my mother who spoke.

'He wasn't a good man,' she said softly. 'But he tried hard.'

And it was right that her mind was on her husband, her dead husband, but I felt a huge, childish rage. She'd noticed something about Keifer! She cared about him! And I realised I would have given half my life right then for her to notice me, care about me. I squeezed her hand with a kind of desperate envy. She did not return the pressure. Then the attendant came back and said, 'Arthur, isn't it?' And I pulled away.

It was only later that I paid attention to what she'd actually said. *He wasn't a good man, but he tried hard.* Would anyone say the same of me?

Mordec's phone went. 'Garvey man, you cool.' Mordec listened intently to whatever Garvey was telling him, then he turned to face me.

'What?' I asked.

'The Bladon boi,' Mordec said, 'he jus died.' My insides gripped hot but Mordec just looked elated, exultant even. 'I'll be there in ten.' He snapped the phone off. 'You comin?' he asked me.

'Where?'

'Bruv – bare madness, dis is beef, it's arms. You backin us or not?'

'In,' I said. And no, Myrtle, I didn't have a choice. After all, as you never tired of telling me, it had been my hand on the knife.

'Ryt, let's move.'

On his way out he leant down and kissed the top of our mother's head. I'd never seen him do that before.

'See you later, Mum,' he said.

And she smiled.

Out in the street, Mordec barked into the phone: 'I said all peeps. And all of us includes Donkey.'

Danny MacMahon's life-support system had apparently been turned off at 4.20 p.m. By 4.22 Danny's cousin Spicer, who knew the O'Dair brothers, had passed the message on. By 4.30 Big Shank was gathering soldjas. Our boys operating just south of Tintagel thought there might be twenty or thirty of them preparing to come into Cornwall.

'We don't,' Mordec said, 'have much time.'

It was less than twenty-four hours since Mordec had pronounced himself leader but he seemed to have total command of geography, resources and men. While I had been busy forgetting about Danny, Mordec had clearly been busy with forward planning. As I listened to him bark orders down the phone, I tried to find, inside myself, a reaction to the death.

My reaction was that the Saxons would bang us hard.

As for Mordec, he didn't just have OG's knife, he also had a can of petrol. He picked it up from a garage on Pels' side of the Estate.

'Wot's that for?' I asked.

'Jus wait,' he said.

There wasn't enough time to brief everyone at the Mill, so Mordec instructed everyone to meet at the playground near Lee's place. This was, in any case, where the scuff was most likely to take place, not because the Saxons had been able to identify Lee as one of MacMahon's attackers, but because this was the only really open space in Cornwall, the only place big enough for a brawl and the only one with six major exits.

By the time we arrived about fifteen Crew members had gathered including Lee and Donkey, Pels, Borz, Garvey, Duane, Elayne and Tanisha. Donkey was sitting astride one of those kids' playthings on springs. It was a duck and most of the spring had been lost so he was flopping heavily back and forth and having to brace himself with his feet.

'I said *at* da play area not *in* it,' growled Mordec. 'Unless you all wanna be sitting ducks' – he paused – 'like Donkey here.'

The Crew laughed, all fired nerves, and Donkey immediately hauled himself to his large feet.

Mordec directed all the male Crew members to the garages at the corner of Summercourt and Helston Street at the southernmost side of the area. The Saxons, he said, would come from the north. Elayne and Tanisha he instructed to stay in the playground area. He wanted lookouts. 'Use the swings. You can see both Atlantic and Gorran Street from there. First decco of anythin, just stand up, that'll be the sign.'

They took up their positions. The rusty chains creaked as they began to swing and watch, swing and watch.

'Right,' said Mordec at the garages, 'Saxon mans gonna be tooled up. What we got?'

Borz had his massive fists and a baseball bat, Pels had a blue sock with billiard balls in it, Garvey and Duane had chains. Donkey had a wooden chair leg.

'Shanks?'

At least half the Crew also had knives. I was one of them. I hadn't even had to put it in my pocket before we left. It was there already. I'd taken to carrying it everywhere with me. I didn't think of it victoriously, as a knife that had already shed Saxon blood. Or even – peace, Myrtle – as a murder weapon. I just kept it by me because it made me feel safe.

As Mordec spoke more people arrived, some of them I'd only seen once or twice at the Mill. I scanned for Quin, but she wasn't there. Some of the younger ones, Tardis and LameDuck, danced on their feet like they couldn't wait, or maybe they just couldn't keep still. LameDuck had been born with one leg shorter than the other and his hopping made me think less of a duck and more of an injured gazelle separated from his herd as the lions approach. The physical edginess seemed contagious and soon there were nearly thirty Crew members jumping and twitching. Still no Quin. Where was she? I called her blowa and it was off. I was glad. I realised I didn't want her here. I didn't want her hurt.

'We won't have long,' Mordec was saying. 'Boydem could be here in five, so we need to smash dem fast and hard.'

In response, Borz mashed his bat on one of the garage doors. The crash juddered and dented the metal. It released some tension and the mob laughed. Borz made to repeat the action.

'No, save it,' said Mordec. 'Save it for the Saxons.'

'Saxon snakes!' yelled someone.

'Rush em!'

'Jack em!'

'Merk em!'

Mordec held a hand for silence. It fell immediately.

'I think dey'll come down Atlantic, could be Gorran. So we'll take Summercourt, Helston, Kelsey and Fistral, surround dem four sides, so dere mans aint jettin nowhere. Afterwards split southside, off skis through all exits. More different ways you run harder for the Feds to catch up. And bell ahead, have a yard to link. Get someone to keep da door open. You won't have time for security locks. Right – Pels, you and Borz stay here and cover dese two exits. Garvey take Kelsey, Duane, Fistral.' He picked up the can of petrol.

'Where you goin?' asked Duane.

'Bladon.' Mordec gave the can a little shake, the petrol sloshed inside. 'Gonna leave Big Shank a personal comin-home present.'

There was a pause, as if Duane was going to challenge Mordec, or at least ask if he wanted company.

But Mordec was too quick for him. 'While I'm gone, Garvey's da main man. Don't go until his signal. Then go together. Strength is surprise and numbers.'

We began to scatter behind the various leaders. I chose Duane. As he left, Mordec called behind him: 'When we've smashed, lie low, we'll link at da Mill 10 p.m. Bring juice to celebrate.'

And he didn't mean orange.

A roar went up round the ground, cut dead by a whistle from Elayne which, forgetting all instructions, she followed with a piercing yell:

'They're coming!'

11

But we would have known without Elayne's scream.

Noise was barrelling down Atlantic Avenue. The Saxons were running, thirty of them, forty of them, their feet so hard on the concrete I swear you could feel the vibrations where we were, the other side of the square. Amid their hoarse and maddened shouts was the sound of metal smashing on metal, chains swung against railings or cars or bollards. The din brought the women out onto the walkways and they began to shout too, or rather to wail, a high-pitched keen of fear.

On a balcony to our right, Lee's twenty-five-stone mother appeared.

'Sweet fucking Christ,' she said.

The first combatants to burst into the square were Hell-Razor, Tractor and the O'Dair brothers. I'd never set eyes on Tractor before, but he was easy enough to identify. He was huge – bigger than Borz – and solid as a tree. His gigantic shoulders seemed to dwarf his small, white head. His hair was pale and closely cropped and he was wearing a blazing red T-shirt. Swinging in his massive right hand was half a plank with nails hammered through at the end. HellRazor was big too, but lean and roped about with muscle, he seemed to be dancing on his feet like a boxer before the bell. I couldn't see anything in his hands, but I didn't suppose he had the name Razor for nothing. Close behind them came the O'Dair brothers, Jimbo and Mack, running pace for pace with each other, as if they were some conjoined Rambos.

They had obviously expected to find us already ranged in the space, waiting for them, but seeing no one in the square but the walkway mothers and the backs of Elayne's and Tanisha's heels (all of us were still southside, packed into Summercourt and Helston and – just – out their view), they hesitated and then came to an abrupt stop.

'Who wants some?' roared Tractor, unable to contain himself and swinging the plank above his head.

The mothers were already on their mobiles. There would only be a moment before there were sirens and we weren't ready. Duane and I hadn't made it to Fistral and Garvey's men weren't at Kelsey. If we all just ran into the square from where we were, then it would be the Saxons who would surround us. There was a breathless pause as we all waited for some miracle – Mordec to reappear with the petrol can and a solution, or Garvey to step forward and take charge. In the end, it was me who spoke.

'Half of us need to cut up westside,' I said, 'take the alleys into Atlantic, come up at them from behind, push them forward . . .'

'Into us,' roared Borz, who couldn't bear the sight of Tractor standing wielding a weapon on Cornwall turf one more moment.

'Yes,' said Garvey at last, 'My mans and Duane's westside, Pels and Borz –'

But Borz had already gone. He simply bawled out of Helston towards Tractor. More and more Saxons were pouring into the ground, but Borz made enough noise for ten men and Pels and the others were right behind him. I didn't see the first smash of baseball bat on plank, but I heard a massive crack, which I hoped was wood and not Borz's skull-bone.

We could still hear the cries as we ran like crazy dogs through the alleys that led to the back of Atlantic. I hoped I'd judged it right, that the last alley would open behind the Saxons, not in front of them. We slowed to the corner. The Avenue looked in a state of shock, like a tsunami had passed. Bewildered kids clung weeping to their mothers' skirts, grown men hid behind wheelie bins, observing the damage to their cars from a stunned distance. But the tsunami had passed, we were looking at an aftermath, the Saxons were ahead of us.

We burst into the street.

A woman screamed and Duane gave a high and wild laugh.

'We're da good guys,' he shouted.

But the Saxons didn't know that. Up ahead of us they slowed and gave some sort of triumphal yell, mistaking us for Saxon bredrins.

And then we got closer.

I shall never forget the look on the face of their back-marker when he realised exactly who was behind him.

'Knight Crew respect!' Duane yelled and the boy fell from pure shock I think.

Garvey kicked him. Lee kicked him. Even Donkey kicked him. Sorry, Myrtle, but I have to tell it like it was.

For the record, I didn't kick him, but probably only because he was pretty much down and out of it by then.

We were near to the mouth of the square, pushing the Saxons towards the play area, which, because of the slope of the land, was slightly raised from the pathways and had railings around it. At one end the drop to the concrete was a few feet, at the other, eight feet or more. Borz, who was still very much upright, was leading the assault outside the railing ring and Pels' men were on the flanks. With us behind them, the remaining Saxons had no place to go but into the ring. They were corralled. Somehow Pels had found bricks and as we pushed the Saxons forward, the Crew rained bricks down on them.

Tractor was also still on his feet and so was HellRazor, but there were men down all around them. Later I heard that HellRazor had personally decked six Crew members. One of the fallen soldjas I thought was LameDuck but I didn't have time to check because a skinny ginger kid suddenly broke from the pack and started towards us. He was swinging a bicycle chain, a long one, mountain bike probably, which meant his reach would be much longer than mine. But in any case, there was a soldja ahead of me, Lee, and he swung the chain at his head. Lee ducked but not fast enough and it caught him on the shoulder. He cried out and staggered backwards. Ginger lunged forward, chain whirling again and then, at exactly the same time I recognised him, he recognised Lee.

'It's him,' Ginger yelled. 'Da boi wot jukked Danny!'

The chain hung suspended in mid-air as forty Saxon faces seemed to turn and look our way.

Lee, who was still staggering, finally lost his footing and sprawled to the ground, his head towards Ginger's already moving right boot.

'No,' I yelled. 'It was me. I did it. I merked Danny Mac-Mahon.'

There was nothing heroic in this, no part of me was owning up, I just said what I said instinctively, to deflect that boot from Lee's head. And deflect it it did – Ginger stopped in his tracks, turned from Lee to me. Which is when, for the first time, I saw his eyes. They were beautiful eyes, Myrtle, the colour of the canal in winter, a deep, steely grey.

Which is when what I had said came back to me as if across a great distance. *I merked Danny MacMahon.*

I merked him.

Me.

It was a shock.

Meanwhile Ginger was still coming, those steely grey eyes all chopped up with anger.

'You,' he said, 'are a dead man walkin.'

The chain had changed direction, it was swaying, jittering towards me. I had my knife out, Myrtle, he was near enough for me to go under his guard. His arm was raised and his heart exposed. It was him or me, Myrtle, and less than three seconds to decide.

Which is when the sirens went off.

And also the fireball.

Turned out that Mordec hadn't gone to Bladon after all, he'd seen what was going down and tracked back round the alleys, just like us. The petrol can had a lighted rag in its throat and he arced it perfectly to land behind our enemies where it exploded in a plume of ginger flame.

I split with Donkey; my place was north of the square and his was south, so it made sense. The Feds were screaming down Atlantic, which was the widest of the narrow roads into the estate, and what with that and the confusion and the fireball the Saxons weren't paying much attention to us. They didn't even bother when we stopped to pick up fallen soldjas. It was LameDuck who'd gone down in the playground and also Tardis, both felled by HellRazor. I didn't know Tardis well, but I knew he'd been named that because his pin-sized head was large inside with *Dr Who* trivia and that made me smile. I lifted his saggy body, carried the weight of him, while Donkey took charge of LameDuck. LameDuck squealed when Donkey hefted him on account of the razor wounds to his upper torso. Tardis was also bleeding from a series of small cuts to his face, but both of them were more frightened than hurt and after a street or two we put them down and made them do their own running.

Donkey lived with his mother, who was out that afternoon, so we just used her flat to wash and bandage up and then drank some of her brandy. After an hour or two Tardis vomited, though it might have been because HellRazor'd also punched him in the head and that, I'd learnt, can make you throw up later anyway.

Garvey called to ask if we had any casualties and tell us that not a single Crew member had been arrested. Lee's mother had, it appeared, been magnificent. She'd hauled herself down to the playground, sat on fallen Saxons until the Feds arrived and then threatened to prosecute everything that moved north of Tintagel. For the Cornwall boys, she'd said, it had been self-defence. You'd defend yourself if someone was coming at you with a six-foot plank, wouldn't you? Apparently even the Feds had had to agree to that.

'How bout yur end? Any mans down?' I asked Garvey.

'Bruises. Bit of banging. Bit of blood. Nuthin serious.'

'And the Saxons?'

Garvey laughed. 'I don't think dey'll be coming back into Cornwall anytime soon. See you 10 p.m. We're gonna blast some serious tunes.' He clicked off.

I paced a little. There was something else on my mind.

Donkey watched me pacing. 'Shouldn't of said jack,' he said. 'Should ya? Bout you being da one who merked Mac-Mahon.'

I thought of Lee's head on the concrete, so close to Ginger's boot.

'I mean, now dey know who to look for,' Donkey continued.

'Thanks, Donkey.' Not such a donkey after all. We were going to have to find a new name for him.

'Although dat boi,' Donkey went on, 'the ginger one, the one wot spotted you, he might not have made it.'

I could have wished for that but I didn't because when I tried to imagine the fireball what I actually saw were those choppy grey eyes.

Myrtle was right about eyes, as she was about almost everything. Eyes make a difference.

'The other upside,' concluded our philosopher, 'is dat the Feds'll have to let OG go.'

That was something I hadn't thought of and I realised then that I didn't really want OG back again. Before that day I'd thought power was a harder fist or a bigger boot. I hadn't understood it could be thinking faster than everyone else, acting faster, as I had thought and acted faster than Garvey. And there was another thing, the feeling of men just falling in behind you as Duane's men had done when they followed me down the alleys. *You could be a leader, Art.*

Was that the beginning of it?

I knew then that I needed to go to the Mill, but I had to wait until the Feds finished their house-to-house. Or, in Cornwall's case, apartment-to-shitty-apartment. I wondered if the pencil-sharpener mouthed Fed who'd come to our place to tell us about Keifer was now knocking on other doors, asking another set of questions to which he'd never get any answers. It was three hours before Garvey phoned the all-clear. I decided to go to the Mill via home, pick up any beer that Winston had missed.

When I put the key in the lock I half-expected to open the door on the funeral party still in full swing, the vicar still

93

drinking tea, Winston passed out on the sofa, my mother staring into space and the attendant eating iced cakes and Aunty Gina tutting. But there was nothing, not a sound in the house, no party, no mother, no Mordec even.

Everywhere was clean and tidy, every crumb swept from the floor and the bins into which those crumbs must have been swept all emptied and the bin-bags replaced with fresh white liners, waiting for whatever new rubbish might come their way. The table had been pushed back against the wall where it belonged and in the middle of the table there was a note in Aunty Gina's black hand. It read:

Dear Mordecai and Arthur
    I think I have done what it is possible to have done in this house, which is no more than my duty. I have done it without a word of thanks from your mother or you or indeed anyone. I do not know what could possibly have been of more importance to you both this afternoon than your father's wake but let that pass too. I have had to return early to Glasgow to discharge obligations to my own father, your grandfather Rory, a grandfather you and your mother have never thought to visit. I do not expect making the journey south again.
    Your Aunt Gina.
    ps I have left eggs and milk in the fridge.

There were also leftover sandwiches in the fridge and I had something limp with ham in while I re-read the note. I focused on Grandfather Rory. I hadn't even known his name.

Rory – the grandfather I didn't know.
Penn – the father I didn't know.

Keifer – the father I did know but who was gone.

It made me think about my mother and all the things – the people – she'd lost too. Her sister. Her father. Gina. Rory. How had it happened? Had they just fallen out? Or had it just been too far, too long a journey for her to undertake, a ticket for which she simply had no money? Or was she ashamed of her new life, her unemployed Jamaican husband, her children, her unkempt house or – when she was sane – her madness?

Or perhaps the split, the distance was deliberate. Perhaps, like me, my mother had spent her childhood years planning to escape. Grandfather Rory and sister Gina belonged together, she did not. And so she'd planned her getaway, planned a new life down south, where she could be whoever she dreamed. And then she'd ended up here. With Keifer. With us. And all her stories, her wise women and her strong heroes had spun away from her.

Would it be the same for me?

There was one, and only one, can of beer left in the fridge. I saluted Winston's restraint, cracked it open and went to sit at the table where Keifer used to sit. It had been a long day.

Oh Myrtle. If only I'd known what was still to come.

12

It began well enough.

I was the first to the Mill, at least the first of the combatants, arriving half an hour before Mordec's appointed time. Quin was already there, sitting on the island side of the canal, talking with Myrtle as if neither had a care in the world. Shaman lay between them and Quin was idly stroking his black head which made me realise that – usually – he only let Myrtle touch him.

'Yur blowa's off,' I said to Quin, interrupting them.

Quin lifted that beautiful, midnight head of hers. 'Mmm?' Clearly the phone wasn't important, she'd let it run out of credit, of charge, it didn't matter. 'Oh, Art. How was the funeral?'

It was clear then that she knew nothing about Danny MacMahon's life-support machine being switched off, nothing about the scuff. And, suddenly, I thought I'd keep it that way, because if I began talking I'd have to tell her about the plume of ginger flames and those canal-grey eyes. And maybe I didn't want to tell her, at least not in front of Myrtle.

'It was a good end,' I said, meaning Keifer's, and I gave some details about the funeral, making it sound as if many family and friends had gathered to say goodbye to the man who was (and wasn't) my father. Why did I lie? Perhaps I just wanted something good for Keifer because, as my mother said, he had tried hard. Or perhaps, I was just speaking about myself, wanting for Keifer what I'd want for myself in the same circumstance, a crematorium chapel full to bursting with people come to pay tribute.

There was a silence and then Myrtle, moving cloths and ivy about her, said: 'When it's my time to go –'

'You're not goin to go, bubz,' Quin interrupted. 'Not for time.'

Myrtle looked at her. 'I'm not afraid of dying, Quin. It comes to us all. As soon as we are born we are dying.' And then she turned her gaze on me. 'It's what we do in our allotted time that matters. It's who and how we love.'

Then she reached inside the voluminous folds of her robes and extracted her soft, leather-bound book. 'So when it's my time,' she began again, 'I want you to have this, Art.'

'Is it worth much, then?' I asked. It was a stupid thing to say, but I said it because I couldn't remember the last time anyone gave me a gift. Even on my birthdays I never got gifts. So it made me want to cry and I couldn't have Quin seeing that.

'It's nothing at all,' Myrtle said, smiling, 'and everything I have.' She tucked the book away again. Shaman nudged up against her. 'Except Shaman,' added Myrtle affectionately, 'and he'll chose his own master.'

If I'd thought to say thank you I didn't have the time because that was when the first shouts of jubilation came across the bridge and Mordec appeared at the head of a riotous number of Crew members. They were waving bottles of vodka like spears above their heads. Some, like Donkey, were slewing towards us, obviously drunk already, and others, like Pels and Borz, just seemed large with excitement. Part of me wished I was slewing over that bridge in the thick of that gang. There's not a lot of time for thinking in a gang.

'What did we do bois?' sang Mordec.

'We rushed em!'

'We jacked em!'

'We merked em!'

The Crew roared and cheered.

Quin stood up, looked first at me and then at the advancing figure of Mordec.

'What happened?' she asked. 'What's going on?'

When he got to the island side, our side, of the bridge Mordec came to a halt.

'You didn't tell her?' he asked me, incredulous. Mordec was not drunk.

I said nothing.

'Knight Crew smashed it, dat's wot,' Mordec said. 'Dem mans got rushed, rushed with flames, an' – he laughed out loud – 'dem mans left were taken by Feds, put in pen!' He mimed the bars of a jail.

'Mordec, Knight Crew Star!' yelled the bois.

'And now it's party time. Big-time party time. Lay it out bois.'

And they laid it out there on the island bank, vodka and beer and cider and food too. Duane and Garvey had arms full of kebabs, Tanisha had burgers and hot dogs and every one of the yungas seemed to have chips and sachets of tomato sauce. While they were unloading the haul, Borz brought out the old Mill jambox and turned it up real loud and argued with whoever was nearest about what music was the most triumphally appropriate. Meanwhile, Pels gathered a few old crates, stamped on them and lit a fire, and someone else fetched some stubs of candles from OG's wheel and lit those too. In the gathering summer dark the lights reflected in the water and the canal side looked spookily beautiful. Mordec didn't take part in these proceedings, just sat on a mound of grass, slightly higher than everyone else, and watched. When the feast was finally ready he jumped to his feet and shouted 'Knight Crew respect!' as though it was the grace before the meal.

Thirty or forty raised fists responded in salute: closed, open, closed.

'Knight Crew, Knight Crew, Knight Crew!' Louder than the music.

Then Garvey shouted, 'Mordec!' And the Crew took up that refrain too:

'Mordec, Mordec, Mordec!' Louder still.

I looked at Mordec and Myrtle looked at me, I could feel her eyes on my face.

The Crew fell upon the food then, some eating hungrily, others tossing sausages in Shaman's direction, which Shaman eyed but only got up to eat when Myrtle touched his collar and gave him permission.

As the drink flowed, Crew members recounted the stories of the night, who they'd fought and who'd been felled.

'That Tractor,' yelled someone.

'More like a combine harvester!'

'Did you see his fists?'

'Did you see his brain?' Pels called. 'Thicker than da plank he was carrying!'

The bois roared with laughter.

'But Borz mashed him, he squealed like a baby!'

'And eyeball this hero!' Someone, Garvey I think it was, pushed Tardis forward into the light of the fire. 'This soldja took nine slashes, nine.' He pointed at the razor cuts on the boy's face, 'and he still came back for more.'

'Tardis – yunga star!' they called and hit him so hard on the back he staggered to the earth.

Myrtle was sitting some way off from the fire, keeping her

own counsel. It was Quin of course who noticed she wasn't eating either and went to offer her something.

'No,' said Myrtle. 'Thank you. I'm not hungry.'

Mordec, who was close enough to hear the exchange, picked some lettuce out of the pitta pocket of his kebab. 'Get some of dis,' he said, 'you'd like dis, baglady.'

Myrtle declined.

Mordec flicked the lettuce away. 'You won't get to be a fighter if you don't eat proper,' said Mordec and laughed.

'I don't want to be a fighter,' said Myrtle.

'You should of seen Mordec's petrol bomb,' said Pels.

'It was beautiful,' Garvey added. 'Beautiful. Saxon mans went up like lil white matches, their heads exploding. Pouf, pouf, pouf!'

'Knight Crew Star,' shouted Donkey. 'Mordec, Knight Crew Star!' And other voices joined in, lifting Mordec's name into the gathering night.

Mordec smiled.

'You're no star,' said Myrtle, and though she was still sitting, she seemed to have come closer to the group, her mud face lit by the fire.

Mordec's smile disappeared. 'What?' he said.

'What honour,' said Myrtle, 'what courage is there in standing somewhere safe and lobbing a can of petrol at an enemy you're not even close enough to see?'

Mordec stood up and even the drunkest and rowdiest of the yungas fell silent. Someone even turned the music down.

'What you sayin, baglady?' He was four or five paces away from her, but his shadow lay across the ground between them.

'I'm saying that if you must fight for no reason –'

'No reason,' interrupted Mordec. 'They were on our turf, my turf. Uninvited. Dat's provocation.'

'If you must fight,' continued Myrtle, closing her cloths tight about her, 'then at least have the courage to get close, look your enemy in the eye.'

'Close?' said Mordec. He drew OG's great Buck knife from his pocket and began to cross the small distance between them. His shadow engulfed her. 'How close?'

Shaman lifted his head and growled.

Myrtle sat unflinching. 'Close enough to see your enemy's soul.'

'Dis do?' Mordec stopped right in front of her, towering, knife pointed.

'No.' Myrtle stood up then too, and Shaman moved with her, as if he was just an extension of her. I couldn't see her feet, but I felt that she had planted them deep in the earth. 'If you kill,' she said, 'you should know exactly what and who you kill.'

She was so much smaller than Mordec but she grew tall in that moment as she lifted her face to his. Beside her the great black dog shook and rippled, but Myrtle shushed him. 'Otherwise,' Myrtle said, her face almost touching Mordec's, 'you are nothing but a coward.'

The Crew held a collective breath.

'You have one sec,' said Mordec, 'to take that back.'

'No,' said Myrtle. 'It's the truth. You are a coward, Mordec.'

The knife moved faster than the dog, the great steel point of it tearing through Myrtle's robes until it was buried up to the hilt. Only when Myrtle began to fall did the dog seem released, letting fly and roaring at Mordec's throat. The speed and ferocity of the attack knocked Mordec to the ground and I thought the dog would kill Mordec there and then, but he did not, just leapt away again to stand over his fallen mistress. No one else had moved, it was all too fast, and in any case we were mesmerised by the dog. I could see the handle of the knife still protruding from Myrtle's clothing and I half-expected the dog to take it in his teeth and pull it free, but something very much stranger happened. Shaman put his muzzle to his mistress's face, his black eyes on hers, and, as all the Crew were held there as if under some spell, Myrtle's soul left her body. Her tattered clothes seemed to suck inwards as though the old woman had breathed in a huge breath and was holding it, and when she expelled that breath, I swear it came not out of her mouth but out of her eyes, like bright smoke rising. But it didn't ascend to any heaven, no, it just entered the black eyes of the dog. He sucked in her soul and then he stood over her body like some guard dog from hell.

Quin was the first to be able to talk. 'Myrtle,' she said, but the heap of cloths was quite still. 'Bubz,' she cried out, 'bubz!'

The cloths didn't move, Shaman didn't move.

Mordec, who realised he was not hurt, only stunned, began to pull himself to his feet.

'What are you on?' Quin screamed at him. 'Look what you've done!'

It was then that I saw two things simultaneously, Mordec moving towards Myrtle, his hand outstretched towards the hilt of the knife, as if he would pull it from her body, and also the muscles of the dog rippling across his body and his haunches crouching and his eyes ablaze once more as he began to spring for a second time at Mordec.

And I knew I could have stopped it, prevented that deadly flight. All I had to do was click my tongue against the roof of my mouth, as Myrtle had so often done, 'Tch, Shaman, tch', and then the dog would have been still, and many things that later happened would not have happened.

But I was full of anger and I let the dog jump.

This time he made for Mordec's face, sank his teeth into my brother's right cheek, gouging his eye. Mordec screamed in pain and only then did I call to the dog, who came meekly to sit at my heels. Later, Quin tried to comfort me, said that I couldn't have known that the dog would obey me so easily. But I did know. Myrtle chose me and Shaman, who I came to understand was indivisible from his mistress, chose me too. No, it was not the dog I couldn't control that day, but my fury.

Mordec was still writhing on the ground. But I didn't care. He had killed Myrtle. Killed that mystical, mystifying, rugged old woman. I never felt closer to her than in that moment. I knew she was dead for I had seen her soul rising, but it was agony to me to see the knife still in her. I felt the sharpness of the blade as though it pierced my own heart. I put my back to Mordec, went to her and pulled the knife out. Shaman never moved.

'Da shank,' someone shouted, I think it was Duane, 'dere's no blood on da shank!'

I hadn't looked at the blade until that moment, my eyes had been on Myrtle's face, the lined beauty of it. But he was right, the blade was a shining strip of clean metal.

'Art for Knight Crew Star,' someone shouted. 'Art for leader!'

And then another voice joined in, hoarse and strange. 'Be it as it is written'. It was like an echo of Myrtle's voice only deeper and throatier and, to this day, I believe it was the dog.

13

If we had dialled 999 then Lance would never have come into our lives. But I made the decision not to call an ambulance for Mordec, partly because it would never have been able to get to the canal bank and partly because we had a dead body to consider. So I made Duane and Garvey carry Mordec themselves, his arms around their shoulders, his blood on their cheeks. Once they got to the main street, I said, they could get a cab to the hospital; it was clear that Mordec needed urgent medical attention and I persuaded them it would be quicker that way. So they went and Lance came. I'll tell that story later, I only mention it here because sometimes I think Lance was the second of Myrtle's gifts to me that night. Only I wasn't to be the only recipient of this gift – he was also given to Quin.

After Duane and Garvey left, I detailed Donkey to go and get a clean white sheet in which to wrap Myrtle, the rest of the Crew I sent home. All except Quin. Everyone did as instructed without murmur. Maybe they obeyed me because of the prophecy, maybe because they saw me take that great knife and put it in my pocket, maybe because the black dog stood with his dripping red jaws beside me. Or perhaps it was because I was the first to step forward, I just assumed command.

Once Donkey had brought the sheet I sent him away too.

I had an urgent need to be alone with Quin. When she'd seen the bloodless knife, Quin's breast had filled with hope and she hadn't been able to stop herself rushing to Myrtle as if, by lifting her head onto her lap and whispering to her, she could bring the old woman back. It took all the time that Donkey was away for her to believe the truth. Myrtle was gone.

'How can it be?' Quin sobbed. She had her hands over the rent in Myrtle's clothes as if she was keeping a wound closed and only shifted her position when I came to sit beside her, which is when Myrtle's book fell to the ground. I picked it up. There was a cut in the soft leather of the cover, the edges of it pushed up like lips in a kiss, and the paper beneath, for maybe twenty pages or so, was also pierced through.

'It was the book,' I said. 'The book that saved her from the blow.'

'Saved her?' wailed Quin. 'Saved her! So how come she's dead?'

I didn't have an answer for that. Not then, not now. A medical person might claim shock and a heart attack, but nothing was ever quite so simple, so rational, with Myrtle.

'Broken heart,' I offered then. 'Because we weren't – I wasn't – good enough. And she gave a shit.'

'No,' said Quin at once. 'No. Myrtle never gave up on anythin, anyone. She was the strongest person I ever knew. Stronger than OG, stronger than Mordec, stronger' – she glared at me – 'than you.'

'Then maybe she chose to go,' I said. 'Maybe she chose this time and this place.' I was sounding madder than my mother but Quin's raging eyes grew softer.

'Did you do that, Myrtle?' said Quin, cradling the old woman's grizzled head. 'Did you, bubz?'

Shaman crept between us then, lay his head close to

Myrtle's on the edge of Quin's lap, and Quin didn't push him away, in fact she stretched out a hand to touch him, because, I think, he was alive, and she needed to feel that life. 'Why did she do it?' Quin said to the dog. 'What did she mean by it, Shaman?'

'Do things have to have meaning?' I heard myself saying.

'This does,' said Quin. 'Everything Myrtle ever did had meaning. So if she chose this, it was as a message. Probly even wrote about it in that blodclaut book. Why don't you look, Art!' And she almost flung the book at me.

Of course she was upset – who wouldn't have been – but I think she was also jealous. Quin had loved and tended Myrtle and Myrtle had left me the only thing she had to leave – the book. But I didn't really want the book, there had never been any miracles in my life and I didn't expect one now. 'There are some things you can control,' that's what Myrtle had said, 'and some things you can't.' But I did want to calm Quin, her agitation was painful to me, so I untied the leather strings. The book fell open at the page to which it had been pierced.

I stared.

'What does it say?' asked Quin.

I had been wrong to think that all the pages in the book were densely written, for here was another one, not unlike the page where Myrtle had written the prophecy, that was blank. Or almost blank. There were two words written at the top.

'The Future,' I said aloud. 'It says *The Future* and it's underlined.'

'There,' said Quin, and she said it with the same emphasis as Myrtle had said 'exactly' that night we were discussing the riddles of the universe.

'There what?' I asked.

'You have to make it,' Quin said.

'What?'

'The future! You're to be king – didn't anythin she said ever mean shit to you?'

'Hang about –'

'No bubz, you hang about – it's time, Art, time!'

'For what?'

'For things to change.' And then Quin stood up, finishing the conversation like Myrtle used to, right in the middle of things. 'But now I need to wash her,' Quin continued, 'honour her.'

I'd never heard her use that word before. Honour. Your word, Myrtle.

'Before I, before we . . .' Quin nodded at the river and then she saw my face. 'Well, it *is* what you got the sheet for, yes? So we can wrap her, put her in the water? We can't bury her. She'd suffocate. She wouldn't be free.'

And Quin, like Myrtle, was right of course, right about the river as she was about many things.

'Yes,' I said, 'of course.' And I got up to help her with the preparations but she pushed me away.

'Myrtle wouldn't like you to see her body,' she said. 'Not butt-naked. I'm a girl. It's different. Let me?'

And I let her. Went to sit at a distance with the book while Quin drew water and began to unfold the many cloths that swathed Myrtle's body. It would have been wrong, I'm sure, for me to have seen – or touched – Myrtle's nakedness, but I wanted to be close to Myrtle that night, as well as to Quin. It would have soothed me to wash her limbs, to do her some service, to give something, no matter how small, back to this woman who, I realised then, had opened my eyes on a different world. And yes, I'd laughed at her, along with the others, and yes, I'd fought her and hated her too sometimes. But she had never hated me. She had always looked at me as if I could be better than myself.

So I sat on the ground with Shaman and studied the book, or rather I looked at that one blank page. There was enough to be thinking about under that heading alone. The Future. It was not something that I'd ever really considered before, I'd existed pretty much entirely in the present. It was enough, I'd thought, simply to get through the day. It was enough to survive. The future – that was for other people.

The Future.

Underlined.

I took Myrtle's pencil and I wrote QUIN on that page and then, beneath it, the word PEACE. I didn't really know what peace I was really talking about then, peace between the Crew and the Saxons, or peace in my own heart, and perhaps it didn't matter because they were probably part of the same thing. Then I took the great Buck knife out of my pocket. It was heavy in my hand. I'd wanted it for so long, dreamt about what it would bring me. Power. Status. Safety.

And here it was in my fingers – the instrument of Myrtle's death.

I put it away. It had come clean from Myrtle and maybe that was a message too. That I had to keep it clean. For her. For the future.

And yet on that page, I wrote *Quin* first. If I'd put peace first, there might have been a different outcome.

Quin was singing. She'd not only stripped the body but stripped herself, using her own white T-shirt as a cloth to wipe Myrtle's face. I was fifty yards or more away but the outline of her breasts beneath her tight vest were painfully clear to me. She leant over her work, singing and using water from the canal. Those full breasts hung above that shrivelled body. Occasionally she'd break off from her labours to stoke the fire as if she was afraid that Myrtle might get cold. And still she sang. It wasn't one of our songs, not some hardcore boombox stuff, it was an African-sounding thing, deep and mellow. It entered you under the ribcage and filled you up with a kind of sorrowful joy.

For as long as I could, I let Quin be, for I knew that she was doing what she needed to do and that that thing was between her and Myrtle alone. But I'd never wanted to hold someone so much in all of my life. And I knew then why I'd hung back for so long – because I'd been afraid. Because I knew that rejection by her, above all the other rejections of my life, was impossible. That it would kill me. But now, as I watched her finally wrap the body in the sheet that Donkey had brought, I knew the time had come. I crossed the divide.

She had left the sheet open around Myrtle's face and the old woman looked as though she had entered a deep, soft sleep. There was even the trace of a smile, or so I thought, about her mouth.

'Quin,' I said, 'Quin.'

She was still singing, though, closer too, it sounded like sobbing and her cheeks were wet.

I took her then, took her in my arms and pressed my lips over hers as if I could take some of the sorrow and that joy in my mouth. She gave herself to me, folded into me, all arms and softness and wanting and no division at all, and that lit something in both of us and we were mad and passionate for a while, tumbling on the earth beside the canal that had been Myrtle's earth and under the stars that had been her stars.

14

We slept that night, but Shaman didn't, he stood guard over the three of us until we woke with the morning dew on us.

We had wanted to put Myrtle in the river and not wanted to. Because it was so final. So there she was, still lying in the sheet beside us.

'At least we gave her the sheet,' said Quin and she laughed because otherwise I think she might have cried again.

I touched Myrtle then, just her weathered face, and she was cold and that made it easier to believe her soul had really gone.

'If you remember someone, then they don't really die,' Quin said. 'Do they?'

And in Shaman's black eyes I thought I saw the silhouette of Danny MacMahon. And that's how it came to be with Danny after Myrtle died, that I began to see him when he wasn't there.

'No,' I said, 'they don't.'

We talked about how we would weight Myrtle's body. There was plenty of rubble around the Mill, but Quin said we should send her off with her own things about her.

'Like the ancient Egyptians,' said Quin. 'We learnt that in primary. People need their own things for the afterlife.'

And I didn't ask 'What afterlife?' because I wanted to

believe it then too, that Myrtle had gone to some higher, some better place. I didn't know then what I know now about the water and the mirrors. So I just said: 'So you think she needs her pink rubber glove? And the Value bacon packet?'

Quin laughed again. It was magical to hear her laugh.

In the end we just chose the heavier things. We tied Myrtle's flattened oil-drum bed to her, and the cement-encrusted tape-dispenser and even the half office chair. She was thin, Myrtle, without her coverings she seemed like some fragile bird. She wouldn't take much weighting.

When she was ready, Quin said: 'I can't close the sheet over her face. You do it, bubz.'

And I did. Only as soon as I'd done it I wanted to flip the sheet open again, so I could see her one last time. But I kept my arms by my sides because otherwise I'd have been opening and closing that sheet for ever.

Together we lifted her to the place where the river was wildest and we knew the tide would take her. We slipped her in and the sheet billowed a bit about her and I was afraid for a moment that it would all unwrap, and she would be naked in front of me after all. But Quin and I had tied tight knots and the oil drum and the office chair began to drag her – oh so slowly – down. We stood and watched her go and there were bubbles, like in the movies, and I was glad because it made it all seem un-real and you could believe for a minute that everything that had happened, hadn't happened. And then Shaman, who had stood by us all this while, suddenly opened his huge mouth and yowled. It was a terrifying, un-earthly sound, but I was glad of it, because it put the truth back in my body and I knew that if he hadn't cried out, then I would have had to.

I would have howled like an animal. No words, you see Myrtle. No words! And I realise I've talked too much about

Quin, about how your death finally brought us together, because we had to fill the gap your going had left and we only had each other to do it. I mistook that gap for love, but it wasn't that, or not only that: no, what I realised that night, that extraordinary night and the morning that followed, was that you were the first person, Myrtle, who ever spoke to the emptiness in me, who thought I had a choice, a future. That I could be a leader, a king.

And also that I could be good.

Me.

Good.

I've done it again, talked about myself when I wanted to talk about you, the quality of your specialness. How you could make a rubbish dump into a place of stars or shine a light into a dark soul and find something bright in the chaos. How you gave hope where there wasn't any.

Gifts, Myrtle.

And what did I give in return? Nothing, not even the simple things. I didn't bring you food, as Quin did, or comfort of any sort. I never even asked about your life, never cared to know what it was that had brought you to the edge of our canal. Quin asked those questions and I was glad – so glad – to know later what she had found out. But I'm getting ahead of myself again. All I knew then, as your body sank, Myrtle, was that Quin was right. If I didn't change, if I didn't write my own future, then you would have died for nothing.

We went to the Mill in silence, Quin and Shaman and me, and we ate bread with mould round it for breakfast as that was all we could find while we waited for the others to turn up as we knew they would. Mordec had been kept overnight in hospital, Duane had phoned that message through, but we didn't know the rest of the story until he and Garvey arrived in person.

The story was a long one. Halfway to the road by Tesco's, Mordec had lost consciousness.

'But he never stopped bleedin,' Duane said. 'Soaked my shirt through. My nice blue shirt gone Saxon red.'

The gathering Crew members laughed.

The journey by car from Tesco's to the nearest hospital was only fifteen minutes but it had taken the three of them the best part of an hour.

'Bastards wouldn't stop, would they?'

'We flagged cabs like they was goin out of fashion. Half of them red-necks didn't stop and those that did – they took one look at Mordec and decided to dash. They thought their cab was worth more than his life.'

'So what happened?' asked Quin.

'Knight in shinin armour,' said Garvey.

'White knight in shinin armour,' said Duane.

And that knight was Lance. He'd been coming out of the supermarket with his father when he'd seen the black boys try, and fail, to secure a cab, and he'd come over to see if he could help.

'What sort of boy?' asked Quin.

'White boy, I told you,' said Duane. 'A cracker, a Milky Bar Kid.'

'A fraggle,' said Garvey. 'Don't know wot's his business and wot isn't.'

'But he helped,' I said, 'he got Mordec to the hospital?'

'Righteous. Got his pops to help an all, they lifted our boy into the car, blood or no blood. Told his pops the blood don't matter. It can be washed off.'

'At the hospital,' continued Garvey, 'Feds were everywhere. Don't make no distinctions, hospitals, Crew, Saxons, they take all-comers, black, white, green. There were bare Saxons and even more boydem, so we had to jet.'

'But not before white knight takes our number,' said Duane.

'You let some any next brere take yur digits?'

'Only for medical purposes,' said Duane and he extracted his mobile from his pocket. 'Take a look at this.'

On his screen there was a text message which read: *Prognosis gd but eyelid 2 swollen 4 full investigation 2nite. M sedated. specialist eye surgeon will visit am.*

Borz had arrived and craned over the phone: 'Prognosis?' he asked, 'Wot's dat?'

'Sedated,' said Duane. 'That's da bit you gotta get hold of Borz, Mordec sedated!'

'Give it ten minutes,' said Garvey. 'Give it five. You can't keep a Knight Crew Star sedated for long. He'll be back soon enough.' He eyed up Shaman. 'Merk the dog and get things back to normal.'

'No,' I said, 'that's not how things are goin to be.'

And, though I didn't command him, Shaman moved to stand at my side.

'Wot?' said Garvey and then, 'Wot you sayin?'

'I'm sayin, Garvey, that if – when – Mordec returns, he comes on my terms.'

'Art's top dog now,' Quin said quickly. Already we were a team of two. 'That's what OG pledged when he signed in blood, whoever drew out the shank clean from a body, he would be king. You all saw it, heard it, and it's written in Myrtle's book. Show them, Art.'

'Wot!' Garvey exclaimed. 'Dat trailor-trash had been loops for time! You can't be serious.'

'Besides,' I added, drawing the Buck knife from my pocket, 'anyone who wants to kill the dog, will have to merk me first.'

There was a silence in which the only thing that moved

was Shaman's head as he swung it this way and that, as if looking for challengers.

Then Duane spoke, as if he was thinking out loud: 'It was Art who cornered da Saxons, Art's idea to use Atlantic and Art who took charge last night.' He paused. 'I say Art for Knight Crew Star. Knight Crew respect.' And he made the salute: closed fist, open hand, closed fist.

Quin was the first to join him. 'In front of you all,' she cried, 'I swear as OG swore and pledge my loyalty to Art and Art alone. If I ever betray that pledge then take that knife, Art, and do with me as you will.'

I write these words down exactly as Quin said them, because they were so strange. They were words that you might have used, Myrtle, and words which would later be used to bring down all that Quin and I were to build. But at the time, nobody even laughed, it was as though Quin's passion brought the Crew to a silence. And I see now what an ally she was, how strong, how intelligent, how quick to spot opportunities. Which is why the throne was never mine unless it was hers also.

As if compelled by her, one by one, the other Crew members, beginning with Duane, began swearing loyalty to me.

Only Garvey held back.

'You gonna sit in dat place?' he challenged me, pointing at the chair lashed to the high wheel. 'OG's place, Mordec's place?'

Thirty faces lifted toward me.

'No,' I said. 'I am goin to sit here, by this stone table.' I motioned to the huge grinding stone that lay on the floor between us. A round of sandstone as broad as OG's wheel had been high. 'And those who have sworn loyalty to me, to the Crew, the best of them, they will sit here beside me.'

I drew up a pallet and sat down by the stone, daring them. How did the idea of that round table come into my head? Perhaps I saw some outline of the heroic, some tale of my mother's with some other knights. Perhaps it was Shaman who guided me, who left my side briefly to stand by the place where I was now sitting. Maybe it was Garvey who showed me the way, the intensity of his anger and his need – I knew what it was like to want power because I had looked at Mordec and wanted it. On OG's wheel there was only room for one man, around my sandstone wheel twelve or more Crew members could gather. Yes, it was certainly an offering to Garvey who, I knew, had become – or could become – my enemy. It was also a reaction to the fierce nod of Quin's head which seemed to say: *One more friend is one less enemy*. Later I found that thought written in Myrtle's book, written a hundred times on a single page, as though the idea had been an obsession. So you were breathing on Quin that day too, weren't you, Myrtle?

'Take a place, Borz,' I said. 'Borz,' I announced to the Crew, 'who led the charge against the Saxons.'

A cheer went up as Borz came forward.

'And you Pels, and Duane, soldjas of that fight, and Quin too.'

'Quin?' demanded Garvey. 'Wot Saxon did she mash?'

'There are those I want about me who are courageous,' I said, 'and those who are wise. Quin is wise. Myrtle trusted Quin and I trust her also.'

'You're chattin shit,' said Garvey.

'The strong don't always use force, Garvey,' I said.

The place I made for Quin was at my right-hand side, so she would always be near me, so they would see us paired together.

'You're chattin breeze,' Garvey raged.

But I was only using your words Myrtle and the memory of my mother's whispers.

Quin took up a seat alongside the men.

'I elect Donkey also,' I continued.

'Donkey's a nuthin,' screamed Garvey. 'Who's Donkey? Donkey's jus a joey!'

'Not any more,' I said. 'I told you Garvey, things are to be different now. I elect Donkey to the Stone for his loyalty to the knights. And to me.'

'Wot!' said Garvey. But I had the momentum.

'And also Elayne,' I continued quickly. 'The Crew's eyes and ears. Is Elayne here?'

Elayne I chose because Elayne had been one of OG's favourites among the women, but the women also respected her. If Elayne was at the table, mouths that otherwise might twitch would be silenced. I also chose her for Quin, so that my queen would not be alone. 'Elayne?'

'She's not here,' said Tanisha, as Donkey took his seat.

'Then I mark a place for her.' I took the Buck 119 blade and carved an *E* into the seat next to Donkey. 'Let that be her place when she returns.' It felt good that my first act with the knife was one of creation, not destruction. But the mark would have been much less sweet if I had known then for what reason Elayne was absent.

Seven places were now taken at the table. I had made Garvey wait, I had watched his eyes as I called the men – and even the women – before him.

'Garvey,' I said then, 'you too have been a leader. You too are deserving of honour. I set you a place at the table too, Garvey.'

The eyes of the chosen were on him, the eyes of the yungas too and also my eyes and Shaman's.

'Garvey?'

He came and he sat. He wasn't smiling, though I was, though my smile was hidden inside me.

'I will call others to the table,' I said then, as the rest of the Crew looked on in hope and envy, 'but not at this time.' I raised the knife aloft. 'Let Quin's pledge be the pledge of those who join the table. If anyone betrays the pledge –'

'Let the knife fall!' said my queen.

15

I walked to the hospital. It was a long walk made longer by the fact that, at first, Shaman followed me as closely as he had used to follow Myrtle and I had to return to the Mill and persuade him to stay there with Quin. But the walk did me good. By the time I arrived at my destination I knew exactly what I wanted to do and say.

I announced myself at the desk and discovered that Mordec had been in theatre that morning and was now on Wycherley Ward. The receptionist gave me directions but I wasn't finished.

'I have another bredrin,' I said. 'He coulda been kept over-night too. He was rushed by a petrol bomb. Do you know if he's about?'

The receptionist cocked her head, pursed her lips. 'Bredrin?' she repeated.

I'd been thinking about the scuff, about Mordec. I re-grouped.

'A friend,' I said. 'His name's Ginger.' I paused. 'On account of his ginger hair,' I added as she rolled her eyes. Now I knew that the Saxon boi could not be called Ginger, that was just my name for him, but I had to start somewhere. 'Please,' I continued, as I saw her about to give up in exasperation, 'I'm worried for him.'

'Can't enter *Ginger* on the system,' she said, 'can I?'

'But was anyone admitted for burns last night?'

'Serious burns cases are referred to the Princess Alice, we don't deal with them here anyway.'

'Minor burns, could have been minor?' I so hoped they were minor, Myrtle.

'How old's your friend?' she asked.

'Don't know – sixteen, seventeen?'

She sighed again. 'Under sixteen and he'll be in children's, seventeen and over in the main hospital.' She pressed some more buttons, then she looked up at me, hard. 'There were three admissions last night, but they're under password.'

'What?'

'Nobody gets to visit without giving the password. Police matter. Your friend was attacked, you said?'

'Yes,' I said. 'Madness,' I added.

She grimaced. 'No password, no admittance.'

I made what I thought was a calm retreat. If I'd understood it right, and Ginger was one of the three, then his injuries couldn't be that serious. That's what she'd said, serious cases went to the Princess Alice. My imagination must have made the flames bigger than they were. And you know what, I was glad about that, Myrtle, glad that that Saxon was going to make it.

There were six beds in Wycherley and Mordec's was by the window. That was good, I wanted as much privacy as possible. He was lying quite still enough to be asleep, the blankets pulled up to his chin. His right eye was covered with bandages which wrapped round the back of his head, but the lower part of the wound was visible, a thin, angry gash of red which extended just below his right nostril.

On the opposite side of the bed from the window, I drew the curtains, doing it noisily, hoping to rouse him. He stirred but did not open his one good eye.

'Mordec,' I said, 'it's me, Art.' There was a chair by the bed but I did not sit down.

'Uh?' was all Mordec said. He was probably still drugged.

'You hear me?'

'Uh.'

'Things have changed at the Mill. I'm top dog now. The Crew have voted me Knight Crew Star.'

The eye opened. It looked slightly swimmy.

'So you aint come to bring me flowers den,' said Mordec. 'Ask how I am?'

'No.'

'I'm shit, Art. I'm grimy. That dog gouged my eye and then they did it all over again. Dem doctors.'

'You're welcome to come back anytime,' I continued relentlessly. 'We . . . I want you back at the Mill, but only on certain terms.'

'It kills,' said Mordec, moaning with pain.

'Shaman –'

'Is dead,' said Mordec. 'At least if he isn't now he soon will be.'

'Shaman is at the Mill, alive and kicking. And that's the way he's going to stay.'

Now Mordec actually turned, moaned again, tried to focus in on me.

'What changed, bro?' he asked.

'You merked Myrtle,' I kept my voice low. 'And I will never forgive you for that. But you're my brother –'

'Half-brother,' said Mordec.

'And I owe you some things. So you're welcome back at the Mill. I'll even appoint you to the Stone.'

'You wot?'

I explained about the sandstone wheel.

Mordec laughed. 'Did you make that up or did our Ma?'

'You on it or not?' I said.

'What does Garvey say?'

'Garvey's with me.'

Mordec shut his eye. 'Move from me, Art,' he said.

And I did. I had, after all, said what I'd come to say. As I passed the nurses' station I heard someone asking for Mordec by name and I turned to see a white boy standing there. He had his back to me, but I could see he was tall and fair and he held himself easily, as if he was entitled to be standing where he was, getting answers to the questions he was asking.

'You see,' the boy said, 'I helped bring him into casualty last night, and I said I'd come by today, see how he was.'

'Lance,' I said.

He turned around. He had one of those strong faces where you're immediately aware of the bone structure beneath the skin, the clear-cut lines of cheek and jaw.

'I'm Art,' I said, 'Mordec's brother,' and I extended my hand. It was a formal gesture and I don't know why I did it, sometimes I think it was just because I was in the hospital and the nurse was looking. Sometimes I think it was because of Lance, because he had a kind of natural courtesy that was easy to play to.

He grasped my hand warmly.

'Thanks for yesterday,' I said.

'It was nothing,' said Lance. 'Anyone would have done it.'

But actually, very few people ever do what Lance did – then, and later.

He saw that I'd come from the direction of the ward.

'Is your brother OK?' Lance asked.

'Yes,' I lied. I really didn't know how Mordec was, I hadn't asked.

'The operation was a success?'

I looked to the nurse for help, as though this was strictly a medical point.

'We'll have to keep him in a few days,' she was gracious enough to respond, 'but yes, the surgeons think they've managed to save his sight. But you can ask him yourself.'

'He's asleep,' I said quickly. 'I think I tired him out.'

'No worries,' said Lance. 'I don't have to see him. I just wanted to know if he was all right.'

My mobile went.

'You shouldn't have that on in here,' said the nurse.

'Yes. Sorry.' I switched it off, even though the caller was Quin.

'Let me get you a coffee.' I didn't want Lance to go to Mordec. I wanted him for myself. Why? I've asked myself that a thousand times, why did I want to be with him, right from the start? I've tried to persuade myself that it was because I was curious, because I wanted to know exactly what had made him come to the aid of a total stranger bleeding in a car park. But there was actually never a moment when I didn't know the answer to that – he had come to Mordec's aid because he was a good person. That's all. He was a shining example of someone being better than themselves – or better than me. And maybe, that day, that's what I was looking for, for a companion on the journey, a fellow traveller on the quest that Myrtle had set for me. *'People can be good, Art, or they can be bad.'* And also, if I'm honest, there was something magnetic about him. It wasn't just Quin who recognised that, it wasn't just a boy-girl thing, it was that when you were near him the world seemed a brighter place.

We went to the cafeteria together. As we queued for coffee, I called Quin back. She was hysterical.

'Dey've nabbed Elayne. Dey've taken her!'

'Who? Who's nabbed her? What are you chattin about?'

'The Saxons. They've got her hidden some place. They're sending someone to the Mill. They want some deal.'

'Any Saxon comes to the Mill, get Duane and Garvey to keep him there. Do nothing until I come, I'm on my way.' I flicked the phone off. 'Sorry,' I said to Lance. 'Coffee's gonna to have to wait. Emergency business.'

'I've got my motorbike here,' Lance said, 'if you need a lift.'

16

Of course, I took the lift.

The last time I'd ridden pillion was when I went with Pels to see the tree around which Keifer had wrapped himself. Pels had come to my place, barely braked, and I just jumped onto the back of the moving bike. I don't think I got a grip on the seat until we were round the first bend. Lance, by contrast, stood and offered me his helmet (Pels didn't even own a helmet) and then climbed slowly aboard and suggested it would be safest if I held him round the waist. I wanted to laugh, I wanted to tell him how it was with machines in the estate, how we raced bikes and cars that didn't belong to us at a hundred miles an hour and did handbrake turns and lit petrol infernos, but I just got on behind him and held on as instructed. I even put on the hat, just to see what it felt like. As I placed my hands around him, I realised I'd never touched a man so closely except in a fight.

We set off down the main roads. Lance didn't take short cuts, maybe he didn't know any, and he didn't jump red lights. I caught myself thinking it might have been quicker to walk. By the time we reached the Mill, my anxiety levels were high. I'd expected that the Crew would have posted lookouts, especially if we were expecting Saxon visitors. But there was no one on the door. I felt my anger rising as I stepped through into the dimness of the building. The first person I saw was LameDuck.

'Door,' I said. 'Get on the door. Now.' My instructions about how to handle any incoming Saxons took less than thirty seconds but it was long enough for the Crew, who were in fact more alert than I'd given them credit for, to launch an attack on Lance.

Which was fair enough given what the Crew saw – or rather what Borz saw: a Milky Bar Kid entering the Mill. And even if that boy wasn't wearing Saxon colours, he was a stranger entering on a day when tensions were running high. Another man might have stopped to wonder why the white boy had arrived with the Knight Crew Star. That man was not Borz. Borz acted first and asked questions afterwards, so he just threw himself on Lance. Or would have done, if Lance hadn't been too quick for him. Lance simply stepped aside and the raging bull that was Borz fell headlong into some crates.

'Stop!' I yelled, rather after the event.

Lance said something that sounded like 'sorry' and Borz moaned and roared from the floor.

'This is Lance,' I began and Duane, who'd come to see what the commotion was, added, 'Knight Crew bredrin, he got Mordec to hospital.' He greeted Lance and then helped Borz to his feet.

Borz dusted himself down. He was scowling but I could see he was also impressed, as was I. Lance had moved like a fighter, and a skilled one at that.

'Where did you learn dat trick, boi?' Borz asked.

Lance shrugged as though it was nothing, which could have infuriated Borz but didn't. Perhaps Borz thought he needed to proceed with care, or perhaps it was the presence of Shaman who emerged from the darkness to stand, briefly, between the two of them. The dog appeared to wait a minute, until certain that the altercation was at an end, and then he turned towards Lance. He didn't sniff at him or wag some doggy greeting, he stood full-square to Lance, lifting his great head as though he was inspecting Lance, judging him, and then he made some soft noises in his throat, somewhere between a growl and purr.

'Art.' Quin arrived and launched herself at me before seeing Lance and the dog and checking herself. 'This is Lance,' I said again.

Quin nodded at him. Shaman was still making the soft noise in his throat. Lance didn't look at the dog, but only at Quin, as did I. I remember noticing the light on her forehead and being struck, all over again, at how very beautiful she was. But if he looked at her that way, that day, then I didn't notice. I had other things on my mind.

'What time we expecting the Saxon boi?'

'He's here already,' Quin said.

The dog moved to my side as there was the sound of scuffle and a slight moan. Garvey and Lee dragged something limp and white into the space in front of me. It was a boy, probably not more than ten or eleven years old, who looked up from the floor with a mixture of fury and terror.

'Get up,' I said.

He staggered to his feet. He'd obviously been beaten and his hands were tied behind his back with a length of rusty wire.

'Who did this?' I asked.

'You said to keep him here,' said Garvey.

'I said keep him here, not beat him here,' I said.

'He's a Saxon,' said Borz.

'He's a child,' said Lance and I saw Quin, with her quick curiosity, turn to look at the newcomer again.

'Who asked you?' said Borz.

And I missed the fact that Lance didn't rise to this challenge because the boy exploded angrily: 'I'm not a child. I'm almost twelve.'

'Untie him,' I ordered.

'What?'

'I said untie him.'

Donkey went to work untwisting the wire and making the boy yelp. When he was loose the boy rubbed his wrists and then let his arms hang, keeping, I noticed, his hands in fists.

'What's your name?' I asked.

'Pug.'

The Crew laughed and his face squeezed up into anger again, a cross little fighting dog. They'd named him well.

'Well, Pug, what have you got to say?'

'I told them. I told them already,' Pug spluttered. 'Big Shank's got Elayne.' He paused. 'And I got the proof.' This was obviously something new. He dipped his hand in his pocket and Garvey, who was closest to him, reacted as if he was about to pull a knife. What he brought out wasn't a knife but it might as well have been. He waved the black and baby-blue trophy triumphantly in the air.

Quin was the first to identify it. 'Elayne's plait,' she said, 'it's one of Elayne's plaits!' She came forward furiously and took it out of Pug's hand. 'Her plait and her ribbon, cut from her head. How dare you!' she said to the boy. And the tone of her voice made him cower.

'Jack im, merk im,' shouted the Crew.

'No,' I said quickly as the crowd moved in on the boy, 'we gotta hear him out.'

The Crew reluctantly stood back, but they were still close and the boy knew it, so I admired the guts with which he lay down his challenge.

'Big Shank says if you don't want her cut someplace else, you gotta give up da boi wot did Danny.'

'Never,' shouted Borz. 'If Shankie's looking for big beef, I'm on it!'

The boy glared up at me. 'But if you give up dat man, then Elayne goes free.'

Lance's cool eyes were on me, and so were the black eyes of the dog – and therefore Myrtle's eyes. You were looking weren't you, Myrtle? Right from the beginning. *You can be a good leader Art, or a bad one.*

I began by calling Tardis and Lee. 'Take Pug outside,' I directed them, 'give him something to eat and drink.' I didn't fear that the boi would run, not without a message to take back to Big Shank. To Pug, I said, 'You'll have your answer soon.'

'Soon?' said Borz. 'He can have it now. We're gonna raid yur manor,' he shouted at the boy's back. 'Blow you off da face of the earth. Go tell dat to Shankie, pug-face!'

'Borz,' I said quietly, 'Elayne's the most important thing now. Her safety. We don't even know where they're holding her.'

'Then come – let's find out!'

I put my hand on his arm. 'The Stone.'

'What?'

'Come to the Stone,' I said. Now I would see if anything had changed. 'I ask all those who are sworn to come to the Stone.'

'We aint got time for all that,' shouted Borz.

'You swore,' said Quin. 'We all swore.' And, very deliberately, measuring her paces, she accompanied me and Shaman to the round stone. That seemed enough to impel Pels and Duane, Garvey and Donkey to follow.

She watched them sit and then sat herself at my right hand. Borz still stood apart.

'Please come, Borz,' she called softly from the Stone. 'We need you.'

And so, gruffly, he came. It's a clever thing to lead so quietly.

The yungas pulled up crates or sat on the floor to listen, keeping quite still, which was unusual. And then it was Lance alone who remained standing.

'Wot bout him?' Pels said, jabbing a finger Lance's way. 'This conversation's private, right? I mean,' Pels turned to me, 'true say he helped Mordec, but we don't really know who he is, where he comes from?'

'If the Elayne you speak of is Elayne Descalot,' Lance said, 'I know her, or knew her. We were in primary together.'

All the Crew knew what that meant. If Lance had been in primary with Elayne it meant he couldn't come from Mount Bladon. He might not be a Cornwall man, but he definitely wasn't a Saxon either, the catchment area didn't extend that far.

'And no one has the right to hold a human being against their will,' Lance continued, and then he muttered something that could have been an oath or an incantation, only it seemed to be in a language I didn't know. So I just listened to the words I did know, the ones you might have used, Myrtle: *No one has the right – the right – to hold a human being against their will*.

He was a stranger among us and yet, with those words, he made himself at one with us, or at least at one with you, Myrtle, with what I knew you would have wanted, valued.

'Stay, Lance.' I heard myself say: 'I'd like you to stay.'

He held my gaze for a moment as if trying to gauge my sincerity and then he nodded and sank very softly to his knees before sitting back on his heels as though he'd just finished praying.

And that was the start of it. If I had let him walk away that day, he wouldn't have shattered my life. But it was me who asked him to stay.

Of course, I've asked myself a thousand times since, what were his motives? Did his heart leap at my queen even then, or was it really that he couldn't stand by when a wrong was being done, could no more walk away from the kidnap than he had been able to walk away from an injured boy in a car park? Perhaps that's why I'm telling this story. Perhaps I need to find that out once and for all.

'So,' said Borz, settling at the grindstone, 'wot we gonna do?'

'It's me they want,' I began. 'Then me they get. Elayne didn't have anythin to do with the Bladon boi. It's right I go in her place.'

'You nuts?' roared Borz. 'You tink dey're just going to give her up, just like that? You go dere and then dey'll have you both. Only thing to do is smash em and smash em hard.'

'I'm with Borz,' said Pels. 'The the only thing they gonna understand is this.' He raised his fist.

'If we attack,' I said, 'they could harm Elayne. It's too risky.'

'Pug,' said Garvey. 'We could trade Pug.'

'Or we could just mash him up,' said Pels, 'get im tell us where they're hidin her . . .'

'No,' I said.

'The future,' Quin said, looking at me and me alone, 'we need to think about the future.'

'One that doesn't reward kidnap,' said Lance from the floor.

'Who asked you?' growled Borz. 'You're not at da Stone, so quit yur chattin.'

'Man's got a point,' I said. I was thinking quickly. 'We need

131

to find a way that frees Elayne now, but protects the rest of the Crew in the future.'

'If Art goes as a straight exchange,' said Quin, immediately picking up the thread, 'what's to stop them taking another Crew member and making some other demand? No one would be safe then.'

'Like we do wot?' asked Pels. 'Dey're not going to sign some letter of agreement, are dey? I tell you, dey only understand one thing.' He shook his fist again. 'Power.'

'Right. Let's show them power,' I said. 'But power on our terms.'

'Meanin?' said Duane.

'They want to scuff, so let there be a scuff, only no tools, one on one,' I said.

Single combat – was that your idea, Myrtle? It certainly wasn't in my head before we sat at the Stone. Or perhaps it was the effect of the Stone itself, how things changed there because it gave you time to think.

'We put up a fighter, they put up a fighter. We meet at some neutral place. If their man wins, they take me. If our man wins, Elayne goes free.'

'I'll be dat man!' yelled Borz.

'They'll put up HellRazor,' said Donkey.

'I'll smash im one time,' said Borz, illustrating his point by punching his right fist into his left palm.

'Not if he dodges,' said Lance, again from the floor.

Borz was out of his seat before the first laugh came. 'You're dead,' he screamed at Lance.

Quin had also risen. 'He's not Crew, Borz, he doesn't know the rules here.'

'And wot,' said Pels. And then, quite suddenly, they were on him, Borz and Pels and Garvey and Duane. They leapt from their places at the Stone with the same sort of fluidity that they'd attacked me on my first day at the Mill. It was four to one but I didn't stop them, because I wanted Lance blooded in. I wanted him to know – and the Crew to see – that he was one of us.

Not even Myrtle could have predicted what happened next. Lance leapt to his feet and a blood-curdling noise came out of his throat, no, not his throat, it came from somewhere deep in his chest, a tribal noise, like that of an ancient warrior going into battle. The noise alone seemed to force his attackers back and, before they had time to regroup, he began whirling his arms as if he was some giant windmill. The rotations were so fast it seemed that he had not two but twenty arms and he turned on the balls of his feet to face each of his opponents in turn. It was blinding, disorientating, even for those of us out of his furious path, and I thought he could not sustain the motion, that he must lose his balance and fall. But he did not. For balance was what he had, he was like a fighting ballerina. Duane and Pels and Garvey couldn't get near him, but Borz, fired by his anger, shoulder-charged the wheeling dervish. The cheers of the crowd were short-lived. Lance was knocked back but not before he'd kicked out viciously with his left foot and brought Borz to the ground.

'Enough!' I shouted, and Lance came to an immediate stop even though his chest was heaving and his eyes were ablaze. He held himself quite still as, for a second time that evening, Borz hauled himself from the floor. He gave Borz a small bow in which there was no malice and no triumph, which allowed me to say: 'You're alryt, Lance. I, and all those at the Stone, welcome you to the Knights.'

'Knights?' queried Garvey.

But it was Quin who voiced my more intimate thoughts.

'I think we have found our champion,' she said.

17

I needed to act fast. As Quin said, a man who could come out ahead when the odds were four to one was a clear champion, but Lance was new and the Crew twitchy and I knew there would be dissent. I called Pug back in, glad that he hadn't witnessed the fight. The Saxons had many formidable soldjas besides HellRazor and, if they agreed to single combat, it would be important to keep the surprise that was Lance on our side.

I told Pug the deal. 'Only let it be a real fight,' I added. 'No tools.'

'You're chicken,' squealed the boy. 'You're scared of da shank!'

Perhaps he was brave that day because he knew I wouldn't harm him.

'One on one,' I said quietly. 'That shows a real man.'

But Pug was right, I was scared. I didn't know whether Lance's skills extended to knife combat. Besides, I still felt the pain of the knife – the one that I had pulled from you, Myrtle.

The bellyaching started almost immediately after Pug left. Garvey, always the ringleader, wanted to go to the hospital, consult with Mordec.

'Just check he agrees the decision,' he said wheedlingly.

'The decision's made,' Duane said. 'It's the Crew's word, Art's word. We can't go back on it.'

That was the first time Duane stood up publicly for me against his brother and his loyalty did not go unnoticed. Not by me, not by his twin. The bitterness that would finally divide my Knights, sworn against sworn, was probably seeded there.

It was Tanisha who mentioned OG. It seemed a lifetime since OG had been arrested, but in reality it had been less than a week. And he hadn't been picked up because of Danny MacMahon, he was actually being held on some charge to do with one of his off-licence protection rackets. If any of us had stopped to think about it for a minute, we would have known that the Saxons would never have named OG as a suspect. The Feds could hammer on Saxon doors for as long as they hammered on ours, and they would never be told a thing. Even the Saxons had that sort of loyalty, respect. No, when Mordec jumped on the wheel and wound up the crowd, it wasn't because he suspected the Saxons of being snakes, it was because he knew what he needed to do in order to stand in OG's place.

Just as I knew now what I needed to do to stand in his.

'Someone needs to try and link OG,' Tanisha continued. 'OG cared for Elayne. He'll know what to do.'

'Art cares for Elayne,' said Quin. 'Art is doing what needs to be done.'

Tanisha became quiet.

I credited the Stone for that, Myrtle, for even when we were not sat about it, it was clear now whose voices counted. Those I had called to the Stone had authority, my authority.

The griping about Lance was stilled by Borz. Borz could be slow and dim-witted, he could be angry and impulsive, but he never bore a grudge. You would have valued that in him, Myrtle.

'Lance is Knight Crew now,' said Borz solidly. 'Show him dat respect.' Borz wasn't a man to shake hands, but he nodded at Lance, asked him gruffly once again where he'd learnt his skills. This time he didn't use the word *boi*.

'I used to do karate,' Lance answered.

I would see him fight many times after that day and some of his moves I'm sure were based on karate training. He kicked and punched – and even sat and stood – like we'd seen people do in martial arts films. But he fought and moved with something else too, a graceful animal alertness, as though he was part lion and part gazelle, the knowledge of strength and speed in every cell of his body.

The night we waited for Big Shank's response was a long one. We'd given Pug a number to call, and I kept the blowa concerned in my pocket, next to my own mobile. I kept fingering it, taking it out and checking if I'd missed something, failed maybe to respond to its unfamiliar ringtone. Sometimes I touched the knife by mistake. Fingered that. Knife, mobile, knife. Mobile. But there were no messages. Not then, not later.

I began to suspect Shankie of mind games. He was making us wait deliberately, keeping the stakes high. Quin, who had initially kept her fears to herself, began to fret openly about Elayne.

'What if they hurt her anyway? They could be slapping her up right now!'

'They're not. They wouldn't dare.' I said this more to comfort Quin than out of any conviction. But nervousness is contagious, it began to spread through the Mill. If the Saxons kept silent much longer we would have no option but to go with Borz's show of force and I didn't want that. In the end I decided I needed to get out, get away.

Away.

I posted lookouts at our back door, in the disused clock-tower and on the bridge over the river, and then I headed home. I posted the lookouts not because I expected an attack on the Mill but because I wanted to keep the Crew members occupied.

Quin and Shaman both came with me and I was glad of them because 'home' is a strange word for the place I returned to that night. The flat was crammed full of things that spoke only of absence. Keifer's worn-out shoes were still in the hall, his jacket half-falling off a peg, his tooth-brush in the bathroom, his CDs stacked on the floor of the living room, as though he'd just popped out for a beer and would be back at any minute. I found myself listening for his key in the lock. And it was the same with my mother. I knew she was in the Hillview Home for the mentally ill, but she was in the flat too, in the scent of the unwashed, perfumy clothes that hung in her bedroom, in the fluff of her towels, in the hair in her hairbrush. Away and not away.

Then there was Danny MacMahon. He was there that night too. If I sat on the sofa, he sat beside me, his blind little face turned towards me, his sightless eyes watching my every move. If I paced, Danny paced beside me.

Shaman paced too.

'What's up with that dog?' said Quin.

'Maybe he smells Mordec,' I said, 'maybe he smells the man who murdered his mistress.'

But actually I think Shaman smelt Danny, who I had murdered.

Murdered. That word crept up on me, stole into my consciousness as quietly as Danny did that night. And murdered is not the same as merked. It's more serious. More dreadful.

I'd murdered Danny.

Murdered him.

137

Shaman continued to pad and pace.

'Shaman,' said Quin, 'for fuck's sake.' Taking charge the only way she could, she went to the kitchen to see if she could find the dog anything to eat. The last of the wake sandwiches were still in the fridge and she divided the remains between him and us.

Still the phone didn't ring.

The doorbell rang once. Through the spy hole I saw the rent man, so we didn't open the door. That was another thing we'd lose, I supposed, the flat. I didn't feel like explaining to the rent man about Keifer or my mother, but if we didn't pay, in time we would be evicted. How much time? I hadn't the brain-space to consider that so I just shut it away with all the other things to which I had no answers.

At midnight the phone finally rang. It was Pug. He left a pause before he spoke, it was only a short pause, just a couple of seconds, but it was long enough for me to feel that he was toying with me, making me wait one final time. I wanted to hit him. Anger, you see, Myrtle, can be in the bone.

'Cemetery,' he said. '8 p.m. tomorrow night.'

'No tools,' I said. 'Does Big Shank agree no tools?'

'Yes,' said Pug, and then he laughed.

'And your soldja –' I wanted to know who they'd chosen for champion, but Pug clicked off.

I threw the phone down.

'Art,' said Quin. 'Bubz.' And she came towards me.

'I should have been the fighter myself,' I said, 'offered myself.'

'You have offered yourself,' she said. 'If Lance fails, they'll take you, bubz.'

She didn't say any more but she didn't have to. If Lance failed I would not come back to the Mill unscathed. I probably wouldn't return to the Mill at all. I'd put my trust, my fate, in someone else's hands. Was that what a leader would do? What a man would do? A good man?

As if to stop these thoughts, Quin put her mouth over mine, kissed me. And I felt hungry for her suddenly. I wanted to touch every part of her body and have her touch me. I wanted to lose myself in her again.

That way I could stay in the present, have a whole night when I didn't have to know what was going to be written on Myrtle's page of the future.

18

The cemetery lay to the west of the estates and, with an exit to the north (theirs) and one to the south (ours), was considered neutral territory by Knight Crew and Saxons alike. The fact that Big Shank had chosen this as the location meant, I had to assume, that his intentions at least were honest.

'I still aint goin without tools,' Garvey said.

I had to agree. Trust is a delicate thing, Myrtle. 'Bring what you want,' I said, 'but keep it outta sight.' A full-scale scuff if it came to that, and I hoped it wouldn't, at a place where the Feds wouldn't find us for some time would be suicide. We couldn't afford to spook them.

Like most things in our area, the cemetery was run-down and even the tombstones looked drunk. I don't think there was an upright slab among them, they lurched wildly to left or right or just lay where they'd fallen, flat on their faces. Lichen ate away at their surfaces and the graves themselves were tangled masses of ivy roots and plants that only you, Myrtle, would have been able to identify.

The only clear space in the cemetery was in front of the tomb of Dr Samuel Watt, Pastor to the Church of Christ, laid to rest AD 1742, aged 86 years. So that's where we headed.

As we walked, I thought how very old eighty-six years was. I didn't expect to live that long.

Shankie's men were already gathered. It was an August evening, and it was still quite light with a peachy glow to the air. It was Quin who drew my attention to the air and the reason I remember it was it was the first time she'd said anything that day that wasn't to do with Elayne. I'm sure that was you in her mind, Myrtle, lingering.

By the time we arrived, Shankie had commandeered the tomb itself and was sitting up high on the greyed marble swinging his legs in a slow, rhythmical way which was menacing in its very nonchalance. His swinging feet covered, and then uncovered, the memorial words: 'Absent from the body, present with the Lord'.

I'd seen Shankie before – of course I had – but only in passing, in a car, on a bike. So I'd never really had a good look at him. He was the mirror opposite of OG. Where OG was blacker than night, Shankie was wormishly pale, as if he didn't get out much, or had spent most of his life underground. And whereas OG had muscles harder and bigger than the gym he trained in, Shankie looked soft somehow, pulpy even. But I saw where he sat, high on the spine of the tomb. And I saw how the others looked at him as we approached and I knew not to underestimate him.

I came to a stop at the edge of the fight ground. It was not a big area, about the size of a boxing ring. Those of the Stone arced about me, Lance the closest (or as close as Shaman would let him) to my left, and Quin to my right. Next to Quin were Duane and Garvey, together for once and, on Lance's side, Donkey, Pels and Borz. For a moment the Knight Crew and the Saxons stood facing each other in silence. I don't know what Shankie was doing, maybe he was checking out Lance, wondering about the white boy he'd never seen before. I was doing a head count. I reckoned that they probably had ten or more men than we did.

I moved forward a pace and, as if in response, Shankie jumped down from the tomb. Shaman growled softly.

'Is it only the dog that speaks?' Big Shank said. HellRazor laughed. Tractor laughed. The O'Dair brothers laughed.

I took another pace forward. 'I'm Art, Knight Crew Star.'

'Knight Crew murderer,' said Big Shank.

'I never meant to merk Danny MacMahon.' And that was the truth, Myrtle, you know that as well as me. It was just supposed to be a nick, because of what they'd done to Lee.

'Too late,' said Big Shank. 'Yur time is up.'

And maybe it was too late. Maybe a man who's murdered can never be good again.

'Where's Elayne?' I asked.

'Hm,' said Big Shank, as if this was an unanswerable conundrum. 'Where's Elayne, bois?'

There were some hoots of excitement and then the O'Dair brothers and Pug pulled something from behind the tomb. It was the slumped figure of a girl, she was wearing a strange, ill-fitting black bobble hat and her hands were tied behind her back. Elayne.

'Oh my god,' breathed Quin.

'Wire,' shouted Pug, joyfully. 'I did her with wire!'

'I moved the wire off you,' I said to the boy.

'Not at first you didn't,' he retorted.

'Move that wire off her!' I said to Big Shank. 'Now!'

'I'll take off the hat,' said Big Shank and he yanked at the bobble.

The shock was electric. They had shaved her head. They had cut not just one of her plaits but all of them and then they'd shaved her. Where her lustrous hair had been there was just a skull of black stubble.

'You're sick,' shouted Quin, voicing what the rest of us were too angry or too stunned to say. 'You sick bastards!'

And then she called out to her friend, 'Elayne. Elayne!'

Elayne did not reply, she did not even lift her head.

'Bitch's hair grows back,' said Big Shank. 'Danny Mac-Mahon's hair – dat don't grow back. Not now. Not never.'

'Take me,' I said then. 'Let Elayne go and take me.' It seemed quite simple in that moment. Just looking at Elayne, Myrtle, and knowing it was wrong. That they had hurt her, Myrtle, and it should have been me.

There was commotion all around the ring. Borz was roaring of course, and Pels too. Quin grasped for my hand but I shook her off. She would understand what needed to be done.

I stepped forward.

And yes, all right, Myrtle. It was also the things about the hair. Big Shank was wrong when he said that Danny's hair wouldn't grow again, it grew right then, right in front of my eyes. For there he was again, standing just outside the ring, a featureless boy with a sudden shock of dark, dark hair.

'Take me,' I repeated.

But my offer had disconcerted the Saxon camp and there was commotion there too. Even Big Shank looked wrong-footed.

'No,' he finally yelled. 'No! We agreed a scuff.' He managed to laugh. 'Then we'll have two of you.' The Saxons began to pick up the beat, to bray with excitement. 'The one that dies at HellRazor's hand and you, Art!'

HellRazor raised a clenched fist and a Saxon cheer went into the air with it.

Stung into action, Duane suddenly shouted: 'Knight Crew respect!' And every single Crew arm shot into the air, clenched fist, open hand, clenched fist, open hand.

'Knight Crew. Knight Crew. Knight Crew.'

Every arm, that is, but mine and Lance's. Lance didn't,

I realised, even know the salute. I looked at him, his eyes could be grey or they could be blue. That day they were blue. It was like looking up into sky that could have been yours, Myrtle, pure and cloudless.

'I'll fight,' he said quietly. 'That's what we agreed. Knight Crew word.'

It was as though he hadn't heard Big Shank saying 'to the death' or perhaps he thought it was just a figure of speech, that Big Shank was joking. Big Shank didn't look like he was joking. There was a malevolent excitement in that pulpy body. Lance, by contrast, seemed calm, peaceful even. And that made my heart sing. I loved that Knight, I think it was that simple. I'd never loved a man before that day, but I loved him. Because of what he was prepared to do, to risk, for a man and a Crew he barely knew, because we'd given our word. And he'd given his. I could use words like 'honour' now, words I later learnt. But it wasn't like that on the day, I just felt a blinding gratitude.

I turned to face the Saxon and the throng hushed. 'I offer myself. You refuse. Come then, we'll fight. But on the agreed terms.'

Big Shank shrugged.

'No tools,' I continued.

'Yur terms,' he said, lightly. 'Yur conditions.'

'Your terms too. You agreed them.'

'Of course. I agree them still. But my conditions are a fight to the end.' He smiled. 'There are plenty of ways to kill a man without a weapon, aint dat right, HellRazor?'

HellRazor didn't answer. He was limbering up, shifting his weight foot to foot, shaking his big hands, loosening them. He was bigger than Lance, much bigger. Lance's prowess, his power, which before had seemed indubitable, now seemed just a few dodges and a kick.

In our silence Tractor yelled: 'Dey're chicken. Dey don't have a man!'

Lance stepped forward. 'They have me,' he said.

There was a moment of stunned surprise and then Hell-Razor said, 'You're on the wrong team, nigga-lover!'

'I fight for Art,' Lance said as though nothing could be simpler. 'To pay the debt.' He paused. 'I also fight for Elayne.'

Elayne lifted her head then. She was bruised around the eyes.

The Crew howled with anger.

'Let it begin.' Lance bent down and removed his shoes.

HellRazor was wearing boots, the sort of heavy boots with which you can kick in a man's face.

'Wait,' I said. 'Pad down.'

It was clear from Lance's face he didn't understand me. I mimed the patting down of clothes: 'Weapons check.'

He looked genuinely surprised. 'We have given our word.'

The Saxons jeered. 'No pad down! Knight Crew word!'

'Him,' said Quin urgently. 'Not you, Lance – HellRazor, we need to check *him*.'

But Lance was already stripping off his shirt and moving forward to stand like a prize-fighter in the tombstone ring. Only he wasn't built like a prize-fighter. In the dusk light he looked pale and insubstantial.

HellRazor gave a huge mocking guffaw and kicked out at a low gravestone. The steel tip of his boot struck sparks and suddenly he was on his way. At once the fight became a spectacle and Crew members and Saxons alike shifted positions, enclosing the space, manoeuvring themselves to get the best view. Our semicircle and theirs were so close and so tight that the bois on the east and western flanks could have reached out and touched each other. But all focus was now on what was happening inside the ring.

Lance neither moved towards nor away from the thundering Saxon, but stood quite still with his knees bent, one arm outstretched and one tight to his side. I thought he would dodge but he didn't, he just stood there and I watched, as if in slow motion, as HellRazor's massive fist came down at him. Hellrazor must have been five inches or more taller than Lance and the wait seemed interminable and then suddenly Lance moved his hands with astonishing speed, doing something with his wrists that not only blocked the blow, but also seemed to propel HellRazor backwards.

There was a roar from the Crew, more of relief than triumph, but HellRazor was quickly on Lance again, his powerful shoulders hunched for a head butt. This time Lance did step aside and HellRazor bellowed as he fell towards his own men, but they were quick to right him, turning him about to face his enemy once more. Lance had not pressed his advantage, not followed his adversary to the rope of human beings.

'Don't just stand dere,' shouted Borz, 'arms him!'

But Lance didn't attack, just waited and watched as HellRazor hulked towards him once more. This time Lance kicked, the whole of his body seeming to pivot on his left leg. The gyration was fast and brought the ball of his bare right foot up almost to HellRazor's shoulder.

HellRazor took the blow but also took the foot, somehow managing to pinion it under his armpit. For a moment Lance was left hopping, off-balance, and the smile on HellRazor's face was broad. But then Lance flipped, agile as a cat, turning over in the air as if gravity didn't exist.

It was then that we saw the blade. HellRazor didn't have to reach for it, it must have been in his hand all the time. A small blade, but with a lethal curve. I saw the flash just before Quin did.

'Mans gotta shank,' she screamed, 'he's gotta blade!'

But already the knife was down, slashing after Lance's moving leg, and catching it, so that as Lance drew away the blade drew too, an arc of red.

The Saxons saw blood, scented victory, cheered on their man.

'HellRazor! HellRazor! HellRazor!'

'Liars,' yelled Quin, losing all her poise to fury. 'Fucking cheats, pussies!'

Lance still managed to land on his feet, but the shock stilled him and as he stared in disbelief at the wound, Hell-Razor struck again, slicing across Lance's bare chest. This time Lance fell.

'Knight Crew word,' mocked Tractor. 'Knight Crew word!'

It was too much for Borz. He got out his chain. 'You gonna get it now!'

'No,' said Big Shank. 'You gonna get it.'

Because the fight hadn't stopped and even Borz was suddenly frozen by the spectacle of HellRazor advancing on Lance as he lay on the earth. HellRazor's feet came nearer and nearer, he was aiming for Lance's head, lifting his right boot with its steel tip and bringing it smashing down – on grass.

Lance had rolled away and now he pulled himself slowly to his feet. He held his position for just a second and then that sound came out of his chest again, louder than if his wound was its mouth. The battle cry of ancient tribes. It was *Kiai*, the spiritual shout, or so he told me later, but to all of us gathered that day it sounded like the earth breaking open on Judgement Day. The Saxons were temporarily silenced, just as we had been when Lance had shouted in the Mill, but HellRazor, deaf with adrenalin and perhaps thinking the battle all but won, was pressing forward again, knife in hand.

The *Kiai* shout came again and again, seeming to carry Lance through his pain and, all of a sudden, it was him advancing. HellRazor had overreached himself and using his opponent's outstretched arm, Lance managed a twist and a throw that brought HellRazor, for the first time, flailing to earth. This time Lance did not hesitate, he jammed his knee into HellRazor's armpit, pulled his arm backwards and the knife fell from his hand. A moment later Lance did something with his index fingers in HellRazor's wrists which made the Saxon scream.

And yet it still did not look like a victory. We all waited for HellRazor to move, to use his weight or his anger or the fact that he was uninjured to throw Lance aside. But he just lay there on the soil, vanquished. I watched a drop a blood fall from the wound in Lance's chest onto the back of his head.

There was a horrified, ugly silence on the Saxon side of the ring. And there was no cheering on ours, we were all caught in the moment, not knowing what could happen next.

Then a voice spoke. 'Merk im.'

Mordec was standing our side of the ring.

His right eye was still covered with a bandage that wound round the whole of his head. He did not look well but someone – I guessed Garvey – had obviously got a message to hospital and he must have discharged himself to come and see the action.

'Shankie said it was a fight to the death,' continued Mordec. 'So you have to merk im.'

'No,' I said, standing against him. 'I say release Elayne. Let it end there.'

There was a desperate pause and a whirl from Borz's chain and then Elayne stumbled – or was pushed – towards us. She ran, a frightened sobbing child, to our side of the ring. It was Quin whose arms were open, who gathered her in and held her tight to her chest, like she was some mother.

It might have ended there but Mordec hadn't finished.

'Big Shank gave his word. Saxon word. A fight to the death. Does Saxon word count for nuthin?'

Forty Saxon faces turned towards their leader.

And then I saw why they were all afraid of that white, pulpy thing.

'Take da blade,' Big Shank said to Lance. 'An do it.'

'It's a trick!' shouted Pels. Although Lance only had one of HellRazor's arms twisted behind his back, he was using both hands to subdue him. If he reached for the knife, he'd have to let HellRazor go.

Yet Lance reached, he picked up the knife.

Hellrazor did not move, he did not dodge. He continued to lie on the ground as if he was still pinioned there.

Lance lifted the knife high above his head. 'The Knight Crew took a life,' he said and, with terrifying force, he dashed the knife downwards – 'and the Knight Crew give a life.' The knife juddered into the dirt to the left of HellRazor's face.

Lance stood up. The knife was still juddering.

'The debt is paid.'

19

What happened at the cemetery brought us the first truce we'd ever known. Big Shank sent word to me and I sent word back: cessation of hostilities. A breathing space. There was no triumph in the Mill though, just a kind of surprise, a joy. Yes, for me at least – joy. There were so many significant words, like bipolar, which had played such a large part in my life without me knowing anything about them at all and now along came this tiny, tiny word, which I thought I knew and understood but which turned out to contain a whole new universe.

Joy.

I don't want to let that word go, I need to mark it, because it didn't stay with us for long. There was a worm in the apple. There is always a worm. And yet the intensity of those hot August weeks made me feel that the joy could last for ever. So I will try and tell you, without bitterness, what beauty that slice of time held for me and all those I cared about.

But first I must tell you about the Stone and also about Elayne. My initial thought was to capitalise on all that had happened. No one could deny Lance, our champion, his rightful place at the Stone, but I was still wary of Mordec. Mordec owed Lance if not his life, then probably the sight of his right eye, because it was Lance who got him to the hospital, but I saw no gratitude in Mordec. I saw him prowling, waiting, biding his time. For what, I didn't know. So I decided to bide my time too.

I watched Mordec. I also watched Lance and Elayne. In some ways she had returned more wounded from the fight than him. His wounds turned out to be superficial and, open to the fresh air, they healed well. Elayne concealed her trauma – and her almost bald head – beneath a silk scarf. And although the scarf was baby blue and tied like a jaunty turban it could not hide her crushed eyes.

Nobody had quite the words to comfort her. Nobody that is, but Lance. He took her aside.

'Your head is beautiful, Elayne,' I heard him say. 'Your shaven hair, their shame. Not yours.' And, very gently, he unwound that turban. She did have a beautiful head – not as beautiful as Quin's – but beautiful nonetheless. You would have thought she would have looked even more boyish without that luxuriantly plaited hair, but actually she looked more vulnerable, more womanly somehow. 'There,' Lance said and, putting the cloth aside, he reached up to touch the stubble. Her face was still bruised and her soul afraid but she smiled then. It was the first time I'd seen her smile since she'd been taken. If my mother had been watching, she would have seen in Lance a prince as well as a warrior. And that's what Elayne saw too. Lance was so easy to love.

I decided to call Elayne to the Stone first. I sent out a message requiring the Knights, the Crew to gather. Yes, I'd begun to divide them in my mind: those of my party who could grow and change and find your path, Myrtle – the Knights; and the rest, who remained Crew. Later that month the idea of the path you had laid for me took on a spectacular, visionary reality – I'll tell that story later – but in those early days it was just a glimmer, a hope, an idea. So I called my men and my women, my Knights and my Crew, together. I wanted witnesses.

I think there were more than thirty people there on the day of the ceremony. And it was a ceremony, we hadn't had so much food or music or beer and wine since the night you were murdered, Myrtle. And just as it had felt good to use the great Buck knife to carve initials at the Stone rather than blood from a body, so it now felt good to celebrate the authority of the Stone rather than the rule of the mob. I was still on my guard though, allowed only a little drink to flow before I began the Calling. I wanted people not only to witness but also to remember.

When I judged the time right, I turned off the music and held the Buck 119 aloft. Silence fell faster than it ever had in the Mill. I barely needed to raise my voice when I stood by the Stone and said: 'You all know what happened in the cemetery,' I said, 'and what we owe to whom. Therefore I'm going to call new Knights to the Stone.' I was addressing the throng but my sweeping eyes were on Mordec.

'And the first of these has her name carved at the Stone already. E for Elayne who bore Saxon treachery and now who holds her head high. Elayne!'

When I had first marked her name, there had been deviousness in my thinking, I'd wanted to stop the twitching of the woman. Now I felt Elayne deserved her place. She'd grown in dignity and she did hold her head high that day, came to the Stone bare-headed, her slight chin jutted defiantly forward. The crowd cheered and, stealing a glance at Lance, her champion, I thought I saw pride in his eyes. Mordec, standing slightly apart, made some guttural, dismissive noise and I wondered – suddenly and stupidly – whether this wasn't actually his grievance, that Elayne had given her heart so fast to the outsider. And of course she had given

Lance her heart. It was clear from the movements of her body, she shadowed Lance as closely as Shaman shadowed me. And who could blame her? Lance had both saved her and made her safe. He had also raised her status in the Crew, our champion was her man, the kindest, calmest man among us. And this fine man had – or so I imagined – given his heart to her. Sometimes you see what you expect to see, don't you, Myrtle? You don't actually see what's there in front of you.

Elayne swore the oath and took her place. There was a moistness to her eyes, I noticed, and that was fitting.

'And now,' I said, lifting the knife for silence a second time, 'I call for our champion, for Lance. Vanquisher of Saxons!'

There was a storm of Knight Crew approval. Though not from Mordec.

Lance came forward, stood before me.

'I swear to Art,' he said, looking me straight in the eye, his right hand laid on his heart. 'And to the Knights. I swear loyalty, now and for ever.'

I remember a lump rising in my own throat then. He seemed so magnificent somehow, so true. A warrior who had fought for me as a virtual stranger. What might he not do for a friend?

Another man, a smarter one than me, standing in that place might have wondered why Lance, who was not of our blood, so readily accepted his destiny among us? I did not think that thought. All of us were running from something and perhaps I imagined he was too. I didn't know he was running towards something. Towards someone.

In the strange solemnity of that moment, Quin spoke: 'And if you betray your pledge,' she said to Lance, 'if you betray Art –'

'Let the knife fall,' shouted Donkey ecstatically, jumping

from his place and making wild slashing motions with hands.

And, finally released, everyone laughed.

Except Mordec.

He waited until the laughter had died down and then he said: 'Boi, you humiliated dat man in front of his crew, do you know how vexed he's gonna be? You should of merked him when you coulda. Dats what a real fighter woulda done.'

There was a tense silence. If Borz or Pels or even Duane had been so accused, there would have been an immediate, and probably bloody, response.

'Mercy is a powerful thing too, Mordec,' was all Lance said.

There was no challenge in his voice, his tone thoughtful rather than provoking, so Mordec, who was obviously spoiling for a fight, couldn't escalate things and just had to stand there while that strange word – *mercy* – reverberated around the Mill.

I knew the moment couldn't hold, so I stepped in quickly:

'The past is the past,' I said to Mordec. 'Today the future begins. It is right that you also come to the Stone.' And yes, Myrtle, I did think that out in advance, as I watched and I waited. *One more friend is one less enemy.*

'Only you have to swear,' put in Duane. 'Swear for the Crew. Like we have.'

'And for Art,' said Quin.

'For Art? For my lil bro?' Mordec spat on the floor.

'And for the Knights of the Stone,' I repeated.

'Never,' said Mordec. 'You could burn alive and I wouldn't stop to piss on you.'

'If you don't come to the Stone,' said Quin, 'you will have no voice here.'

Quin – ever my queen.

'No one gives me permission to speak,' said Mordec. 'If I wanna chat, I chat.'

Shaman growled softly.

'I mighta mashed my eye,' he said, scowling at the dog, 'but there aint nada wrong with my voice.'

I took the knife and carved an *M* into the Stone next to where Duane sat.

'This is your place, Mordec, a place at the Stone ready for you when you are ready for it. That is my word.'

'Yur word,' sneered Mordec.

But the Knights had heard and the Stone was true and I knew who had the power that day.

POWER.

MERCY.

I added those two words beneath *Quin* and *Peace* on the page of the Future. Perhaps I shouldn't have put power. But there is power in mercy as Lance had shown that day in the cemetery. Mordec was not to be placated but the rest of the Crew – the Knights of the Crew – understood what had been achieved that day.

What followed were undoubtedly the happiest weeks of my life. As I said, it was August and hot and we lay by the water – river and canal – all day and sometimes all night too. We began to communicate in a way that we'd never done before. We talked about important things, intimate things. It would be easy to say that this was yet another effect of Lance's coming, but I don't think that would be wholly true. I think it was about, for the first time in our lives, feeling safe. Not having always to look over our shoulders. I like to think that this was my gift, what I gave as king. I began to build a place of safety. If you've ever been really scared, not just scared to go out or be on the streets alone, but scared to live inside your own skull, then you'll know what I mean.

Until that time, no one had really opened up, talked about themselves. Details of our lives outside the Mill were deliberately left sketchy, as though we had no existence except our Mill one. There were reasons for this. Our other lives were often painful and we had to assume those of our fellow travellers were painful too. Often it was better not to know and it was certainly better not to tell. That was just stirring pieces of glass in the heart. Besides, the more people knew about you – even among friends – the more you could be hurt. Some of us had had enough hurt. I can say this now, but of course it wasn't so clear then, not at all. We were only children after all.

But in those hot August weeks we lay and talked, especially me and Quin, Lance and Elayne. While the truce held, while the Saxons were at bay, we seemed have an urgent need to know each other: *Look at me! This is who I am! Who I might be!* The four of us lay together, five if you counted Shaman, who always lay with us. The talking began though, as so many things began, with you, Myrtle. Quin told us the story of your life, the story you'd shared with her as you'd sat together, heads bowed at the fire. How you really did have that big house and that swimming pool in Jamaica, a big farm in fact with a hundred estate workers. And also a child. You had a child, Myrtle, a boy called Deangelo. You weren't a baglady then, you were a wife and a mother and a landowner. You wore jewels and fine clothes and helped run the farm. That's why you were away when the hurricane struck. You were in Canada buying agricultural machinery. Of course you phoned home, but the lines were down. Of course you tried to get home, but the airport on the island was closed. It was a week before your feet touched island soil again. At the airport you hired a driver to take you home, not knowing what you would find there. You'd lived on that land for forty-five years and yet you thought the driver had taken a wrong turn, driven you somewhere else, somewhere you didn't belong and had no connection with. There was no big house any more, no smaller, estate workers' houses. They were piles of rubble, flat to the ground. There were no estate workers. There was no husband.

And there was no Deangelo.

Of course you went mad, why wouldn't you? It took you two years even to admit that Deangelo was dead. He was fifteen when you saw him last and he was to remain fifteen for ever. There was no body to bury so you buried part of yourself instead. And when the pain still wouldn't go away – because nothing ever goes away, does it, Myrtle? – when that pain stayed, you moved. You came to England. You tried to start again, a new life, a small life where no one knew what you'd been through, where no one could open the wound. But the wound opened all by itself, it opened at night when the dreams came and in the daytime when you stood in unfamiliar supermarkets and cried among the mangoes.

Eventually you arrived in a psychiatric ward. It was only then that you remembered how strong you were. When you discharged yourself it was not to return to the small, English life, but to come here to the canal. If you had nothing, then nothing could be taken from you. You could never hurt that much again. It was a conscious, deliberate choice. *Some things you can change, some you can't. Some things you can control, some you can't. The past – that's gone, but the future – it's all in your hands.*

Is that why you left that page blank, Myrtle? Because you didn't know how far you could go with your own future? I want to think you wrote that title for me, but of course you didn't. You were just working things out for yourself, how you could live a life that made sense, how you could look forward, not back, up not down. How you could still take pleasure in stars and red campion. How you could dream a different sort of dream.

'She didn't think she'd stay here for ever,' Quin finished. 'And then you came, bubz.'

'What?'

'Myrtle's husband was an Arab, so Deangelo was mixed race. Like you.' Quin paused. 'She stayed here because of you.'

'Did she say that?'

'No, but she didn't have to. I could see it in the way she looked at you. She was propa loved up with you, Art.'

I was lying on my back, Shaman beside me, and at that moment the dog lifted his great black head and laid it on my chest. As I stroked him – and he didn't always tolerate stroking – I thought how that made three people who had loved me in my life: Myrtle, Quin and my mother. Four if you counted Lance. If you've been loved, you can give love, isn't that right, Myrtle? And if you haven't, you can't. You just don't know how it's done. Just like if you're around good people, it's easier to be good. You were a good person, Myrtle, you were one of the best people I ever knew.

'I wish I'd known her,' Lance said.

'You didn't need to know her,' I said, more sharply than I intended.

Lance twisted around to look at me, but he didn't say anything and I didn't elaborate. Perhaps I resented Lance's natural goodness, perhaps it was just that I wanted to keep some part of Myrtle all to myself. A leopard cannot change his spots, not all at once anyway.

'Still,' said Lance mildly, 'it sounds like she was someone you could learn from.'

Quin sat up then.

'Why are you never angry, Lance?'

I'm not sure he knew what she meant at first, but I did and it was typical that it was Quin who put her finger on this strangeness – this specialness – about him. In the Mill, most of us were angry most of the time. We fought and sparred like we breathed, without pause. Small things brought us to the brink of fury. But Lance: he was like some huge calm lake you had to throw a rock into to get so much as a ripple. Even when he'd been jumped by the Crew, by Pels and Borz, Garvey and Duane, he didn't seem to resent the fact that it had been four to one. Same with HellRazor. The Crew had been burnt up about the use of the knife. Not Lance, though it was his flesh that had been cut, Lance defended himself as best he could and moved on. He didn't bear a grudge, he didn't blame.

'How do you do it?' pressed Quin. 'How do you keep so calm?'

Lance considered that, as though it was the first time anyone had required him to think about that part of himself.

'I'm not sure,' he said at last. 'I suppose I don't feel angry. If I don't feel angry why should I act angry?'

'You were vexed for me,' said Elayne. 'About me.' There was adoration in her eyes. And the pain that that girl would go on to endure was in direct proportion to that adoration.

'I was angry that they'd taken you,' was all he said. 'That wasn't right.'

'Weren't you vexed inside?' pressed Quin.

'No. Well, yes.' Lance put his hand over his heart – 'Not angry here but here' He tapped his head. 'Because it was wrong.'

You know, Myrtle, I'm really glad you never got to meet Lance. You would have loved him so much more than you ever loved me.

'Bad luck to HellRazor if you'd been really militant on him then,' said Elayne softly, teasing him.

'You can't fight if you're really mad,' said Lance seriously.

'Can't you?' I remembered back to the time when I was blooded in. I fought out of anger then, didn't I? But then, of course, it was partly because of Mordec hitting me. Because of the injustice of it. So perhaps that was what fired me up, made me strong – not the anger but the injustice. That was a new thought.

'If you're angry, you lose control,' continued Lance. 'Or that's what they teach you in karate. It's all about control.'

That's when he told us about *Kiai*, the spiritual shout.

'Kee-eye, Kee-eye!' shouted Elayne. 'Did you do it to scare HellRazor?'

'No.'

'But it did scare him!'

'The shout releases the air in your body, so you don't get winded if your opponent lands a blow.'

'But it's more than that, isn't it?' said Quin.

'Yes.' But he didn't go on, he didn't have to. I knew what that shout was, it was power and soul and it came from a kind of Myrtle place, a place beyond the things you knew.

'What else do they teach you?' Elayne asked. It was as though she never wanted the conversation to end.

'Meditation,' said Lance. 'They make you get up at sunrise, clear your mind.'

'Clear your mind?' questioned Quin.

'Yes. Try and let go, think about nothing.'

'What's the point of that?' asked Elayne.

Lance shrugged. 'It's part of the training.'

'I wanna know,' Quin persisted. 'Tell us.'

'I'm not sure I know,' said Lance.

'Please,' said Quin and she laid a very soft hand on him.

Or maybe it wasn't so soft, maybe that's how it looks to me now, as I remember from beyond the mirrors. But she definitely touched him and then he told us.

'You have to sit,' he said, and he got back into the position he'd adopted in the Mill, where he looked like he'd just finished praying and sat back down on his heels. Then he put his right hand under his left hand and let his thumbs touch. 'Then you close your eyes and listen to the sound of your own breathing.' He closed his eyes and we watched him breathe in and out.

'That's it?'

'If thoughts come, you have to try and let them go.'

'Why?' asked Quin.

He opened his eyes. 'It's about attachment. If you get too attached to things – to people' – he looked her right in the eye then, just as he'd done with me when I called him to the Stone – 'then you'll suffer. Pain. Loss.' He closed his eyes again. 'If you let things go, you can be free.'

'I still don't get it,' said Elayne.

'Why don't we try it,' said Quin suddenly. 'The four of us? Why don't we wake ourselves at sunrise and try it?'

It was a mad idea, stupid, but that was the sort of mood we were in in those weeks. Something, somewhere, had changed and we were grabbing on to things we'd never experienced before, new things. And we were laughing, so much laughter we had that August.

Of course we didn't know exactly when dawn was so we set our mobiles wrong and it was pitch black when we awoke.

'Well, if it had been light,' Quin said, 'we'd have missed it, wouldn't we.' And it wasn't really that funny but we all laughed anyway. There are no street lights down at the canal, so dark is really dark and there wasn't even a moon that night.

But gradually our eyes adjusted a little and we crept over the bridge that divided our island from the mainland, because Lance said he thought the sun would rise from behind the Mill and it would be good to look at it beyond the water.

'But we'll have our eyes closed, won't we?' said Quin and we all laughed again.

The bank was damp and Quin said we should huddle together for warmth. So we did, sat in a row, first Shaman, then me, then Quin, then Lance and then Elayne.

Yes, she was very close to him that night.

Lance sat on his heels and we tried that too.

'I can't do it,' said Quin. 'I can't even do the sitting.'

Nor could Elayne and nor could I.

'It doesn't really matter how you sit,' said Lance. 'Just be comfortable.'

So we did, all of our bodies touching, kneeling thigh against kneeling thigh.

'Shut your eyes,' instructed Lance.

'Why?' said Elayne and giggled. 'We can't see anythin anyway!'

We were like schoolkids being naughty, and that alone felt good, Myrtle, like we had let go of something already.

I shut my eyes. And actually I saw more with them shut. I saw spots of light and also lines of light, although that might have been eyelashes, but there were patterns there beneath my lids.

'Breathing,' said Lance, 'try and forget everything but your breathing.'

I slid my arm around Quin.

'No,' she said, wriggling, 'that makes me think of you. I'm supposed to be thinking nada.'

I took my arm away, but my leg was still right up against hers. And it was sexy there in the dark.

Her other leg must have been right against Lance's, but I never gave that a moment's thought.

I concentrated on my breathing, drawing the ins and outs more slowly than normal, listening to the sound of myself. And to the sound of the dog. I couldn't quite shut out the noise of his snuffling beside me. Lance had told us that the state we were trying to get to was something like that moment just before you fall asleep, when you're awake but suspended between reality and dreams. Or I think that's how he put it. Although it sounds more like something you would have said, Myrtle. Because in the midst of the dark and the breathing it was you I was thinking of, Myrtle. And I tried to clear my mind as instructed, but you wouldn't go away and actually I didn't want you to. I didn't want to let you go from my mind any more than I'd wanted to close the sheet on you that day at the canal. If that's attachment, that's all right by me. I never had so much in my life I could afford to let go of anything I loved.

Quin.

Oh, Quin.

Of course I thought of Quin too that morning, conjured her dark and glorious face behind my eyelids, tried to hear her breath too, inhaled in case I could catch some of her sweetness. And perhaps I was suspended between dream and reality then, only I wanted the reality, so I opened my eyes. What I saw was the dawn.

It was transfixing. At first there was just the faintest tinge of something in the sky, a pale rim of light which made the Mill building look all the blacker, and then, in moments, it was a real outline. You could see the square hugeness of the Mill with its derelict bell-tower suddenly lit like in a film, and for the first time ever, I saw the old bell itself, black against the coming blue. Because it all went blue then, baby blue, Knight Crew blue, the rim tracking higher and taking in the great conical towers of the brewery beyond. And I remembered that first day I'd come to the Mill when the mists were looming and how I thought of it as a great castle. And here it was again, my Mill, my castle and your sky, Myrtle. I was looking up, not down, and the sun was rising higher, coming over the roof-line of the Mill and all of a sudden its reflection was in the water, and I saw a great golden path open out across the river in front of me. And I – who was not supposed to be thinking – thought: *I should walk that path. I should walk towards the sun.*

I was aware then that I wasn't the only one with my eyes open. Quin and Elayne and even Lance were watching the sun rise. And nobody was laughing. Maybe the sun walked towards them just as it walked towards me, maybe it held them spellbound too, because we didn't speak. And I can't really explain exactly how I felt in that moment, except if it was gratitude. Yes, maybe I felt grateful to be alive. As though just being alive was enough.

I don't know how long it was that we all kept the silence but I do know that it was Quin who finally spoke.

'In Nigeria,' she said, 'the sun is so bright, you think there can't be darkness anywhere in the world. Even in the bush where it's dense and thick, there's sand beneath your feet. Bright, bright sand. And there are birds as common as sparrows with tails of blue and green and green lizards with red heads and claws, which if they scratch you sting like pepper. And there are oranges in the trees and spiders, hundreds and hundreds of spiders, like tiny crabs, shells on their backs.' She came to a breathless stop, suddenly embarrassed by the spill. 'Or that's what I remember, from when I was four.'

But I didn't want her to stop. I had no idea that her head contained such dazzling things.

'Only spiders don't have shells, do they,' she added more slowly, 'so that can't be right, can it? But I had to go and get the oranges, or maybe they were tangerines and I was afraid, because of the spiders, because I thought they'd fall on me.'

Afterwards I asked myself whether these words, the ones I've written down, were the actual ones Quin used? Maybe, I thought, I didn't hear the words, just saw the pictures, a little black child in that gorgeous, gaudy place? But I don't think so. I think these were Quin's exact words. Words which opened us up, made our lives bigger, just as Lance's word *mercy* had. And none of this will surprise you, Myrtle, but it surprised me.

'You were brought up in Africa?' said Lance.

'Till I was five. I came here when I was nearly five.'

And I hadn't known that and it made me feel I didn't know her at all. But I did, because I'd always understood her largeness, the part of her which (as with you, Myrtle) seemed beyond the things that you could count or see.

'My mother gave me to her sister Abeni and her husband,' Quin continued.

'Yur mum gave you away?' said Elayne.

'It's not so uncommon in Nigerian culture. Abeni was too old for kids, and my mother had four already. I was the fifth. Quinta. My mother was glad to see me go. "You're going to a better life," she said.'

I re-visualised that bright sun and the bright sand and the bright birds and tried to see the bright black mother holding Quin in her arms and whispering about the better place, the better life. Only when I tried to picture that black mother, I could only see my own mother, the long-ago one, holding me in her arms and whispering fairy tales.

'My mother gave me away too,' said Elayne. 'Put me in care.'

165

And of course that wasn't so uncommon either, not among our fellow-travellers. Yet I hadn't known that either.

'You OK, bubz?' asked Quin.

'Yes,' said Elayne. 'You?'

'Of course. I call Abeni Mum, she is my mum. Dayo's my mad. A mum and a dad,' she looked at me. 'I'm blessed, right?'

'And me too,' said Elayne. 'Cos my grandma came for me. Took me back.'

'Your grandma,' repeated Quin. I had her hand in mine by then and, it may have been my imagination, but I thought I felt her fingers tremble. In any case, she pulled herself upright. 'It's blitz. We should go in.'

Shaman rose too, shook himself. It was cold, despite the coming sun, but I hadn't noticed it till then. The damp of the ground seemed to have seeped into our bones.

Back at the Mill the others were still asleep, but we couldn't sleep. Lance and I broke up a pallet and set a fire close to the grinding stone, for warmth.

We sat and watched the flames as we'd sat and watched the path of sunlight across the water.

'In the village,' said Quin, 'there's no electricity. At night just fires and torches. That's it. The rest is as black as Shaman.'

'So what do the people do?' Elayne asked. 'Like at night?'

'Sleep.' Quin paused. 'And sing. My grandma was always singing.'

'Do you remember the songs?' asked Lance.

Quin didn't answer him, kept staring into the flames. And I thought of the song she sang to you, Myrtle, as she washed you and wrapped your old bones in the sheet. Is that why she took such care that night? For you, Myrtle, but also for the memory, for the loss of her own once-upon-a-time grandmother? I wanted Lance to leave my queen alone.

And he didn't ask her again. Instead he picked up an old oil can, held it upright on his knee and, very softly, began drumming. The sound wasn't like fingers on tin but like the beat of blood in your veins, it flowed in and through you, warm as your heart, regular as your breathing. At first he drummed slowly and all of us seemed to relax and expand but then his fingers began to hit harder and stronger and Shaman lifted his head and I thought that great mouth would open in a yowl again, but it was Quin's mouth that opened. The sound that came out was as tribal as Lance's *Kiai*, yet soft, so soft, a rhythmic chant of mythical words.

Words, Myrtle. There were so many beautiful words inside that girl and you released them with your death and he released them with his drumming.

Agbe gbé mi délé oò-agbe
Agbe gbé mi délé oò-agbe
A kì í ràjò ká máà délé oò
Agbe gbé mi délé

Elayne and I sat there stupefied as Lance matched his beat to her beat and then began to join the song, singing in response to her, as though she was leading him, guiding him. And the sound was more lovely than anything I'd heard in my life and yet it made me ache inside.

And it made Elayne ache too. That was quite clear, she looked at Quin with jealousy and Lance with longing. Because she wanted to sing the song too and she couldn't.

And nor could I.

When they came to a stop Quin's eyes were shining.

Lance lay down the oil can.

'How did you know that song?' Elayne challenged Lance. He shrugged. 'I didn't.'

'You sang it!'

'Quin sang it. I copied her, that's all.'

'You knew the beat,' Elayne pressed.

He shrugged again. 'Quin found the beat.'

'What did it mean?' I said, suddenly furious. 'What do those words mean?'

'*Blue toraco lift me home,*' said Quin dreamily.

'Blue toraco?'

'It's a bird,' Quin continued. 'With tail feathers of blue and yellow. People take them for good luck.' She glanced at Lance and began humming again. '*A kì í ràjò ká máà délé oò. One does not go on a journey and not return home. Blue toraco carry me home.*'

And her faraway face and Lance's near one and the notion of a place you could call home, a place which called to your most secret soul, all that so balled the loneliness inside me that when Mordec emerged from the shadows, I was glad of him.

'Hush up yur mouths,' he shouted. 'Some of us here are tryin to kip.'

20

Mordec.

While Lance's wounds were healing, Mordec's were festering. Lance had a thin line of red above his right ankle and another arced on his chest, but they were quiet and covered-up injuries. Mordec's eye, now he'd torn away the bandage, was an angry thing. He could see well enough but the flesh over his cheekbone and around the eye socket was raw and inflamed.

'Bubz, I think they let you out a bit early,' said Quin. 'Get that hospital to check you out.'

'Wot?' said Mordec. 'You don't like da way I look? I'm gonna look like dis till I'm six foot under.' He flung an empty beer can at Shaman. 'Thanks to dat fuckin furball.' It was not the only object he'd thrown at the dog, but Shaman had an almost uncanny sense of Mordec's movement about the Mill and his guard was always up. The beer can, like many others, missed.

'You shouldn't have knifed a defenceless old woman,' I said. And that's what I sometimes thought when I looked at him, that his crime was written on his face for all to see. But though the crime was his, the injury was down to me, wasn't it, Myrtle? Because I could have stopped the dog and I didn't. Lance would have stopped the dog, Lance would have controlled his anger, shown mercy. But I had been without compassion that day and, though I didn't know it then, that lack would cost me dear.

Quin kept on about the hospital but, despite all her persuasions, Mordec refused to return. I began to believe he was deliberately nursing the wound, letting its poison course round his body, feed his resentment. In his mutterings against me, I felt he used his disfigurement as a kind of proclamation: *Look where my brother's leadership has brought us.* He took Pels aside, he whispered with Garvey, he even muttered with some of the yungas – Tardis and LameDuck among them. I never heard his actual words, but I didn't have to. Things filtered back to me: the truce couldn't hold, the Saxons would come back at us, mercy was nothing, I had been weak, Lance had been weak and, finally, what sort of leader lies by a canal and sings?

Perhaps I could have stopped the twittering, called Mordec to account, made him come to the Stone and speak out loud. But I didn't. Maybe that was a mistake. I suppose I felt I had time on my side and, more than this, that I had Lance on my side. That was the beginning and end of it really. With Lance beside me I felt I could keep us all safe, not just physically safe, as Elayne felt for instance, but morally safe. I think that's the first time I've used that word, Myrtle. Moral. It's one of the words I found in your book. Hard not to find it, you wrote it so many times. What do I mean by this word? Only this, that when you had Lance beside you, you felt you would always have right on your side. That his soul was brighter and purer and more powerful even than the blade of the Buck 119.

And it wasn't just me who felt his strength. It was Borz too and Donkey and Duane. The kingdom was mine, but Lance was the jewel in the crown. So we were all stunned when he stopped coming to the Mill.

We made no arrangements about the Mill, never promised to be there or not there, but there was a rhythm to our comings and goings and one day he just wasn't there.

There was no prelude, no announcement, no indication and no reason I could fathom for his absence. People looked to me as if I should know something, but I didn't.

The gap he left was monumental.

People called him of course, starting with Elayne. But he didn't answer his phone or he had it turned off.

'School started, has it?' jeered Mordec. 'Mebbe he went to get an exam.'

And it was September by then, I think, and maybe the schools were back, it wasn't something we were used to paying attention to.

'He'll come Saturday,' I said to Elayne, 'Sunday.'

But he didn't.

'What if they've taken him?' Elayne cried. 'The Saxons. What if they've nabbed him?'

'How could they nab him?' said Quin. 'Borz an Pels and Duane an Garvey, the four of them could take him.'

'If they'd taken him, we'd know anyway,' I said. 'The Saxons would rave about it, they'd want us to know.'

But I still made enquiries, got Donkey on the wires to see who was talking to who.

'Nada,' Donkey said. 'No man knows nada.'

'You can never really trust a Milky Bar,' said Mordec.

'You could trust Lance,' said Elayne. 'Lance was different.'

Mordec laughed. 'He was never really one of us. Jus take one look at the cracker an you could tell.'

'He was blooded in,' said Elayne, 'he was Crew.'

'He was a champion,' said Quin. 'A Knight of the Stone.'

'Stone!' Mordec spat.

'Why's everyone saying *was*?' asked Elayne, her voice suddenly going high and tight. 'Why am I saying it? He is our champ. *Is*!'

'Not if he aint here,' said Garvey, appearing from nowhere to stand at Mordec's side.

I felt exposed. The tide that seemed so easy to stem with Lance beside me, now seemed to wash dangerously about me. With Lance the Stone seemed to represent something solid, something achievable, without him everything was suddenly flimsy.

'We'll find him,' I said. 'I'll find him.'

'You don't even know where he cotches,' said Mordec.

It was true. We'd always met here, at the Mill. But I knew I had to find him. Elayne's distress had become Quin's. And I loved my queen for her fretting because I believed it meant she knew how much I missed and needed Lance, how central he was to my hopes and dreams.

And it was Quin who suggested he might have left his address with the hospital.

'When he picked up Mordec, maybe he left it as a contact?'

She was right, of course. How well she understood him even then. Lance, giving his address just in case because, with a father dead and a mother locked away, there was no one to stand next-of-kin for Mordec.

I left Shaman at the Mill with Quin and went to the hospital alone. Quin had wanted to come with me but with the unease, I thought it better if one of us remained at base. Her instincts were mine, I trusted her implicitly.

At the hospital, I spun a story about needing the address to send our family's thanks to our good Samaritan. The nurse smiled approvingly as she wrote out the address in loopy blue biro: 12a Cardon Avenue. I knew Cardon Avenue, it ran parallel to the main thoroughfare that divided the estates from the rest of the world. The road was numbered from 1 at the southernmost end to about 200 at its northernmost reach. That meant that Lance's address, number 12, fell at the southern end which, although Cardon wasn't part of the estates, still made it closer to Cornwall than Mount Bladon. That felt good.

I was there in less than an hour. The flat wasn't in a block, but occupied the first two floors of a three-storey house in the middle of a terrace. The door was painted green and had a discoloured brass knocker in the shape of a lion's head.

I knocked.

'It's open!' shouted a voice.

At my place in Cornwall we had three separate locks on the door (one of which was a deadlock), plus a spy-hole and a chain. When people were really scared – like Lee's mother – they also fitted iron grilles or gates in front of the door.

'Come on in,' said the voice.

So in I went, just pushed the door very lightly and there I was, in Lance's home. The hallway was narrow, made narrower by the piles of paper to left and right, magazines or posters of some sort. I hesitated.

'In here,' called the voice. 'Kitchen.'

I followed the sound forward and then down two steps, careful of my footing among the papers..

'Adele!' the voice greeted and a middle-aged woman in a floating purple dress appeared at the kitchen door. 'Oh, not Adele. Sorry, I was expecting someone else.'

'Art,' I said tentatively. 'I'm a friend of Lance's.'

'Hib,' she said, offering me her hand. 'Hibiscus. Child of the Sixties.' I must have looked blank because she went on: 'Never mind, I never got it either. From the club, are you?'

'Club?'

'Karate.'

'Oh,' I said. 'No. I mean, yes.' The lie was probably unnecessary but automatic anyway. It seemed simpler. 'I mean, we used to link at the club . . . but I'm not there now.'

'Oh – so you've given up fighting, have you, Art?' she asked. 'Good for you. I never see why men have to fight all the time. We're not Neanderthals any more. We're civilised people. At least some of us are. Lance!' She suddenly yelled at the stairs. If Lance was up there, he didn't reply.

'Still,' Hib went on, 'I suppose I was glad he had the training when that knife maniac attacked him the other week. Did he tell you about that?'

'Er . . . yes.'

'Animals. I know we're not supposed to say that about our young people but honestly those boys on the estate, they're just animals! Animals! I blame the fathers. A father should be about for his son. Right?'

'Right,' I said.

'Lance!' She yelled again and when he still didn't appear she just shrugged and said: 'Tell you what, as you're here, wouldn't mind doing me a favour, would you? I need a pair of fresh eyes.' From the piles of newspaper cuttings on the kitchen table she pulled two large envelopes.

'What do you think of this?'

From the first envelope she drew out an A4-sized poster which had a picture of what I thought was a newborn baby on it. Only the baby was covered in blood and had one of its little legs pulled off. Above the picture ran the words 'Your choice', and below it: 'His death, Sammy, aged twenty-three weeks.'

'Grimy,' I said.

'Grimy?' she repeated.

'Disgusting.'

'Oh good,' she said. 'Excellent. And this one?' The next poster was just the bloody head and neck of a newborn, held by a pair of forceps as if the baby had been ripped so violently from the womb he – or she – had come out in two pieces.

'Worse,' I said. 'Sick.'

'Interesting. I prefer the one without the leg, myself.' She looked at my face. 'Sorry to do it to you, love, but killing people is wrong. As in right and wrong. Right? And words don't do it, do they? You've got to see the pictures. I mean, *foetus* – people can't get their minds round that word, doesn't conjure anything. But this little boy, Sammy, he's a real baby, a real person. And they killed him.'

I began to wonder if she was bipolar and, if she wasn't, how much more extreme she could be if she was.

'What do you think?' she asked.

'About what?'

'Abortion, of course.'

'I think,' I said, quite slowly, 'that if you're going to merk – kill – someone, you should look them in the eye first.' I don't know why I said that, Myrtle. You probably do, because I expect it was you who also suddenly lay sightless Danny MacMahon with his shock of black hair on the table, naked and covered in blood like a big, big baby.

'Oh very clever,' she said and then she laughed. 'I might use that idea. That'd shake them up.'

I needed to get out of there.

'Is he upstairs?' I asked.

'What?' she said distractedly. 'Oh Lance. Probably. Probably got his music on too loud. Can't hear us. Why don't you go up and see? It's the room straight in front of you.'

I went up. His door was shut and there was no music unless he was on earphones. I knocked, I did that because I thought, if he'd been in my house, that's what he would have done. There was no answer, so I called to him and when he still didn't reply I went in.

'Lance?'

It was a small, sparse room and he wasn't in it. I felt a great wash of disappointment. How could he not be there! I realised then that I'd had expectations of this moment. In my imagination I'd seen him waiting for me, getting up to embrace me (yes – I imagined Lance embracing me), glad that I'd come for him. Next, he'd tell me whatever it was that had kept him from us, and we'd laugh about it, and then we'd walk out the door together and back to the Mill. And everything would be all right again.

Only he wasn't there.

I should have left right then, but I didn't, I went into the room and shut the door behind me. It felt wrong but I was curious. I realised I wanted to look at his things, see how he lived when he wasn't at the Mill. There was little enough to look at, a bed, a desk, some shelves, but the feel of the room was very different from the ground-floor spaces of the house. Downstairs there was chaos and mess, paper and clutter, here everything was neat and carefully arranged. The bed was made (not something I could imagine paper-strewing Hibiscus being bothered with), the wastepaper basket (Lance had a wastepaper basket!) emptied, his small collection of books lined up tidily. The only thing that seemed slightly out of place, slightly too colourful, were the three drums by the desk. Not Western drums but African ones, different sizes but each the shape of a large goblet with skin pulled taut across the top and secured with beads and string and rope. I picked one up, remembering how his hands had thrummed the oil can, and I began to beat the drum as he had the can, only the sound I made was hollow. I put the drum down.

On the desk was a notebook with a blue hologrammed cover. If I shouldn't have gone into that room and shut the door behind me, I certainly shouldn't have looked in that book. You need permission for notebooks, don't you, Myrtle? But I picked it up and opened it. It was book of songs, every page written in his neat hand. There were songs about fighting men, about rivers and journeys, there were poems about loneliness and missing parts of oneself. And then there was a love song, the last thing to be written in the book. It was titled *Blue Toraco* and it was about a girl who was afraid of spiders with shells on their backs.

'A girl,' went the song, 'brighter and more beautiful than the Nigerian sun.'

21

I needed to leave.

I wasn't going to say goodbye to Lance's mother but there she was in the hall greeting a woman I presumed was Adele. They were standing at the bottom of the stairs kissing. It was only a kissing of cheeks but the noise of it was loud.

'Oh,' said Hib, when she noticed me. 'You off already?'

'He's not in,' I said.

'Oh,' she said. 'Well, I'll tell him you stopped by.'

I went out onto the street.

Kissing.

I tried to keep calm.

Kissing!

That flesh-to-flesh smacking sound.

It was just a song, I told myself. Just a few words (words, Myrtle) on a page. What did that prove? I mean, if you write a song about a river, it doesn't mean you're in love with the river, does it? Besides, Quin *was* brighter and more beautiful than the Nigerian sun. You would have to be a stone not to see that. And Lance wasn't a stone, he was flesh and blood. Handsome flesh, red blood. Why should he not admire the beauty of my queen? It wasn't a hidden thing, it was there for everyone to see. But, of all men, Lance. The only man I think I'd ever cared about and who had cared for me. Lance, who'd come into my life because of his concern for a blood-ied stranger – my brother. Lance, who'd offered me a lift on his bike because he intuitively understood my urgency, my need. Lance, who'd stood up for Elayne and been prepared to die for me in a fight that wasn't his, because he believed kidnap was wrong and besides, we had given our word. He had given his word. Lance, who was the best of all my Knights, the most shining example of all that was possible. Lance who was sworn to the Stone. And to me.

So why did I need to hear Quin's voice?

My phone was off, I'd obviously failed to switch it back on after being at the hospital. There were three messages. The first was a text from Elayne: 'Saxons nabbed Lance. They got him!' The second was a voice-mail from Quin (her voice, her beautiful voice): 'Pick up babe, pick up, we need you.' And the third message was from Duane, but I didn't get to listen to that one before he called again.

'Art? Art! You gotta come, man.'

'What?'

'It's all kickin off in Tintagel.'

'Whoa – slow down.'

Duane was breathless and incoherent but his urgency was compelling. I was twenty minutes' running time from Tin-tagel but I began that run. Running pumps your body and clears your brain.

Babe.

We need you.

We?

'Wah blow, Duane?' I repeated. 'You gotta tell me.'

Duane's words were fast, a jumble about how the Saxons had taken Lance and were holding him in Bladon.

I didn't believe it. 'Did Pug come, was he the messenger?'

'No.'

'Who was then? How do we know it's true?'

'Mordec said.'

'Mordec!'

'Can't explain,' said Duane, 'but it's startin, it's gonna start.'

'What, Duane? What's gonna start?'

'Mordec said we should get tooled up and go straight into Bladon, cut em down. He'd lead the show. He was on it, Art. I said we should cotch an wait for word from you. But yur blowa was off – where de hell have you been? Borz said I was a pussy, Lance was our champ, if he was in danger we should go to him. And Elayne wouldn't cotch either. Elayne said she knew where they held her and she guessed they'd hold him there too and even Mordec didn't want that, but while they were arguing, she just jetted. She's gone to Bladon, Art, she's gone on her jays!'

That last was clear – Elayne by herself in enemy territory. 'Where are you now?' I asked Duane.

'Fickling Street.'

'So you'll be at Tintagel in ten,' I calculated. 'I'll be there in . . . seventeen.' But only if I kept running full pelt. 'And Mordec?'

'He's gone ahead with the others, but dey're stopping for tools.'

'Do we know where Elayne's headed?'

'Essex Street. Dat's where they kept her. Mack and Jimbo's place on Essex Street.'

'I'll be there.' I clicked off and dialled Elayne. Maybe I could head her off. Elayne alone in Bladon was suicide. But there was no reply. No reply! Just a disembodied voice: *The Vodaphone you are dialling may be switched off.* May be switched off or actually switched off? And who had flicked that switch? Elayne's actions were mad, she'd gone insane.

But then Elayne loved Lance, he filled her big adoring eyes. And if you face losing the thing you love, it can make you mad, can't it, Myrtle? Can't it!

I dialled Mordec. No reply. But I didn't expect a reply. I expected him to flick me away. He had what he wanted. A fight on his hands and the troops lined up behind him. My troops.

I was still running.

I did not call Quin. I could feel my own madness rising. *If you're angry, you lose control.* Lance, ever my tutor. If he'd touched her . . . but of course he hadn't touched her. It was just a song. Not even a love song. I had given it that name, I had named it a love song, because Quin was my love. He had just written about spiders with shells on their backs. Lance was good: a good warrior, a good friend, a good man. I needed to hold on to that.

And I needed to be calm.

I tried to concentrate on the Saxons. Some part of me still didn't believe they'd taken Lance. It smelt like a trick, only I didn't know whose trick, the Saxons' or Mordec's?

Mordec's probably. The imminent scuff was certainly his doing. The man couldn't wait, not one hour, not one minute. I'd been away such a short time and already he was undermining the authority of the Stone. I'd thought the Stone was a place of shared authority and also of peace, somewhere I could go to think things through. It was only at that moment that I saw it for what it was, a place of order. I thought back to Lance's pristine bedroom. His neatness was the same thing writ small, a way of keeping his mother's chaos at bay. The Stone was my way of keeping chaos at bay: the chaos of the Mill. The chaos of my life.

And here was Mordec, crashing into that order with his violent, violating desire for power.

And I was doubting Lance.

I had arrived at Tintagel.

What I saw would haunt me for the rest of my life. It happened in slow motion, or perhaps that was just the effect of my legs suddenly becoming still, so that everything around me seemed to slow down too. I stood there heaving and panting, unable for that split second, to shout, to intervene, and this is what I saw: Mordec, at the junction of Camcaid and Tintagel, brandishing a knife. Not the Buck knife, not my knife, but a big knife nonetheless. He held it like a gloat above his head. Behind him were others of the Crew, prominent among them Garvey and Pels, Tardis and LameDuck. The Whisperers. Tanisha was also there. Tanisha! Although Tanisha had been OG's main girl, I always thought of her as more Knight than Crew, I had not appointed her to the Stone but she had been part of my hopes.

Opposite them, in the mouth of Essex Street, stood a band of Saxons. I didn't recognise the front men – Tractor wasn't there, or HellRazor or the O'Dairs – so it must have been mainly yungas but they were still red in their roars, red in their flags and soon, I thought, to be red in blood. I was perhaps twenty foot from the combat zone and, because the road sloped where I was, slightly higher up, I had the sensation of looking down on the action as though it was a film, an unreality, a lunacy.

If I'd had had to guess what would happen next, I would have imagined Mordec yelling, leading a charge, but all at once there was a Saxon in the road, a young boy, slight as a girl, pushed out from the crowd and then suddenly running towards the Crew, towards Mordec's knife, with an astonishing and foolhardy courage you had to admire, because nothing distracted him, he just ran straight at Mordec and he didn't even seem to have a weapon. He was dressed head to foot in red, the clothes all seeming a little jumbled, a little big on his light frame, and the red and white scarf about his head jaunty as a pirate's. As he ran he shouted something I was too far away to hear and, if Mordec heard it, it made no difference to him.

Later they told me that she shouted 'Lance!' For it wasn't a Saxon boy, it was a girl who ran onto to Mordec's vicious knife. And, despite her calling, Mordec still stabbed out, gave a great whoop of triumph as that red figure fell. And just before he punched I knew who that child was – knew before she fell and the scarf came free from her head and she landed on her back, face upturned, hair stubbled about her scalp.

'Elayne!' screamed Tanisha.

And yet he'd stabbed, the bloodlust so high in him he'd just stabbed anyway.

I don't really know the order of what happened next except that I was suddenly beside her and so was Quin and so was the ambulance. There was someone shouting. It was Mordec: 'She was wearing red. She was wearing red!'

Which was a lie and I hated him for it.

Then he was gone, they were all gone – Crew and Saxons. If the ambulance was there it would only be a moment before the Feds were too.

Only Quin and I remained, Quin kneeling on the ground, cradling Elayne's head in her lap, holding her one more time, as she had that day in the cemetery. Only my Queen did not look strong any more, she looked all choked up. 'Stay with me, bubz,' she was whispering. 'Please stay.'

'They haven't got him,' Elayne said dreamily, eyes closed, 'they haven't got Lance after all.' And then she seemed to drift from us.

The first of the ambulance men was big and fat.

'Move out the way, love,' he said to Quin.

'Tell me she's going to be all right,' Quin said.

'No one's all right in this estate,' said the ambulance man. 'Sometimes I think we shouldn't come 'ere. Just leave you to it. More of you dead the better.'

He was pulling at Elayne's clothes, finding the wound, which was in her stomach.

'Jesus Christ,' said the ambulance man. 'Tom,' he called to his colleague and then, to me and Quin, 'Get back, get out of the way!'

They worked on her, stuck needles in her, hitched her to drips, loaded her into the van.

'Can I come?' asked Quin.

'Only family allowed,' said the ambulance man.

'I am family,' said my queen.

He sighed. 'Get in.'

The door slammed. Quin didn't look back at me, all her focus was on Elayne.

By the time the Feds arrived and asked for witnesses there weren't any. Even I'd begun walking, though not to anywhere in particular. I didn't know where to go or what to do. I felt as if I was drowning, as if I'd fallen into the river beside the Mill and water had closed over my head. I didn't want to go home – there was no one and nothing for me there. But I didn't want to go to the Mill either.

In retrospect, I think I should have gone to the Mill, retaken control, stood in my place at the Stone. But seeing Elayne like that, at the end of Mordec's knife, ripped the spirit from me. Suddenly nothing seemed worthwhile any more, as if all that I'd dreamt we could do or be had gone, disappeared with Lance, run with Mordec, ebbed with that wound. Elayne was one of us, of the four who, together, I'd thought could build something from the truce, from the power of my Stone. The four of us who'd found some brief happiness as we'd lain by water and thought of things bigger than ourselves.

And then there was Mordec himself. I did not trust myself with him. Could not be certain that my knife hand would not make one more blood-soaked wound that day.

So I just wandered not paying attention to the roads I took or the turnings I chose. Eventually I realised I'd wandered far away from the estates and I was afraid because away was where Keifer went on the night he lost my mother and found a tree. But there loomed in front of me not a tree but another castle, the huge edifice of a church, St Michael and All Angels. And I went in. Don't ask me why. Perhaps it was because it was getting dark and there was a spill of light from the entrance and that light, just for a moment, looked like the golden path that had trod to me across the water. Perhaps I was driven in by rain or simply by the need to be somewhere where I wasn't known, so I could rest.

It was a cavernous building but not gloomy, lit as it was with candles, and the flickering light made me think of OG and I almost (almost) wished him back at the Mill, so someone else could be in charge, do the thinking, and I could just let go, drift away like Elayne.

A man came up to me then, his black robes swishing at the floor.

'Welcome,' he said and gave me a smile and a sheet of paper. 'Welcome to our Church.'

And I felt stupid tears prick behind my eyes again, not for the bit of paper which was just some service sheet but for a welcome that came with a smile not a punch. Such small gestures to make a heart lift. The man swished away and I took a seat. I chose a place in a pool of dark behind a column, but I could still see the quivering light of the candles and it made me feel strangely at home. Maybe, I thought, people came to this place as they came to the Mill, because they didn't have anywhere else to go. The sheet in my hand said 'Evensong', so I supposed it was a Sunday. I'd lost track. People began to file in, most of them elderly, old women with woolly hats and clumpy shoes, old men with grey hair and worn-out overcoats. They paid no attention to me, just nodded at each other in a slow, shuffling way and then dotted themselves about the huge space.

After a while somewhere else in the building, unseen by me, someone lay soft hands on the organ and the church was suddenly full of this great lifting melody. I'd heard an organ before of course, but I'd never actually been in a place where one was being played. As well as the music, I could hear puffing and clanking as though the organ was some huge, lumbering beast, some dragon of my mother's imagination with a deep memory and many loves and many wounds to recount. The old people didn't listen as the great beast sang, maybe because they'd heard it all before. But the song was strange to me and stirringly beautiful, and I ached to have Quin beside me, because I knew she would hear what I heard.

A little while later, the priest went up to the altar in his golden robes, the beast wheezed and roared a more familiar tune and the old people began to croak out a hymn. The service proper had begun. The hymn was printed on the sheet but the words meant nothing to me and I was thinking I should leave when I noticed the name of the person scheduled to read the first lesson: Alice MacMahon.

And of course Alice MacMahon could not be related to Danny MacMahon. She couldn't be his mother, she couldn't be his grandmother. There were so many MacMahons in the world what was the chance of this MacMahon, Alice Mac-

Mahon, having anything to do with young, dead, Danny? No chance. No chance at all. Yet still the adrenalin flicked in me so I stayed, stayed in the church of St Michael and All Angels because of that name, because I wanted to lay eyes on Alice MacMahon.

As I waited the old people prayed, the priest intoned, the monstrous organ breathed and I thought of you, Myrtle. How God had seeded a hurricane in your heart, killed your husband and killed your child. And how you'd risen from your crushing, how you'd looked up again at the stars and held red campion in the palm of your hand. And I thought then that maybe you'd led me here (because you did lead me here, didn't you, Myrtle?) so I could rise too, rise above the chaotic, malevolent Mordec, above the leaving of Lance and the wounding of Elayne which was also the wounding of all my hopes and dreams. So I tried to be as I was the night you showed me the stars, I tried to look up and not down, to open myself to where I was and why I was, to see things I'd never seen before, hear things I'd never heard. But in that church there was just a robed priest and a dark window and some rituals that weren't mine.

Then it was time for the reading. The lectern was a huge brass eagle with spread wings, polished till they shone. I moved along the pew so as not to be behind the column, so I could see Alice MacMahon as she came to the eagle. She was not an old woman, she didn't shuffle or stoop, and her coat was bright red. But she wasn't young either, not too young to have had a son Danny's age anyway. Her hair was dark and short and her face pale and shadowed in the flickering light.

This is the gospel of our Lord.

She began muttering words from the big book, only I didn't hear those words, or maybe I didn't understand them, because I wasn't looking at a woman with a red coat any more but a boy with a red knife sticking in him. And when I looked at him that time in Bladon I hadn't seen him, Myrtle, that's the honest truth, because he was enemy and enemy always looks the same. Enemy is blank face and hatred and that's what I saw that day. But when I looked at Alice MacMahon, it was Danny who was standing there. He was a small boy, Myrtle – did I ever tell you that? A small boy with a pale face and a neat nose and that dark, dark hair. He was staring straight out at me and for the first time, Myrtle, he had eyes. Clear, light hazel eyes, too light and too piercing for that shock of hair. And I suppose his mother and his father thought that they were beautiful eyes. But he wasn't an angel, he wasn't St Michael and All Angels, Myrtle, he was, after all carrying a baseball bat. But he was a child, Myrtle. Just a child. And I was a child too. Only I was the one with knife and I stuck it in his side and the blood flowed out into Alice MacMahon's red, red coat.

And suddenly in that dark flickering place with the red coat and the monstrous breathing dragon, I'm on my feet because I realise it's not Mordec or Lance or Elayne I have to rise above but myself, my careless, care less, murdering self and I'm shouting. *'I'm sorry. I'm sorry, Danny. It was wrong. I was wrong.'*

And of course I wasn't thinking about the reaction of anyone around me because, at that moment, there wasn't anyone around me, there was just Danny and the Mill and my life and where I'd come to and the red knife and the sleeping dragon and you, Myrtle, perhaps you. I was probably shouting to you. To make it up to you. To make it up to Danny.

Only there is no making up to a dead person, is there?

I don't know how long I stood there before I felt the stares of the old people and the hand of the priest and heard the gentle but insistent question, 'Are you all right, son?'

I had no idea whether I was all right. But Danny would know. Because you see he didn't just have eyes that time, Myrtle, he had a mouth, a little, tight mouth, and he looked at me with those clear eyes and that tight mouth and he said just one word:

Justice.

Then the child in me, who probably wanted something to end and knew then that it wouldn't, began to sob.

22

Alice MacMahon went on reading, reading and reading as if nothing had happened. Some of the old people tutted though. They didn't like the outburst in their quiet, holy place. When they looked at me they saw enemy, I suppose, a young mix-raced kid from a life that wasn't theirs. But the priest, he still leaned over me.

'Can I help, child? Can I do something?'

But nobody could help and there was nothing to be done, so I just mumbled and said I would go home.

'Where's home?' the priest asked. 'Can I take you there?'

'No,' I said. 'Thanks.'

'But will someone be there for you?' he pressed.

'Yes,' I said. 'Someone will be there for me.'

It turned out not to be a lie. When I got to our walkway landing, Shaman was sitting right outside the door of our flat. He must have walked from the Mill by himself, found his way by himself. Unless, that is, you guided him, Myrtle.

The great dog got up, shook himself and came to greet me. The night was dark and he was warm. He put his muzzle in my hand and I felt under his neck where he might have had a collar but didn't. I thought then what an extraordinary thing a dog is. How they love you despite everything and how you can actually feel the weight of that love. So I was wrong when I said it was only my long-ago mother, and you,

Myrtle, and Quin who'd loved me. Because Shaman loved me too and, I realised then, I loved him.

The dog and I went into the house together, tripping over the mail that had built up behind the door. I was glad of the mail though, it meant that we were ahead of Mordec, we had the house to ourselves. There were letters for my mother and there were letters for Keifer. Keifer's looked like final demands and another night I might have been angry that there were people out there prepared to pursue a dead man, but that night I was just glad that no one could make demands on Keifer ever again. I threw Keifer's letters in the bin. My mother's I took into the kitchen.

My mother.

Since Aunty Gina's departure there had been no word from my mother. No word on how she was, no word on how long she would remain at Hillview. Maybe Hillview thought there was no one home to send word to, and maybe they were right. But my mother herself? I wondered briefly if she thought about us at all, if she puzzled about my life, or Mordec's? But those thoughts were painful so I stored them, along with the letters, behind the toaster to wait for another day.

I realised I hadn't eaten since breakfast. The only thing I could find in the house was a jar of frankfurters, which I shared with the dog. That took up three minutes of the hour I had to wait for Quin. She'd texted from the hospital to say that Elayne was OK and she was on her way.

What did 'OK' mean?

I turned on the television, found myself watching a murder mystery. A killer was about to be brought to justice. Justice. I switched channels: a game show, a news programme, an American film. I wanted to lose myself in the telly the way Keifer used to. Perhaps I needed a beer, only there wasn't any beer. I switched off the television, time was moving slowly, oh so slowly. Shaman dozed and I envied him, watched his ears twitch as he dreamed.

Finally the bell rang and I opened the door on my queen.

'Art,' she cried, 'Art!' And she flung herself at me, pressed and buried herself in my chest, her head at my shoulder, her cheek to my neck, the taste of her hair in my mouth. I held her tight and close.

How could I have doubted her?

'Tell me,' I said.

Of course I wanted her to speak of us, of our love, make a mockery of Lance's song, but she spoke of Elayne, which was right too.

'She's going to live, bubz. They took her straight into theatre, operated straight away, but they said she'd be OK. "Not life-threatening", that's what they said.' Quin pulled away a little. 'Only I'm afraid . . .'

'About what, babe?'

'About Lance.'

I felt myself stiffen when she used his name. I couldn't help it.

'Elayne woke in the ambulance,' Quin continued, 'began just babblin. All bout Lance. Chattin shit mostly but, oh bubz, I think if Lance doesn't link Elayne she'll die but if he does, she'll be all right. I know this is madness but that's what I feel. That we have to find Lance.'

We broke the embrace, her eyes were full of wanting. I kissed her and she returned that kiss hungrily. My jealousy was misplaced. She only wanted Lance because he could make her best friend well.

Beside us the great dog shook for a second time.

I ushered Quin into the sitting room and the dog followed. 'I went to Lance's place,' I told her. 'He wasn't there but his mum thought he was. So he can't have jetted too far.'

'So why don't he answer his blowa?' wailed Quin.

'Does he know about Elayne?'

'Yes, I texted him from the hospital. I mean she went to Bladon cos of him, she risked everything cos of him!'

'Did you tell him that?'

'Course, bubz.'

We sat together on the sofa and I was glad that the night was coming and that soon we could lie together again.

I took out my phone. 'Bell him again,' I said. She almost grabbed the phone from me. I was about to tell her the speed dial number but she was already thumbing over the keypad, she had his number by heart.

'Pick up,' she said. 'Pick up!' Then, a moment later: 'Lance!' And she turned towards me, her face lit like a sun. 'It's him!'

'Lance,' she breathed back into the phone, 'oh, where have you been?'

I'd like to tell you I just felt elation, relief. And I did. But I also felt that old tightening rope of red – he'd taken her call! Then I realised it was my phone she was using, my number that would have flashed up in front of him. Lance hadn't taken Quin's call. He'd taken mine.

'Give the blowa to me,' I said.

But Quin was burbling, she was telling him everything that had happened in a mad rush as though he might disappear again and never know the end of the story. 'So Elayne needs you,' Quin concluded. 'You have to come. If you don't come she'll die.'

'Pass that blowa to me,' I said again and this time she did.

'Lance,' I said. I'd missed saying his name. 'I came for you.'

'I know,' he said quietly. 'I'm sorry.'

'Sorry?'

'Sorry about my mother anyway.'

He was sorry about *his* mother!

'She told me she'd shown you the pictures . . .'

And there would come a time – when Quin lay so still in the hospital – when I would finally understand why he'd raised this issue, why the pictures mattered, why it was that his mother couldn't bear a single child dying anywhere in the world.

'Whatever, man, it's nada,' I said. And it was nothing then. 'Where have you been, Lance? We've needed you.'

'I'm sorry,' he said again. 'But there were – there are – reasons.'

He left a pause and I left it too. If he wasn't going to tell me, I wasn't going to ask. We were brothers, we were sworn. It should be enough.

'But you'll come for Elayne?' I asked. 'She needs you, Lance.'

'Yes,' he said. 'I will come for Elayne.' He paused a second time. 'But I don't love her, Art, you know that, don't you? If she has expectations they are hers not mine.'

I heard truth in what he said, but it was not a comfortable truth.

'What's he sayin?' asked Quin.

'That's not the point,' I said more harshly than perhaps I had intended. 'You owe her.'

'I understand that,' said Lance. 'What she did was foolhardy but incredibly brave. I honour her.'

We talked hospitals and times and then I rang off.

'Wah guan, bubz?' Quin repeated.

'He said we'd link at the hospital midday tomorrow.'

'Oh, thank god!' Quin clapped her hands together, overjoyed.

'And he also says he doesn't love her.'

'What?'

'He doesn't love Elayne.'

I watched my queen carefully as I said this, and I saw the effect of my words on her. She looked astonished and then shocked.

'But, but, he said all those things, bout her hair, bout how proud she should be an he sat by her, at the river . . .'

'And he also risked his life for her in the fight, the one-to-one.'

'Why did he do those things?' Quin said. 'Why did he do any of them, if he didn't give a dee?'

'Honour,' I said.

'Respect?'

'No, honour,' I repeated. Your word again, Myrtle. 'That's it. That's all. He did those things because he just thought they were the right things to do.'

'Oh Art,' she said, 'let's go to bed.'

And we did and she kissed and kissed me the whole night through as though she was the happiest person in all the world.

23

Quin and I arrived at the hospital just before twelve. I said maybe we should visit later, give Elayne some privacy, let her see Lance alone, but Quin was insistent.

'Elayne might need us afterwards,' she said. 'I mean, when Lance jets. And neways, you want to see Lance too, don't you? You need him back at the Mill.'

I couldn't deny that.

I couldn't deny Quin either. She'd taken time to re-braid her hair that morning and looked, I thought as we walked through the hospital together, more beautiful than ever.

Elayne wasn't in a general ward, she'd been put in a side room by herself.

I half-expected Lance to be with her already, but he wasn't.

'Don't worry,' Quin said, seeing me consult my mobile as we entered. 'We're early.'

Elayne was wired up to a drip and she seemed to be asleep. People always commented on how very light-skinned she was for a mixed-race kid. That day she was like chalk.

'Elayne,' said Quin softly, obviously shocked. 'Bubz, it's me.'

Elayne didn't reply.

We stood beside the bed a moment, uncertain whether to wake her, and then Quin said, 'She looks a bit like Snow White, doesn't she, like she's waiting for the prince to come and kiss her awake.'

'The prince already came,' said Elayne and she opened her eyes. Her face was etched with pain but she managed a kind of dreamy, slightly other-worldly smile.

'What?' said Quin.

'He came,' Elayne said. 'Lance. My prince.'

'How do you mean he came?' said Quin sharply. 'It isn't twelve, he said he'd come at twelve.'

'Is it? Did he?' said Elayne. 'Mmm. I've lost track.'

'Are you OK, Elayne?' I asked.

'I am now,' she replied and her eyes closed again. I thought she was probably drugged, high on painkillers.

'He came,' she continued, 'and he leant very close and he said how brave I was, what a hero.'

'A hero!' said Quin.

'Heroine,' Elayne corrected herself. 'Heroine, yes. For goin to Bladon because of him. It was all wrong, he said. He was s'posed to rescue me, not the other way round. That Lance, old fashioned.' She made some soft mumbling noises, a little riff of happiness. 'Lance,' she murmured and then, as she turned slightly, she gave another moan of pain. A few low cries followed as she tried to get comfortable and then her breathing became slightly heavier and it seemed that she'd simply fallen asleep again.

'Are you still with us, bubz?' asked Quin. 'You still in dere?'

I motioned to the drip.

Quin looked at me. 'Maybe it was a dream,' she said. 'Maybe Elayne was in la-la land?'

'La-la land?' questioned Elayne, surfacing again. 'It felt like a dream. It might have been a dream. But then he lipsed me, and I woke up.'

'Kissed you!' repeated Quin, and there was an edge of steel in her voice.

'Yes,' said Elayne, 'yes. And I didn't mind if I was ill for ever if he kissed me. In fact I wanted to be ill for ever. Aahhh. Lance . . .' The mumbling began again and then she seemed to slip back into her pained but smiling sleep.

'Elayne,' I said, 'Elayne?' But there was no further reply.

We waited there some while, both of us, for different reasons, unwilling to leave. Eventually Quin said: 'Do you think it's true? I mean . . . the things she said?'

'No,' I said.

'No?' Quin took my hand, and I saw something new in her eyes then, something I'd later realise was hope. She led me to the nurses' station. 'Did someone visit before us?' she asked, checking.

'I'm sorry?' The nurse looked up from her notes.

'A white boy? Did a white boy visit Elayne Descalot?'

'Oh him,' replied the nurse brightly. 'Yes, great kid. Lance, wasn't it? Boyfriend is he? She called his name in the night. Over and over again. Very fitful. But since he came, well, you can see for yourself. She's very much calmer, more relaxed. It helps, you know, in the healing process.'

Quin's hand tightened in mine. 'Thank you,' she said and we walked away.

'You were right then,' I said, wanting to release her. 'He did make a difference to her, just like you said.'

'And you were wrong,' she said. 'You said you didn't believe her.'

'I didn't mean I thought Lance hadn't come here,' I said. 'I meant I didn't believe he kissed her. That can't be true.'

'It can't?' Again that look in her eye.

'Lance couldn't just kiss any girl – not unless he loved her. That's sort of how he is. He jus couldn't do it.'

'Not even out of kindness?' she pressed. 'To make someone well?'

And I didn't ask why it mattered so much to her, perhaps I was doing with my thoughts what I'd done with the letters and the toaster. Or perhaps I just wanted to speak up for Lance, after all my doubting of him, because part of me needed him to remain invincibly pure. 'He's safe. That's it,' I said, 'the most honest man I ever met.'

'So bout the lipsing bit . . . You're saying that bit never happened, she la-la'd it, right?'

'Yes,' I said. 'They are pumpin drugs into her.'

Quin smiled at me. 'An you can want something that much, can't you?'

'Yes,' I said, and I leant to kiss her. 'You can.'

She moved her face a little, so I caught her cheek not her mouth. 'I'm happy for Elayne,' Quin continued, 'if that's what she thinks, then cool. The truth doesn't really matter, does it?'

But the truth always matters, doesn't it, Myrtle?

'Getting Elayne well,' is what I said then, 'that's what matters.'

'Yes,' Quin said. 'And jus cos we didn't see Lance doesn't mean he's not comin back, does it? I mean he belled last night, and he came to link us today. So we haven't, can't, won't lose him.' She stopped before adding quickly, 'I know how important he is to you.'

And I didn't say 'And also to you', I just left the issue beside the toaster.

You see, Myrtle, the closer the horror came, the more I hid from it.

We left the hospital, collected Shaman and returned to the Mill. I felt ready to face Mordec but he was not ready to face me. He was passed-out drunk.

Quin looked at him lying on the floor among the Tennent's lager cans.

'How long's he been like that?'

'Da boi was overcharged last night,' said Garvey. 'Probly still spinnin.'

Mordec's mouth was slightly open and he was snoring. He was also still wearing the clothes he'd been in the day before. There was a dark splash of Elayne's blood on his jacket. We had a few blankets in the Mill, the odd duvet, but Mordec was sleeping hard to the stone floor. I hoped he'd wake stiff and cold, I hoped he'd hurt real bad.

Quin was more charitable. 'Maybe he was propa para,' she said. 'When he realised what he'd done. So he drank to blot it out.'

But if that was true Mordec would have to have had some kind of a heart, and the more time passed the more I suspected Mordec had no such thing. The brother I'd looked up to, the one who could care for people, who'd looked out for me when I was a child, he was long gone. In his place was this impetuous, violent man. That I should be standing over him, looking down at him, seemed a statement about how things were between us now.

The general mood in the Mill was subdued, sombre even. With Mordec out of the equation, it was easy enough to regain the ascendancy. I called the Knights to the Stone and they came willingly – even Garvey. The yungas also complied immediately with my demand for silence. Partly, I think, they genuinely wanted to hear about Elayne and partly – or so I believed – they'd missed the structure of my leadership. With me, they knew where they were. When I gave the news that Elayne would live, there was audible relief.

'And Lance,' I added, 'he visited her this morning too.'

'Lance?' said Borz. 'So he's back, you found him?'

'He found us.'

'And he's comin back to da Mill?'

'Yes.' I said, feeling Quin's eyes bore into me. 'Yes.'

'Yeh!' said Donkey.

'Why did he go?' asked Garvey. 'Where's he been?'

'Not with the Saxons,' I answered, skirting the question. 'Who chatted that shit?' I heard myself sounding like Mordec, like Garvey. That's what anger can do to you, make you into something you're not. I needed to be careful, to control myself. That's what would mark me out from the lesser men. 'Who told the Crew that Lance had been taken into Bladon?'

There was general murmuring. No one seemed quite to know.

'Bruv – wot's yur point?' asked Pels. 'You think it was some sort of Saxon plot? Dat the Saxons wanted us to go up Tintagel, have a scuff?'

'No,' I said. 'If they'd have wanted that, they'd have been waitin for us.'

'Dey were waitin for us!' said Borz.

'Not the main players. Not Tractor. Or HellRazor, or Jimbo or Mack,' I said. 'It was jus the yungas, wasn't it? Do you think if Big Shank was in on it, they'd have stopped at just dressing Elayne in red and pushing her back? It was yungas havin a bubble, because Elayne had wandered onto their manor.'

There was a silence.

'Blood, what you saying den?' said Garvey at last. 'You thinkin dere's a snake? You blamin Knight Crew?'

'I'm just askin,' I said.

'Askin who, bro?' said a slurry voice. 'Askin who exactly?'

Mordec had somehow staggered to his feet and was propping himself up against the lower treads of OG's old wheel.

'You're not at the Stone,' said Quin coldly, 'so don't speak.'

'Then I'll come to the Stone,' said Mordec and moving stiffly (and yes, I was glad about that) he came forward, lurching towards the place I'd marked for him. 'There,' he sat down heavily. 'Now I speak.'

'No,' I said. It seemed to me suddenly revolting to have him there, a blasphemy against all the Stone stood for. 'You're not sworn.'

'We all swore,' said Duane. 'You have to, too.'

'To the Knights,' said Quin. 'And also to Art.'

'Oh Art. My lil bro.' Mordec conjured a non-existent glass. 'Here's to you, lil bitch.'

I took out the Buck knife. Only my control, I told myself, only that separates me from him. I held the knife aloft. I had after all marked his place myself, I too had made a promise, given my word. 'Swear, Mordec.'

Mordec swung his head, left and right, looking for support, for rebellion, but there was none.

'Swear,' said Borz.

I lifted the knife higher, where it glinted above his head. Even drunk, he still wanted that knife but – for the time being – it was still in my hands.

'Alryt,' he said. 'Alryt!'

'*I pledge loyalty to the Knights and to Art*,' said Borz. 'Say it!'

'I pledge my loyalty to the Crew,' Mordec said.

'To the Knights,' I corrected. You have to hope, don't you, Myrtle? You have to see the seeds of good, the possibility of change.

'To the Knight Crew,' said Mordec.

That had to be sufficient. I let it pass.

'And to Art,' pressed Quin.

'And to Art.'

There was still a sneer in his voice but I said quickly: 'I appoint you to the Stone, Mordec,' and then I brought the knife down. It would be safer, I knew, to have him bound to us.

'And if you betray that pledge, if you betray Art –' Donkey began.

'Then da knife comes down an all dat bullshit,' Mordec drew an imaginary line at his neck. 'I know dat, Donkey boi, so hush yur mouth.'

'Respect,' I said, putting the knife away. 'We give respect to all those at the Stone. That includes Donkey.'

'Yeah,' said Mordec. 'And where's my respect, huh? Like who you sayin nabbed Lance?'

'Rumours are easy enough to start,' I said carefully.

'But where was yur man, get me? If yur big champ had jus cotched in da Mill, there couldn't of been no chattin.'

I ignored that. 'You shouldn't have taken troops to Bladon without my say-so,' I said. 'We agreed a truce. My word on it. You – you could of kicked everything off again.'

'Truce!' said Mordec. 'You were a ghost. Yur blowa was off. What did you want us to do, leave Elayne to dem blodclaut Saxons? The Saxons don't do mercy, remember? Dat's yur golden bois department.'

'It was you who almost killed her,' said Quin furiously.

'You mad?' Mordec retorted. 'I jus jukked any old Saxon. She was wearin red, all-over red. Any mans with half the balls woulda done the same.'

'I wouldn't have done it,' I said. 'I would have used my eyes. If you don't look, Mordec, you don't see.

'See what? There was nada to see but a Saxon.'

'She called out, Mordec. She called.'

'Lance,' interjected Pels. 'She shouted *Lance*.'

'Yeah, like wot was dat supposed to mean?'

'And if you couldn't hear her voice, you could have seen that she didn't have a tool,' I said. 'You should have clocked on, Mordec – no blade.'

'HellRazor didn't have a shank, until it jus appeared,' Mordec said. 'An den he had a nice sharp curved one. Bro, I was at da beef at Tintagel. You weren't.'

'And even if you didn't know it was Elayne,' I said and I paused. 'Couldn't work it out –'

'Den wot?' he said quickly. 'You saying I knew it was Elayne? I jukked one of our own? You're crazy.'

'I'm sayin you lost it, Mordec. I'm sayin you let the blood get in yur eyes.'

'No, you've lost it bruv, dem Saxon mans dere de enemy.'

'I'm also sayin that even if it had been a Saxon, Mordec, it was clearly a yunga, barely a child. You should have shown mercy.'

He got to his feet then. 'Mercy? You're like Mum – in some nex reality. You're a pussy, you gone spell-bound wid dat old baglady's scrap book. You lost Lance and now you've lost da plot.'

That was a challenge that, in previous times, I might have had to answer with a blow. But it was Quin who answered him.

'Is it only women you knife?' she asked.

There was a hideous pause.

Her probe, as usual, had gone right to the heart of things.

'You wot?' said Mordec.

'First Myrtle,' she continued quietly, 'and now Elayne. Is that the sort of man you are?'

Mordec lost it all over again then, roared at her, but he was still unsteady on his feet, and it was nothing for Garvey and Borz, who were closest to him, to hold him back. Which was lucky, because Shaman jumped too, landed between Quin and her – and his – old enemy and I only just had time to make the soft 'tch tch' noises that stopped Shaman springing a second, and probably fatal, time.

As the hackles lowered on the neck of the black dog, Mordec screamed, 'I'll merk im. I'll merk dat dog!'

But that was not what would happen to Shaman.

'Sit,' I said to Mordec. 'Be still.'

And, because of the restraining hands of my men, he sat. But he was not still. Not then, or ever again. His resentment against Quin, which was born then, grew day by day, week by smouldering week.

Sometimes I think it would have been better for me to have died in that moment than live to see how Mordec would take his revenge on my queen.

24

I don't know how I would have survived those late September weeks without Duane. In the absence of Lance – and Lance continued to be absent – he became my right-hand man, my eyes, my ears, my rock. Of all the Crew members, it was Duane who most easily understood how it was with Mordec and me, perhaps because of his own troubled relationship with Garvey. It was sometimes hard to remember that Duane and Garvey were brothers, let alone twins, but why should I have been surprised? I'd learnt that there was more to brotherhood than blood.

As Duane and I tightened our bonds, so his brother knotted more closely with mine. Duane believed (as I did) that Lance would return, Garvey (like Mordec) scoffed at the idea, saying that Lance was a Milky Bar Kid who'd had his moment of glory and had now returned to Milky Bar Kid things. One place to which Lance had not, however, returned was the karate club. It was Duane who discovered that; he asked about, got the name and address of the club, went there alone one morning to check. Lance hadn't been seen in the club for nine months or more.

'But he will come back,' said Quin, who was also keeping the faith. 'I know he will.'

'Yeah,' said Mordec, 'when Elayne's out of hospital, maybe. Not much good havin a gash who's always dozin.'

He and Garvey laughed.

'It's not like that between them!' said Quin.

'No?' said Mordec. 'So how come he links her but not us?'

'He visited her once,' said Quin. 'Just once.'

Quin knew that for a fact as she went every day to the hospital to see Elayne. She was the most diligent carer for her friend. Each night she'd give me the news.

'Not today,' she'd say, 'not today.' And you didn't know whether she was talking about Elayne not being discharged or Lance not putting in an appearance.

I began to wish that I'd asked Lance, when I had the opportunity, why he was keeping away. I could have gone back to his house but I didn't – perhaps I was afraid of that hologrammed notebook. Instead I speculated about his family, about other reasons why he might have gone to ground. I knew he had a father – it was his father who'd driven Mordec to the hospital that night. But then there was his mother and the bloodied babies. *I'm sorry about my mother.* That's what Lance had said. Perhaps he wasn't talking about the gory pictures but about his mother herself. Perhaps her obsession had precipitated something in his family just as my mother's kiss with the spotty man on the sofa had precipitated something in mine. You can twist things up, make them up, can't you, Myrtle? When you don't want to see what's staring you in the face.

At the Mill Lance's absence had consequences. Quin's moods could be black. Once, when she was very down, I suggested we try Lance's thinking – or non-thinking – technique, get up early, watch the sun walk across the water again.

'What would be the point of that?' she asked.

Her low moods seemed to parallel dips in Elayne's progress and that's the way I explained them to myself. When, after four long weeks, Elayne finally got out of hospital, I told myself, things would begin to pick up.

And so they did.

Elayne's mother, as we knew, was long gone but we didn't know until then that her grandmother, with whom she lived, was disabled. Late onset diabetes had apparently all but put her in a wheelchair. She could barely care for herself, let alone a recuperating child. So it was Quin who accompanied Elayne home, took charge of changing her dressing, counted her painkillers. Quin who still spent time with Elayne every day.

'She needs me. They need me,' said Quin. 'I can help them.'

'Bet you cook em dinner, don't you?' said Garvey.

'I open tins,' said Quin.

'Girl, you never opened no tins for me when dat mutt did my eye,' said Mordec.

'You can look after yourself,' said Quin.

'Yeah,' said Mordec. 'Too right.'

He was always finding things to needle her with, mainly about Lance.

'You found him yet?' he'd call when she passed. Or, 'Looked under any big stones lately?'

'You wouldn't say that if he was here,' said Quin. 'You wouldn't dare.'

'Girl,' said Mordec, 'get dat through yur thick skull he *aint* here. Dat mans jetted, gone, off skis!'

'He'll be back,' I said.

Gradually, as the weeks passed, Elayne got stronger and Quin's mood lightened. One day I heard her laugh – it was a big sunny sound and one I realised I hadn't heard for a very long time. It was the same with the songs, or rather with the humming. I'd catch her about the Mill, just humming.

'What you hummin? What's the song?'

'Dunno,' she say and she'd kiss me. But I knew. It was another of her African songs, something quiet and deep. 'Just feel haps, bubz.'

She re-braided her hair more frequently, came from Elayne's wearing fresh clothes.

'You're so beautiful,' I said.

'Oh Art,' she replied and put her finger on my lips, as if it was a secret between us.

Then one day Mordec came to me also with a smile. Only his was a twisted smile. I was sitting at my place at the Stone, which I sometimes did when I wanted to think, to be left alone, for people had learnt not to disturb me there. It was one of the only places, I realise, where I did not feel vulnerable.

'You were right,' Mordec said, intruding.

I was never right with Mordec, so I was on my guard at once.

'About what?' I asked, some foreboding urging me to my feet.

'About Lance,' he said. 'He's come back.'

'Where?' I said stupidly, casting my eyes around the Mill as if I expected Lance to appear right in front of me like some genie. The only thing that appeared was Shaman, who came to stand sentinel beside me.

'Oh – he isn't here,' said Mordec, clearly enjoying himself. 'Lance hasn't come here.' He sniggered.

'Where then?' I asked, feeling my insides beginning to knot.

Garvey had come up behind him and he was smiling too.

'Why don't you tell him, Garvey? A man has the right to know where his bitch is.'

'Lance,' I said as solidly as I could, 'we were talking of Lance.'

'And Quin,' said Mordec. 'You see we found em together.'

My brain turned somersaults, my heart crashed in my chest.

'Didn't you know?' He continued with a gargoyle grin. 'Dey've been linking for time.'

The only thing that held me upright in that moment was the weight of Shaman's body stood against mine.

'An all dat Florence Nightingale stuff,' Mordec shook his head. 'All dat going to visit Elayne at home. She hasn't been dere for weeks. She's been down at the old lock-keeper's cottage. With him. And whatever dey've been doin I don't think it's doctors and nurses.'

I struck him straight across the face, picking the side where his eye was damaged.

He recoiled in pain, but he did not strike back, not with his fist anyway.

'So much for mercy,' he said. 'Mercy.' He laughed. 'But I'm only the messenger, you need to save yourself, bro. For them.'

'Are they there now?' I asked. And you'll note, Myrtle, that I did not disbelieve my brother. Not for one moment did I disbelieve him. Because what he was telling me was already carved on my soul.

'Yes,' Garvey said. 'We've jus come from there. Good decco we got through da window. Curled up together like kittens.'

My hand was already on the knife.

'Do you want to go get em?' Mordec said. 'Or shall we?'

The lock-keeper's cottage was a derelict building on the canalside about half a mile away. I wanted to take the great Buck blade, run the towpath and plunge it into both of them. Take them in the act, cut those sweaty little kittens apart. But Duane, who'd come up behind me and heard the whole exchange, spoke: 'I'll go,' he said. 'Take Borz and Pels and Donkey and some of the yungas.'

'An us,' Garvey, meaning himself and Mordec.

'We'll bring em to you, Art,' Duane continued. 'Bring em here to the Stone. That's the right way to do it. Dis is where we all swore.'

'Oh yes,' said Mordec, 'dis is where we swore. Any disrespect . . .' Mordec drew a knife arc across his neck. He was clearly enjoying himself.

'Just get on it,' I shouted.

Duane knew, you see, that I would not have been able to control myself, so he let me off the hook. I could have chosen him as my loyal, my most trusted man. But I had chosen Lance.

When they'd left, I left too, left the Stone anyway. What use was the Stone now? I climbed up high. I went to the gallows place where OG used to sit with his feet hanging over the water. I went partly because you could see the towpath from there but also because the beam was high and narrow and you had to concentrate to sit there in case you fell. And I needed to concentrate on something other than Quin, otherwise I would fall. And not just into the river. I would fall and never rise again.

Yet all the time I sat there on that high gallows' beam, I just heard her hummings, her Blue Toraco songs. Her happiness.

With him.

And I thought of all the weeks and months I'd hung back from Quin, waiting to be sure, to know that I could cross safely into her carefully guarded self. And here he was, after just a moment, riding straight into her heart, straight between her legs. And she had let him. She had welcomed him in.

211

Her song was so loud in my ears that I almost didn't hear the shouting of the returning Crew. Perhaps I had closed my mind to the jubilation I knew I'd hear in Mordec's voice. So it wasn't until they were really close that I heard, not jubilation, but shouts of rage and saw that there was blood on some of the Crew and that others were limping.

'He got away,' shouted Duane. 'Lance fought his way out, he's off-skis, jetted!'

And do you know what, Myrtle? My first reaction was gladness, pride even. He had not disappointed. He was a warrior still. God damn my heart, I loved him even then.

'But we got the ho,' said Mordec. 'We got her.'

Quin's hands were bound behind her back, with wire, no doubt. Mordec would have taken wire and bound those hands tight.

'Art,' Quin cried up at me.

But I turned away, put the distance back between us.

25

I spent the night in the bell-tower. The floor was only about five foot across so there was no room to lie down, but I wasn't going to sleep anyway. The tower itself was roofed above where the old bell had hung, but otherwise open to the elements on all sides. I went there because I wanted to see the stars and to listen to the river. But there were no stars that night, Myrtle, the sky was completely clouded over. There was one seagull wheeling, he was far too far inland, so I thought he must, like me, be lost. I concentrated on the river, tuned in to its sounds so as not to hear Quin's. One note from my queen's voice and I might have weakened.

Shaman sat close beside me, his body keeping me warm as the night deepened. But his was not the only company I had: they came at me time and again, climbing the rotted stairs to beg or argue. The first was Tanisha. She was red around the eyes from crying.

'Please, bubz,' she said. 'Don't do it.'

'Do what?' I said coldly.

'The blade. Do whatever it is with dat blade. Mordec's chattin like you're goin to merk her. That you have to merk her.'

'That so.'

'But dat shit Donkey was chattin bout the oath an all dat

breeze, dat was jus air, weren't it, Art? You're not actually on it, are ya?'

'Jus words you mean?' I said. 'It was all jus words?'

Words, Myrtle. Words!

'But Quin,' said Tanisha, 'you can't hurt Quin. Not yur Quin.'

'She isn't mine any more.' That was a stab, self-inflicted. 'She thinks she's above the law. The law we made, we swore to each other. Is she alone to be above it?'

'Art –'

'No, Tanisha. Leave me.'

'But I have to know.'

'You'll know tomorrow. I'll tell every man at the Stone, tomorrow morning. Tell everyone to be there.'

The next to come was Borz, solid, stalwart, impetuous Borz.

'Bruv,' he said, 'you should come down.'

'Should I?'

'Mordec's chattin breeze. There are those who want not jus Quin's blood but Lance's too.'

'And you think I don't want Lance's blood!' I said, and even Shaman woke and growled at the tone of my voice.

'Every man acts a fool, get me,' said Borz. 'But Lance – we need him. Need him against the Saxons. Without him . . .'

'Yes?'

'Get me?' He shrugged hopelessly.

'Yeah,' I said. 'One rule for Quin and another for Lance. Because she's some gash, because she don't beef?' Here was the fury again, dragging me down. 'You're on that? That's right?'

'Bruv, you're doin my head in,' said Borz. 'All I know is what's goin down here is shit, nada. True say, I'm sorry about Quin an dat, but dis is all a minor compared with beef wid dem mans. The Saxons, Art, dere da enemy.'

But the Saxons didn't feel like the enemy that night. The enemy felt like my heart which was tearing itself in two.

Borz had barely been gone five minutes when Donkey arrived. I was surprised at Donkey.

'Quin,' he said, 'she's asking for ya, Art. She says, if you would just speak to her, with her.'

'Wot?' I said feeling the anger rising again. 'She can explain, can she?'

'No,' said Donkey, who was no donkey, 'she's whipped over you, Art, she loves you up, man.'

And that was it, the beginning and the end. She loved me, and I loved her. I still loved her!

'Get out, Donkey. Leave me alone.'

Only Duane was brave enough to come after that and he alone did not press me to his point, just asked if he could stay with me a while. We leant against the parapet together, looking out over the river, hearing the sound of it slap, slapping against the bank. How long had that river been flowing? Since long before my birth, for all of time probably, and it would continue to flow. Flow, flow, flow. After my death. After Quin's.

'So wah guan, bruv?' Duane asked finally.

'I'll do what I must,' I answered.

Duane looked at me then. 'You may trust me with yur life,' he said then. 'I'll back yur end, I'm wid you on the Stone. But I aint gonna lay one finger on her head. Sorry, man. I jus can't. '

And I saw then that even he loved Quin, and I knew that there were many among my Knights for whom that would also be true and in that love was the seed of destruction that I would sow if I let the knife fall. But there are things that are right and things that are wrong. That's what you taught me anyway, Myrtle.

After Duane left, I took your book, scanned and scoured its pages for some aid, some comfort that night. But there was nothing among your scribbles about mortally wounded love. You left me alone that night, Myrtle, and I had to think for myself. So I returned to the page of the future and underneath the words *Quin* and *Peace*, *Power* and *Mercy*, I wrote JUSTICE.

Because justice is important, isn't it, Danny?

I was still awake when the sun rose the next day. Only this time, instead of looking across the river at the Mill, I was standing with my back to the sun, so its path led away from me. Maybe that was a sign too, Myrtle. I was looking for signs, I suppose, clinging for something in the wreckage. Because I knew in my heart everything was moving away from me.

It was Tanisha who finally came to tell me that the Crew was all assembled at the Stone.

'Take Quin out of the Mill,' I told her. 'Let LameDuck an Tardis stay with her.'

I could not afford to see her before I announced my decision. To see her would undo me. One call for mercy from her and I would have given in.

I climbed down into the morning darkness of the Mill, dark enough for the Knights to have lit candles at the Stone, one beside each place illuminating their faces: Duane, Borz, Pels, Garvey, Donkey. Mordec. And one set at my place too. The yungas sat in concentric rings about the Stone. It was a beautiful, a moving sight to see so many gathered there, as many I think as witnessed Lance swearing loyalty to me, *for now, for ever*. Yet the candles made me think of an altar on which there was to be a sacrifice. As I approached a silence fell.

The only true Knight missing from the Stone was Elayne.

I wondered then if she would have spoken up for Quin? I thought of her lying recuperating at her grandmother's. Maybe no one had told her of Lance's treachery, maybe that was a secret she still had to learn. I would like to have believed that, despite her own love for Lance, Elayne would have spoken for my queen. But I don't think she would, I think Elayne would have been as emptied out as me.

Mordec was twitching, the silence getting on his nerves. 'Come now bro, you're takin time,' he said. 'We know wot we have to do.'

So I held the pause, didn't sit immediately.

'It's Art's decision,' said Donkey, 'and Art's alone.'

They all shifted uncomfortably, willing some action, some release.

'It's the Crew's decision,' said Mordec. 'Dem mans at da Stone, we all gave word, get me, we all agreed da penalty for snakes, for betrayal. Any cockroach need crushin. Dead it.'

Some of the yungas couldn't help but cry out, as if it were them that were under his heel.

I sat then and the silence resumed.

'The penalty,' I said carefully, 'is the fall of the knife.'

'Meanin?' said Garvey suspiciously. 'Dun try an slime yur way out of it.'

'Mercy,' said Duane suddenly. 'Mercy! Since Lance, I thought we had new rules?'

Oh, Lance had his rules all right. But debts have to be paid, right, Danny?

'Rules?' Mordec repeated. 'Like wot? Like you can jus link any mans gash, even Art's' – and here he made filthy thrusting motions with his body – 'and dat's it?'

Another day I might have taken the Buck knife and pitched it into his breast. But my fury was all but spent that morning. 'Knight Crew law,' I said, 'is Knight Crew law. We are all sworn as Mordec says. But the fall of the knife does not mean death.'

'Oh – jus a slap on the arse, yer?' Mordec challenged.

'Yeah!' called out LameDuck from the floor and was hushed immediately.

'Cutting,' I said.

'Cuttin? Cuttin wot?'

'Her face,' I said.

There was a horrified gasp, as though cutting was sharper than death, worse than death.

If it was mercy it was a brutal thing.

One of the yungas – a girl – gave a long, low wail.

'Ah,' said Mordec, 'cuttin her face.' He was savouring it, rolling it around in his mouth. 'That'll make hero Lance think twice bout her.'

'Dis aint,' said Duane, finding his voice at last and looking me straight in the eye, 'da word of no man.'

'No,' I said. 'It's the word of a king.'

The wailing stopped. You could have heard a pin drop. I waited for a further challenge but it didn't come. That was the bitter respect I was afforded that day.

'Pass me da shank,' said Mordec then. 'Give me da Crew knife. I'm on it. I'm on it now.'

'No,' I said. The eagerness on his face revolted me. 'I appoint Garvey.' The least I could do was save Quin from Mordec's savage hand. Garvey would wield the knife, but not so deeply.

Garvey stood up, took a flick knife from his pocket, made the blade spring. And I was glad he didn't ask for the Buck knife, with its eight-inch curve of steel.

'Is now the time?' he asked.

I asked him to wait, just five minutes. Why? I don't know, even to this day. But those five minutes were to change everything because they allowed Duane time to contact Lance. Another treachery, but one born of decency. And so your rights and wrongs, Myrtle, continued to tangle.

Tanisha was sobbing and so were other of the girls. Borz, who hadn't spoken at the Stone, looked stunned. Donkey was simply bewildered, moans of disbelief coming from his mouth. Mordec was slavering, urging Garvey to the task, running his finger along the flick-knife blade. I knew if I stayed downstairs in the Mill, I might change my mind. I might thrust myself between that knife and my queen. So I tore myself away, climbed to that high gallows place, where you have to concentrate. Forgetting (or perhaps not forgetting at all) that Quin was outside. That I'd be able to see her.

LameDuck had tied her to the railings of the bridge over the canal. Tanisha, who was now hysterical, ran out to deliver the verdict.

'Untie me,' I heard Quin say softly. 'I won't run.'

LameDuck and Tardis seemed so astonished by her calm that they stood back while Tanisha fumbled with the wire. When her hands were free Quin rubbed her wrists.

'Who will do the deed?' she asked. 'Will it be Art?'

'Garvey,' wept Tanisha. And it was Quin who put out a steadying hand to her bredrin, as though it was Tanisha that needed support. 'Shh, babe,' she said, and only when Tanisha had quietened did she draw away and say:

'Let him come then. I'm ready.'

And I do not know how Quin had spent her night and what thoughts had been hers as she sat in the dark of the Mill, waiting to know her fate. But I never saw her more of a queen than in that moment. Nor did I ever love her more, or hate her more.

Mordec came out in front of Garvey of course and he was jeering again. 'See this,' he yelled, pointing at his eye, 'you'll think me beautiful after what Garvey will do to you! Make it good, Garvey! Make a cut for me!'

Quin looked at Mordec but said nothing and then she began to walk, not away from Garvey but towards him, towards Garvey and the blade. She stopped just a knife's length from him.

'Do it,' she said.

But he hesitated, stood there looking, as I looked, at the continent that was Quin. The blinding light of her sun, the proud black tilt of her head, the song that still sang in her silence, and the million brilliant spiders which carried her shells on their backs. My love, my Quin.

And also his.

For there he was in a cloud of dust, motorcycle dust, helmet on. No speed limits that day, he simply roared over the bridge, putting his bike between Quin and the knife. And at the same moment Garvey fell, knocked by the bike, Quin rose, Lance lifted her up as if she was just smoke and air and he put her astride the bike behind him, and then he turned so fast OG would have been proud of the manoeuvre, and he was away, revving over the bridge and into a distance.

Mordec screamed with rage, Garvey remained motionless in the dust and as for me – I laughed for joy.

Yes. Joy.

26

The first thing we had to deal with was the injury to Garvey. From where I'd sat on the gallows I thought he'd just been winded by the encounter with the bike, but when I got to the bridge I found him still on the ground, his leg lying at an odd angle.

'He rode straight at him, straight over him,' Mordec shouted at me. 'Dat's yur champ, yur Mr Mercy.'

But it was not Mordec who frightened me. Duane was kneeling by his twin brother and as I came to a stop beside them he looked up at me, his face rigid with rage. 'Lance don't show no respect. Not for you. Not for the Stone. Not for no man.'

Beside Duane, Garvey cried out in pain as he tried to lift himself up.

'Mans right,' Mordec said. 'Pure disrespect. If dis was to leak to dem Saxon bois, we'd look like pussyholes.'

Duane stood up. 'Art?' He challenged me. 'Art?'

'We gotta bring dat boi down,' said Mordec, 'show him who da big men are round here.'

'No,' I said. I was bone-tired.

'So dat's it, is it?' said Duane.

'I didn't say that.' There would be time enough to deal with Lance. And deal with him I would, but at a place and a moment of my choosing. 'But it's not the most important thing now. Mans gotta bust leg,' I added, indicating his brother.

'If we don't jet after dem now,' said Mordec, 'dey'll go into a safe-house. Dey'll be off skis.'

'There is no off skis, Mordec,' I said. 'No away. No place to run.'

And, for the first time perhaps, my heart understood why Keifer had driven at that tree that night.

Garvey moaned again.

'Take him,' I said to Mordec. 'Go with Duane and get him seen too.' I needed some space, needed to be alone. 'Lance won't split, I give you my word on that.'

Reluctantly they lifted our fallen soldja. I didn't care how they got him the attention he needed, I just wanted them to be gone.

When they were out of sight, I went back into the Mill, lay on the jumbled bedding which had accumulated behind OG's wheel. It was good to lie down, to stretch full length. I did not mean to sleep, I believed I had too much on my mind for that. But I hadn't rested for thirty-six hours and sleep clawed and gnawed at me, weighted me down until heaviness lay in every limb of my body. And so it was that I sank into some deep place where, for a time, it seemed that I lay down my burden and dreamed of happier times. Someone sang to me and someone held me, a woman's soft hands, but not Quin's. It was my mother and I was a child again and nothing mattered and nothing hurt.

It was hours later when I awoke and my real life came crowding in again. Duane was standing over me, flicking ash from his cigarette. It must be the afternoon, I thought, for him to be back.

'Let's plan dis shit,' Duane said.

'Garvey?' I asked, coming into myself slowly. 'Is he all right?'

'He'll live.' Duane stubbed out the cigarette and I found myself liking him for being angry on Garvey's behalf, for the reassertion of his kinship with his twin, but I also felt jealous. I could imagine no hurt to my brother that would alter my feelings towards him.

'Lance,' Duane continued. 'We have to find him.'

'Duane,' I said. 'Duane, you have always been my wingman, these last weeks, I've counted on you more than anyone. But this is my battle. Can you see that? It's between me and Lance alone.'

I thought he would talk about Garvey, I thought he would play the brother's card, but all he said was, 'You're not tonk enough to take on Lance alone.'

And maybe I wasn't strong enough. 'But I have to try,' I said.

'If you fail,' Duane said, 'it will be the end of the Stone.'

'I know.' Which is why I knew I'd go through with it, whatever the cost.

'Mordec's already stressin,' continued Duane.

'About what?'

'A new Knight Crew Star.'

'Did someone call?' Mordec appeared out of nowhere, looked down at me among the covers. 'So wah guan with da nomads? Dream anythin useful, did you?'

I stood up. 'I'll find them,' I said.

But it turned out they weren't hiding. While I'd slept I'd had a text. It came from Lance's phone but it was signed by Quin: *at lock. come. Qxx*

Two kisses.

They wanted to be found, they wanted an ending too, I suppose.

I should have shared the information with Duane, but I didn't, partly because I knew he wouldn't let me go alone

223

and partly because I didn't want Mordec to get wind of where the fugitives were. Instead I set up search parties, tasked Mordec with watching Lance's house, asked Borz to take men to Quin's.

'Wot bout the lock-keeper's cottage?' asked Donkey.

'Dey won't have gone dere,' mocked Mordec. 'A mouse don't go to da same trap twice no matter how dum dey are.'

'But I'll check,' I said casually, 'just to make sure.'

'I'll come wid you,' said Duane.

'No – you try the karate club, Duane, see if anyone's heard anythin.'

'He hasn't been dere for nine months!' protested Duane.

'Exactly,' I said. 'That's why he might think it's safe.'

'And if we find em?' asked Borz.

'*When* we find em,' said Mordec.

'Do nothing,' I said, 'until I get there.'

So it was that I set out along the towpath alone – except for Shaman. As ever I was glad of his company, his trotting beside me made the walk seem a natural rather than a cold-blooded thing. The handle of the Buck 119 was chill, even though it lay against my leg. I gripped and – re-gripped – its black weight as I walked, then I ran my fingers along its spine, pressing my thumb down to feel the blood gutter. I didn't try the blade. I knew that was sharp.

I passed the scrap yard from where we stole the pallets we sat on at the Mill, passed the concrete indent where you slept sometimes, Myrtle, and on to where a once proud in-dustrial barge had been left to rot just below the surface of the water. I stopped a moment to look at that boat, delay-ing perhaps my arrival at the lock. But the lock came soon enough and the lock-keeper's cottage.

That cottage, with its porch and its brick chimney, would once have been a pleasant, workmanlike place but now, like so much at the canal, it was abandoned, broken down. Trees grew at its ground-floor windows and the roof had rotted in. Much of the window glass was missing and I imagined it would be damp in there as well as dark.

Yet they had lain together there, made it a nest of love, warmed it with their passion, a secret, treacherous, beautiful place.

I stood at the door, but there was no door. Maybe the door too had rotted or maybe Mordec had kicked it in. I wanted something solid to bar my entry, but everything solid had fallen away.

I went in.

It was dark inside – though not as dark as the Mill – and it was also small. I could hear the two of them talking, not urgent talk, just quiet and simple conversation. I couldn't hear exactly what was being said, but neither of them sounded afraid, neither of them were thinking of me entering the house with the great Buck knife blade flush to my thigh.

There were only three rooms on the ground floor, two in which they were not and the one back room in which Shaman and I found them.

They'd been sitting, how closely I couldn't tell because Lance leapt to his feet.

'Art,' he said at once. 'Art, oh my friend – forgive me.'

There was a shining sincerity to his words, his face upturned, his hands outstretched towards me, as though he was a child, as though it was that simple.

'And please don't blame Quin,' Lance continued. 'Everything that happened was down to me. It was wrong. I was wrong. I'm so sorry, Art.'

Only sometimes *sorry* isn't enough, is it? I felt my tight little mouth twisting up just like Danny's did.

'That's why I tried so hard to keep away.' He was speaking again. 'I tried, Art. I knew if I came back, if I saw her just once . . .'

A moral man, you see Myrtle, trying to conquer his own base desires, trying to keep his hands from my beloved. Oh yes, I was sure he'd tried. For remember he was, unlike me, always the good man.

Quin rose from the floor behind him then, leaving behind the three African drums that had lain there with her, the hologrammed notebook and the print of two bodies in the duvet. So close those prints, so very close you couldn't tell where one body had ended and another begun.

I leapt at Lance then, beat him with my fists. The knife was still in my pocket. I realised I needed to feel my flesh hard against his, my bone to his bone. I hammered my knuckles against his shoulders, his neck, his cheekbones. I knew with one turn of his forearm he could have deflected me as he'd deflected so many others before me. But I had the power of rage and righteousness and had he been ten men I would have crushed and beaten him. Or so I believed as my fists landed time and again. Afterwards I wondered if he'd let the blows rain down on him, accepted them as his due, for he knew in his soul he was guilty, that much I learnt that day.

Quin did not stand idly by, she screamed at me to stop, she tried to get between her old and her new lover, but there was no space for her, no space at all. I was locked with Lance as though it had been we who were the lovers, my arms about him as they had been that day on the motorbike.

It might have ended thus, but when he still stood despite all my blows, then I reached for the knife, held its great heaviness in my hand. It seemed then almost too heavy to lift, but I did lift it, held it above my head and brought it down towards the dearest friend I'd ever had.

At last he reacted, shouted his deadly, holy shout:

'*Kiai!*'

He span and kicked and the knife was knocked from my hand. We both looked at it a moment as it gleamed and skittered on the floor and then Lance, always quicker than me, reached for it. In one swift movement, the blade arced from the floor to my throat, the point against my windpipe.

He held it trembling there.

'Do it!' I shouted at him. 'Do it! You have taken everything else from me.'

'Never,' he said, his chest heaving above me. 'Never.' And he threw the knife down. 'I'm sworn to you, Art. And I'm sworn to the Stone.'

Then he embraced me.

Do you know how many other men have held me in my life, Myrtle?

Not one.

Then I allowed myself to remember one other song in the hologrammed book. It was called *Without Limit* and it spoke about men, the passion of the unnamed bond between them, so that one man would kill and another die for his friend. And there was guilt in that song and heartache too, but that wasn't what I remembered, I just remembered the bond, the strength of it which I felt now in every muscle and sinew of his arms. And I knew no man would ever love me the way he had loved me, or give me what he had given me.

I pushed him away.

'I'm leaving,' he said then, 'going north.'

I didn't believe him.

'My parents – they're separating. My father's moving north and I will go with him. You will never see me again.

There was a cry of anguish from Quin.

227

'Only I beg you,' he said, 'take Quin back. She loves you. She will always love you. Isn't that so, Quin – isn't that what you've said a million times?'

Quin was crying, she was sobbing.

'Please?' said Lance, and then he simply walked out of the cottage.

27

L ance's departure, as always, left a gap.

Quin and I had to look at each other, speak to each other. But there was nothing much to say. So I just picked up the knife, sheathed it and put it away, so she would know at least that I no longer wished her harm.

'Bubz, I know I don't deserve this,' she said when she'd stopped crying, 'but . . .' And she came to me and laid her head against my chest, as she had so many times before, so that her cheek touched mine and the fragrance of her hair was in my mouth. I put my arms about her, of course I did, but it was a hollow thing.

He was still in the room.

We should have left that place, but where was there to go? I couldn't return to the Mill and admit to losing Lance a second time; nor could the two of us go unobserved through the estates, I had posted men everywhere. So we stayed by his drums and his notebook in his love-nest.

And, eventually, we lay where they had lain, printed ourselves on that same coverlet. Yes, that's where I took Quin that day and it was a spiteful taking. I punished her – breached her again and again – and she endured it.

'What we gonna do?' she asked afterwards.

But I didn't know.

Shaman howled at us both. Perhaps he was hungry. I

couldn't remember when I'd last fed him, or myself indeed. And perhaps it would have been hunger that finally drove us from that place but, as you know, Myrtle, although I didn't have a plan, someone else did.

Mordec.

I always knew there would be a time when Mordec would move from whispers to action, but I wished it had not been this time. It was Duane (ever my faithful Duane) who called to give me the news. Apparently Borz had gone with Mordec to stake out Lance's house, and when no Lance was to be found, Borz had got restless, questioned (as he had done with me the previous night) whether Lance should be punished at all.

'The Knight Crew. We need him.' I can just hear Borz saying it, playing up to Mordec. *No top man of dis crew should value some gash over da Crew No. 1 Gangsta.*

If you fail at this task, Duane had said, it will be the end of the Stone. And I had failed, had allowed Lance to walk free a final time.

Free.

No, maybe he wouldn't be free, *not now, not ever*. I wasn't free. The wrong I did Danny continued to stir in my heart and the wrong he'd done me, I knew, would continue to stir in his. That's how it is. There is no away. Not if you stand in front of a mirror just once and look yourself in the eye.

'Mordec's on his way back to da Mill,' said Duane. 'He's gathering troops. He's saying if you want to remain leader, you'll have to arms him for it.'

'Fight him?'

'Yes! Beef him an bare heads.'

'What bare heads, Duane?'

'The Crew,' said Duane. 'The Knights. Dere's bare backing his side now.'

'Who?' I asked, though part of me didn't want to know.

'Borz,' he said. 'And Pels. And LameDuck and Tardis.'

Borz. Of course Borz, considering what he'd been saying. That I could deal with. And I wasn't unaware of how Pels had been gravitating towards Mordec. But LameDuck and Tardis, Tardis who I'd carried on my back away from the fight on Atlantic.

'And Tanisha,' Duane added.

Tanisha, who should have been a Knight with us, I'd let her slip too. Let her down.

'Because of Quin,' said Duane. 'Because of what you did to Quin. An also Lee.'

Lee. My first ever comrade in arms, my bunking-off childhood friend.

I'd heard enough. 'And for us?' I asked. 'How many for us?'

'Me,' said Duane, 'and Donkey.'

Faithful Duane, faithful Donkey.

'And some of the yungas.'

Pitifully few. 'I'm coming,' I told him. 'We'll link on the towpath.'

Quin had heard only half the conversation, but she guessed at once what was going on.

'Lance,' she said, 'bell Lance.' She pulled at her mobile. 'He'll come back for you. Fight for you. I know he will.'

And I felt full of hatred for her, because I knew what she said was true.

'Lance! Lance!' I shouted. 'Can't you forget him for one second?' I tore the mobile from her hand and flung it through the smashed glass window, heard it splash into the canal beyond.

'Don't ever say his name again,' I told her. 'Don't ever think I need that man for anything!'

The journey back along the towpath was made in angry silence. But at least, for a little while, Quin and I were travelling in the same direction.

Duane was waiting by the scrap yard, just downstream of the Mill.

'Dey're back,' he cried, 'dey're back already.'

Shaman, who had walked the whole way with his nose to the ground, suddenly lifted his head. He smelt what I saw, Mordec gathered with what looked like an army about him in front of my castle. Shaman yowled like they were his enemy not mine.

I looked at Duane and the sorry band behind him. There were not ten men standing there for me. Mordec had gathered twice that number. Out front was Borz and his baseball bat.

'It's lost,' said Quin quietly. 'It's all lost, Art.'

And her eyes were on me, but her mind was on Lance. I knew that because my mind was on him too. If Lance stood with our ten then Mordec's twenty would be nothing. He alone could turn defeat into victory. He was just a phone call away. A call I'd never make.

Yet still his name hung in the air.

Lance.

Lance.

Shaman swung his head, as though the name was in his ears too, looking first at Mordec's troops and then at ours. Then, without a backward glance, he took off towards the underpass which led away from the canal. I watched his going with disbelief. Since Myrtle died, he'd hadn't voluntarily left my side for a moment, he'd been with me at the flat, at the Mill, in the bell-tower, walked with me, tracked me, slept by me.

'Shaman,' I cried, forgetting everything in my sudden need to have him by me now. 'Shaman!'

But he never even turned at his name, didn't hesitate at all, just went on walking.

I felt astonished and bereft and also betrayed.

Of course I didn't know then, Myrtle, where the dog was going, his nose still to the ground as if he was following a scent.

The yungas murmured, they didn't know what the dog meant to me but the omen was clear and it was bad.

'We'll be slewed,' one of the yungas suddenly said. 'Slaughtered!'

'Get Mordec on the blowa,' I said quickly. 'We'll talk. He can't really want this fight.' And to tell the truth, Myrtle, I did not want this fight either. It was one thing for Duane to have told me which of the Knights had gone over to Mordec's side, it was quite another to see them standing there. Borz, Pels, Tanisha, Tardis, LameDuck and even Lee. This enemy standing the other side of the canal were the only family I'd ever known.

They'd seen us now of course, seen the dog leave, seen Quin and me arrive. The shouts were coming thick and fast.

'Even his mutt's jettin!'

'Got yur ho back have you?

'Where's Lance? Where's yur hero now?'

Mordec refused to discuss things on the phone, cut the conversation short, suggested we meet in the middle of the bridge – alone – but where everyone could see us, talk there.

'I don't trust him,' said Duane.

'Make him go unarmed,' said Donkey.

'No.' The truth was, I didn't want to go unarmed myself. If I was to face Mordec, I wanted the Buck 119 in my pocket. Out loud I said: 'He'll never agree to it.'

233

'Then we must have a signal,' said Duane. 'If you need us, if you want us to come onto the bridge.'

'If I reach for the blade,' I said, 'if my hand goes to my pocket, come then.'

I turned to Quin, kissed her quite deliberately on the lips, in front of my own men, and Mordec's. I didn't think of it as a goodbye then, but I knew that I needed to touch her one more time. I also wanted those of Mordec's band who cared for Quin – which was almost everyone – to know how things stood between us, that she was still my queen and my love.

She returned the kiss with a kind of defeated longing and then I walked to the bridge. Duane came with me, but only as far as the beginning of the railings, and Borz, who was accompanying Mordec, stopped at the opposite end of the bridge, leaving Mordec to come forward alone. We walked pace for pace together, Mordec with a little swagger, and me perhaps more tentatively, but we still reached the mid-point at the same time.

Behind Mordec the Mill and the brewery with its conical towers loomed above the waters and were reflected in them. It was still my castle, I thought, my home. The place where I'd been happiest.

We brothers stood facing each other, only a knife-hand apart.

I knew it was going to be the end but some faraway part of myself still hoped for a beginning. There was so much that still needed to be said.

'Do you remember,' I began, 'how our mother used to tell us stories of castles and of heroes?'

Whatever Mordec was expecting it wasn't this.

'Bruv, wot you on? You're chattin breeze,' he said.

'And she asked us to hold those stories in our hearts and told us that one day, one day, things would be better?'

'No,' said Mordec. 'No, I don't remember dem times.'

Is it possible she never said these things to Mordec – or just that he never heard, never listened?

'And after the stories, long after,' I said, 'there was the sunrise and the stars. Do you ever look at the stars, Mordec?'

'Bruv, I aint no cracked mystic,' said Mordec. 'Now – da business.'

'This is the business, Mordec. What we do in our allotted time. Who and how we love. Did you ever love anyone, Mordec?'

Mordec paused. I don't think he'd ever thought about this before. 'You,' he said at last.

That shocked me to a silence of my own.

'But that was one long, long time ago,' Mordec continued. 'I gotta look to the future now.'

'What future?' I asked.

'One with you erased from memory, bro. You're standin in my light.'

'So what is it you want, Mordec?'

'Old school, bruv. Only where OG cotched – I'm goin to sit dere, bro. Tonk leader, buff Crew. Knight Crew ten, Saxons nil. Get me?'

I said nothing.

'So I jus need you,' he continued, 'to kneel down, right here,' he said, pointing, 'right here at my feet where everyone can see you, and swear out loud to me, new Knight Crew Star.'

'And if I refuse?'

He gestured at the bank behind him. 'Plenty of soldjas to help you change yur mind.'

It was then that my phone went off. It was on vibrate and I felt it tickling in my pocket. So my right hand went, as it had done a hundred thousand automatic times before, down to that pocket.

Later, very, very much later, Lance would tell Quin that he had made that call. That Shaman had tracked him, smelt him almost to his door and when Lance, for the first time, had seen the dog without me, he'd known immediately something was wrong. And if he hadn't understood, Shaman would have made it clear by his barking, he was barking at Lance, jumping at him, howling at him. So Lance put in a call to check if I was all right. On that agreed signal the battle began.

And so it was that my friend undid me one final time.

28

I saw my mistake in the look of outrage in Mordec's eyes and heard it in Duane's throat as he roared forward to defend me. Mordec, believing himself under attack, reacted with the instinctual quickness of the natural fighter. He drew his own knife, a small steak knife with a serrated blade. One of the knives that had lain in our kitchen drawer, the knife perhaps that had killed Danny MacMahon.

My hand had barely moved from the phone when that knife came whipping down, entering the side of my body somewhere below the ribs. If there was pain, I didn't feel it there, not in my side. It was my head that exploded and I found myself falling forward, but by that time I'd got the Buck 119 in my fingers and it was falling too, with all my weight behind it onto – into – my brother.

I don't know where I caught him, because I was still falling, but a great '*oh*' came out of his mouth as if I'd punctured all the air out of him. Then he fell and, in doing so, pulled the kitchen knife from my side and I felt it jagged there and then my heart pumped and pumped as if it would send all the blood in my body to tend that wound, but the blood just leaked out, out, onto the concrete beneath me.

I knew it was a death wound, saw my life spilling there. And after a while – quite a short while – the pumping slowed, as though my heart had given all it had to give. What was a boy who'd never much thought of the future to think of death? They say when you die violently all of your past flashes before you. It wasn't so for me. I just thought of the sun and how I wouldn't see it rise again, how I'd never go to Africa and see those spiders with shells on their back, or how, for me, there would never be another night sky drilled with stars. Even so I wanted to continue looking up, and I did, Myrtle, up into the late afternoon sky, where, just a moment before there had been a huge expanse of blue. But now that sky was blurring, bubbling and frothing with tiny spots of red. I blinked my eyes as if that would clear the haze, but it didn't. Which is why I didn't see – although I heard – Knight attack Knight, Crew attack Crew. How, as Mordec and I lay together on the ground, closer in our dying than we'd ever been in our living, they fought on the bridge around us. Duane against Borz, Pels against Donkey, their yungas and ours cutting and hacking each other and also my dreams, everything I'd hoped for, Myrtle, all cut and hacked on that bridge.

I thought of you then, Myrtle, how the blade never touched you and I was glad of that. How the book lay on your chest while Mordec stabbed and you took your own death inside yourself. I hope it was a quiet death Myrtle. I hope you lay on the ground and felt Deangelo about you, felt you had a home to return to. *A kì í ràjò ká máà délé oò. One does not go on a journey and not return home. Blue toraco carry me home.* Then my wandering mind found Danny MacMahon and I wanted to imagine how it was for him as his life slipped away, only I couldn't because I knew nothing about him, nothing about his life. I'll killed a total stranger. And maybe, in his dying, he'd wished me dead and here I was bleeding away at the end of the same serrated knife. *Justice,* that's what I wrote in the book of the future, Myrtle.

Justice.

Danny, I hope this is justice enough. I hope you feel the debt is finally paid.

And I hope you have some peace.

I wanted Quin then, wanted her close in those dying moments, wanted her to hold my head as she had yours, Myrtle. But there were too many men on the bridge, the fighting too dense, it would have been dangerous for her. But just to touch her hand, just to hear her voice. And then I heard her voice.

'Lance!' she called. 'Lance. Lance!'

Of course Lance.

Others took her up her cry, and I heard Shaman bark and I knew why Quin called, my dog had brought my friend. But it was too late, way too late.

The scuffling about me stopped, men fell back and I waited for whatever it was that Lance would do. But it was Quin who acted. She ran onto the bridge and pulled the great Buck knife from Mordec's body. And I wish beyond anything I'd had the strength to stop her taking that knife, but I could barely move then.

'Look what we've done,' she screamed, 'Look, Lance, look what you and I have done to Art. To my beloved!'

To my beloved.

My beloved.

'Let go the knife,' I whispered. 'Come to me, Quin.'

I don't think she heard me, so furiously was she standing there, wielding the blade above her head.

'Art to whom we both swore,' she said, 'and both betrayed. Art and the Stone. We have done wrong, Lance.'

Then she moved and where the sky had been I saw only her face, it was bleeding red, slashing red and I thought at first it was my eyes, the red froth in them that so blinded me but her arms were in that bloody picture too and the curve of the Buck knife and she was ripping and slashing her face harder and deeper than Mordec would ever have done.

And where was Lance that final time? I couldn't see him, couldn't see anything beyond the spreading film of red. Maybe he was just too far away to put himself once more between her and the knife. Maybe he was standing stunned, as they all were on the bridge. For there was no noise anywhere.

Somebody came to me then. It was Duane, knelt or fallen beside me, I didn't know which.

'Take the knife, Duane,' I whispered. 'Put the knife in the river. On your oath, Duane, put it in the river.'

And he said: 'My lord.'

Or that's what I thought he said. 'My lord.'

As if I was a king after all.

29

No. I had never thought about death, but if I had, I would have thought of it as the end of things, a place of blackness but also of peace. There I could let go and be let go of. I could be nothing, so nothing could touch me. Like the womb before birth, only in retreat, me getting smaller and smaller until I ceased to exist. I was unbegun. I didn't think of that state as heaven – how would I have deserved heaven? But it would have been heaven compared with the place of mirrors.

They put us in the river, Mordec and me, and I don't know whose hand it was that tipped us into the water, but I know it was done without ceremony. There was no washing for us, no sheets, no tender Quin singing over our souls. But then Quin, alive but unconscious, was moving on a different path.

They put us in together, or perhaps my splash was a little before Mordec's, so when I found myself where I found myself, I half-expected him to be with me. But he wasn't. Which makes me think perhaps there are individual hells and this is mine. To see everything but to be able to touch nothing, as if the river is a pane of glass beyond which my old life lies. To cry out and to have no one hear that cry. Everything refracted, reflected back at me, seeing it again and again, mirrors within mirrors until what, until when?

Until I understand?

What if I never understand, Myrtle?

I've called for you so often, thought maybe you of all people would find me here, Myrtle. But maybe they put the ones like me, those of us who have killed, out of reach. Put us in a place without a future, so all we can do is look back, revisit the past.

How much time has passed since I came to this place? I don't know. Time moves and does not move here, my mind advances sometimes, or so I think, and then it sticks, I stick, I remain hopelessly locked inside a time which is no time. Which is why I wanted to tell this story, to try and get it straight once and for all, to put it down not distorted through the mirrors, but as it happened for good or for ill. I feel when I've put it all down, when I have relived each joy and each horror one more time, then, then I will get some rest. Murderer that I am.

Murderer and king.

Lover and killer.

Knight Crew Star and fatherless child.

No – no self-pity. Return to the story, get to the end. Because events didn't stop when I stopped, no, they went on, I saw it all unfold beyond the mirrors. Saw that at precisely the same time as Quin arrived at hospital my mother – Mordec's mother – left Hillview. No one accompanied our mother home, so she opened the door on that flat all on her own, walked in the hallway, all on her own. Called our names:

'*Arthur!*'

'*Mordecai!*'

'*I'm here. I'm well. I'm home!*'

No one replied. Which wasn't unusual, so she didn't feel the dread seeping through her, not at first. It was only when she moved around the flat and saw how unused, how cold it looked, how the fridge was empty and the dirty dishes in the sink crusted hard, only then did a small flake of panic fall in her. But she wouldn't panic, of course not, she was well now, such a small thing as her sons being out when she arrived home was not going to render invalid all the hard work of the previous weeks (or was it months?) when she'd been away and Gina had been in charge. Hadn't Gina been in charge? Where was Gina?

Days passed. Days of phone calls to my mobile and to Mordec's, both unanswered. Calls to Gina, answered but not with the information my mother wanted to hear. And the steadily growing alarm and the fact that there was no one with whom she could share her fear. There was no Keifer. If the absence of her boys, her sons, left a hole in her, the absence of Keifer was a canyon. She went about the flat searching for him, she knew he was dead – she'd been to the funeral after all – but still she tried to smell him out, she lay on the marital bed, she pressed his pillow over her face. But it didn't smell of her man – it smelt of the cheap washing powder Gina used and also something else, some other unfamiliarity. Someone had slept in the marital bed (it was me of course, it was Quin, and the bedclothes smelt of our sex). My mother retreated to the flimsily built bedroom wardrobe where Kiefer's shirts still hung and his leather jacket still stank of his beer and his tobacco and his sweat. Blissful sweat. Known sweat. She wrapped herself in that jacket, sat in that flimsy wardrobe, clutching at one of her three missing men.

Eventually, keeping the jacket round her (it was a cold day, the autumn closing in) she went out, bumped into Lee, who she recognised from some long-ago time.

'Mordecai?' she said to Lee. 'Arthur. Do you know where they are?'

243

Lee saw her shivering there, despite the jacket, took her home to his twenty-five-stone mother. Mrs Lee had the weight for the job, she would be able to say what needed to be said.

Mrs Lee made tea and looked at my mother with pity but, as she stirred, she couldn't help saying, 'It was plain as day, they were running wild.'

My mother did not believe what she was hearing. A fight at the Mill – what Mill? A child, a girl, in hospital with slashes to the face? Many beaten and many wounded and Mordecai and Arthur, gone?

'Gone where?' she asked.

Twenty-five-stone Mrs Lee shrugged. 'In the river,' she said. 'That's what they say.'

My mother went to the river, she stood on the bridge where Mordec and I had bled and bled. She couldn't have known she trod on that spot. The red had washed away and what was left was muddy brown. She looked over the railings at the river running by. And by. And by.

Shaman emerged from the Mill and went towards her and I wanted, needed, him to warm her as he used to warm me. But Shaman didn't know my mother and all he was doing was keeping guard. But his barking did bring Elayne out, Elayne whose grandmother had begged her not to return to the Mill, but the Mill (Elayne said) was, despite everything, where she belonged, where she was most at home. Elayne recognised my mother.

'You're Art's ma,' she said, 'aren't you?'

And my mother was glad to be known, to have her existence confirmed, she'd begun to think she'd slipped through a net into a different world.

'Yes,' she said.

'Art was a star,' said Elayne, 'Art was a king.'

'*Was?*' said my mother.

And then Elayne realised my mother didn't know so she told her, told her how her sons had fought and died on that bridge. It was the truth, wasn't it? She kept back the bit about how Mordec had also stabbed her, that day on Tintagel. Perhaps Elayne thought – knowing her own grandmother – there was only so much a person could take.

'Why did they fight?' said my mother, bewildered. 'For what?'

And I wanted to shout – in fact I did shout – for honour and hope and mercy and love and the castles of the past and the castles of the future. Your castles, Mama!

And also for justice.

But my mother couldn't hear me.

'I don't know,' said Elayne. 'I think it was a mistake.'

Another mother might have called the police, the authorities, had the story checked, the river dredged. That mother was not my mother. My mother was afraid of those in authority, afraid of their power, afraid of being locked away one more time. For she was mad. Very much madder than she had been before. Who wouldn't be mad whose only children had killed each other and been thrown in a river?

But if she chose (and she did choose) to refuse the information, if she never told a living soul what people were telling her, then she could continue to hope, couldn't she? She could imagine that, if she just stayed long enough in the flat then we would return, she'd hear our keys in the lock. Which is why, when she got back that evening, she jumped at every shadow that walked on the balcony and why in the days and weeks that followed, she so rarely, so very rarely, went out. For how would it be if we returned and she was out? And so she sits there still, drifting. Sometimes she takes her pills, sometimes she lets them drift too, because without her pills, she occasionally has a high, occasionally feels happy again.

As for Duane, for all he called me 'my lord', he did not honour his oath. He picked up the Buck knife, wiped the blade, and would have put it in his pocket (thinking perhaps *there will always be enemy*) if Lance hadn't wrenched it from his hands and, with a cry of anguish, flung it into the river himself. The knife that had sliced my beloved's face floated harmlessly down through the water like a silver fish. As far as I know it lies on the river-bed still. As for Mordec's ser-rated knife, I don't know who took that, but I expect it's back in a kitchen drawer. Waiting.

I didn't see how Quin got to hospital, but it was prob-ably Lance's doing. He would have crawled there on his hands and knees carrying her on his back if that's what was needed. He was certainly by her when she first woke. They had stitched – and stitched and stitched – her; closed those angry, criss-cross wounds, put dressings on her bruised and swollen face, sedated her. And he just sat and sat until she awoke. Her aunt Abeni came and so did her uncle Dayo, but they went away again. Lance didn't. Or if he did (because of course he had too) he was always first back, waiting and waiting for her to wake.

And she did wake eventually, although she didn't open her eyes.

'You've been here all the time,' she said, 'haven't you?'

'Yes,' he said.

'You've been here and so has Art.'

'Art?'

'In my la-la land, he's always there, watching me. Watch-ing over me.'

'I'm glad,' said Lance, and perhaps he was. He moved closer to our beloved.

'Don't,' she said.

'What?'

'Don't come near,' she said. 'Not near enough to touch. We mustn't touch, Lance. Not now, not ever.'

More honour she gave me in death than in life. Quin – my proud and forever queen.

Lance was brought to a whisper. 'Quin . . .' he began.

'Promise me,' she said. 'You have to promise.'

His hand rose towards where her hand lay soft on the sheet, as though he would touch her right there and then, as though it was impossible for his hand to keep from hers. Then his hand dropped away.

'I promise,' he said. 'But I swear it not for you, but for Art. As what I owe him.'

And I would have forgiven him then – if I hadn't, even in my hatred, forgiven him already.

'Thank you,' Quin said, and sank back a little into her pillows.

And so they sat a little while in silence and I thought, he too is punishing himself. Quin cut her face and he is cutting his heart, for I'd never seen him look so hollowed out. And that made me wonder whether I had been punished enough. Me, who never spent a night in a jail cell, never had to sit in a room opposite Danny's parents, never had the guts to take a knife to my flesh as Quin had done to hers. Yes, Quin punished herself all right. Of all of us, only she had that bravery – that grace.

A little while later Lance said: 'Is there anything, anything, Quin, I can do for you?'

'No.' And then, perhaps hearing his distress at her answer, she added, 'Except a mirror. Bring me a mirror?'

And he didn't ask why she wanted that mirror, just said 'of course' and then: 'Can I sit with you, can I still sit by you?'

'Oh Lance, you are my closest bredrin. Our bredrin. Art's and mine.'

It wasn't an answer but he let it be one, and next time he came he brought the mirror, a small green one that flipped open. He put it on the bedside cabinet beside her rather than into her hand, so as not to have to touch her.

'Thank you,' she said.

She waited until he was gone for the night and then, with the hospital curtain shut around her, she flipped the mirror open. She looked first at her eyes, which were still her eyes, and then at the shape of her face. The swelling had gone down, though it was difficult to tell by how much, swathed as she still was in bandages and dressings. So she began to peel off those dressings and when they didn't come easily (because they were stuck with plaster or blood) she pulled at them, she wrenched them off, one by painful one. When her face was clean of the gauze she looked at the welts and the slicing, and she was pleased. Pleased with red-raw lines of disfigurement. As she was disfigured – even the nurse who found her was shocked.

But Myrtle, the light was still on her. In every one of my thousand, thousand mirrors she was beautiful. It wasn't her black skin raised red I saw, it was her shining soul. And if I could have kissed every one of those wounds, I would have. Kissed them and loved them as part of who she was and all she had suffered.

The nurse was of a different opinion.

'What do you think you're doing?' she shouted at my queen. 'Do you think I've nothing better to do than patch you up? We should send you home, your sort are a drain on resources.'

But she patched her up, nonetheless. And upped her medication, to keep her in bed, to keep her quiet.

So she was silent the next time Lance came and sat so close (but not close enough to touch) beside her bed. So, as she slept, he began to talk.

'All my life,' he said, 'I've been half a man. No, half a human being. You see, I was born two, one of twins. But my twin, a girl called Cara, she died. Lived and died in four minutes, the cord around her neck. And I survived, big and healthy and strong. And my mother looked in the cot and she loved me. And also hated me because I had survived and my sister hadn't. And I didn't know why she looked at me the way she did, why she gave me hoovers when other boys had trucks. Not that I didn't like the hoover. I did, it was one of my favourite toys for a while. But I still didn't understand that look, that said I wasn't enough, never enough. She didn't tell me about Cara, not at first, but I felt Cara nonetheless. Her absence. I was always looking about me as if I'd lost something, only I didn't know what. I always felt I wasn't exactly who I saw in the mirror. And then one night, years later, when I came back from the karate club all full of the fighting, my mother finally lost it, she shouted for the daughter she'd only had for four minutes. My sister. Then I knew what the gap was, Quin. And nothing and no one filled that gap until I found you. And it was as though, for the first ever time, I was complete. I didn't need to look any further, any more.' He paused. 'Only you were Art's.'

Quin never moved a muscle at this revelation, for she was still asleep. But I heard it and I realised then that whatever Lance had said those blissful summer weeks at the Mill, it had not been this. He had held all that pain inside him and never said a word.

A word, Myrtle.

So many things we don't know about each other as we plough on regardless through our lives.

Lance left before Quin woke that night and when she woke, she pulled the bandages off all over again. This time the nurse was angrier and not so prompt. Which is probably how the infection started, germs seeking open wounds, germs under fingernails, germs floating in the hospital air. Within a day the poison had spread, raging through her blood, making her hot and mad. She sweated in the bed, she moaned and cried, she dreamt wild dreams. I was in those dreams, I know because she shouted for me.

'Art,' she shouted, 'come for me.'

And I would have crossed every continent of the world to get to her but I was sunk in the river, imprisoned beyond the mirrors.

She called for him too: 'Lance, Lance, where are you?'

'I'm here,' he said into her darkness. 'I'm by you.'

But he kept his cruel promise, never once leant over as she raved and put a comforting hand on hers. So how should she know he was there, how should she know anyone was there for her?

She was moved to intensive care. There was a soap dispenser at the door to the ward, all visitors to wash their hands before entering. Lance washed his hands, scrubbed them white, so as to carry no new germs in his touch. Only he didn't touch.

She was attached to a drip, wired up to a machine that monitored her heart. How could any machine, I thought, be big enough for that job? A different nurse came up to Lance, watched him watching her.

'She pulled her tubes out last night,' the nurse said. 'Does she want to die?'

'Die?' said Lance.

He didn't believe that Quin would die. I didn't believe it.

Later that day Quin stopped raving but her pulse was feeble, her breathing shallow.

'Do you have her parents' phone number?' the nurse asked.

'She doesn't have parents,' said Lance. 'Not in this country.'

The hospital phoned Aunt Abeni, they phoned Uncle Dayo, but neither of them arrived in time.

The heart monitor dipped and beeped.

'None of it was your fault,' Lance said to her. 'Why shouldn't you have loved two men? And why couldn't we two have loved you together? There was so much to love.' He heard himself use the word *was* with shock.

But she was still alive. Her midnight body lying on those white, white sheets. And she looked so feeble there, so cold, and I wanted the sun, the great bold African sun, to burst into that ward and warm her, to bathe her in its golden light, to put her to her rightful place amongst extravagance and colour and life. But she lay alone in that chill white bed.

'Lance,' I shouted then from beneath the river, 'for God's sake hold her, Lance. Take her in your arms. Warm your queen!'

But he wouldn't. He had given his word and he wouldn't. Not even when her breathing changed, when it became harsher and louder, sobbing in her throat.

'Lance, Lance, take her, hold her, hold our girl!'

The nurse unhooked her charge, told him to say his last goodbyes.

'If you ever loved me Lance, hold her!'

The nurse gave him privacy, she left the room.

'Goodbye,' Lance whispered over Quin's exhausted body. 'Goodbye, my missing piece, my better self, my perfect, beautiful, only one.' His hands went up like a prayer, like hands that would finally cup themselves around that perfect disfigured face, but then they fell away again. They fell away!

And she breathed out and not in again. And the silence in that room screamed.

He stood, too stunned to cry. And I thought that her death – for she was dead – would release him. That now he would at least lean down and kiss her one last time, speed her on her journey.

But he did not.

And the whole of the river heaved with my howl.

30

At the Mill, the physical injuries from the fight on the bridge were healing, but the mental wounds were not so easy to bandage. Without Mordec, without me, there seemed no point to Borz and Duane being enemies any more, but they weren't friends either. Their two factions continued to circle each other with a kind of exhausted suspicion. As for Garvey, his leg was still in plaster from his encounter with Lance's bike and he limped around the Mill, growling purposelessly. Donkey made one or two futile attempts to gather everyone around the Stone but nobody seemed to have the heart for it any more. They were all drifting, except perhaps the girls.

'I didn't say goodbye,' Elayne told Tanisha as they stood and looked over the glum river one late afternoon. 'To Quin. I never said goodbye.'

'I thought you went to hospital?' Tanisha said.

'I did,' Elayne said. 'But he was there. Lance. Quin was asleep and he was sitting right beside her. So close. And I just couldn't go in.' She paused. 'And now she's gone.'

Tanisha put her arms around her friend, such a simple gesture.

'I wanted her dead, of course,' continued Elayne. 'There were times when I could have squeezed the life out of her with my bare hands.'

'Cos of Lance?'

'Course cos of Lance,' Elayne said sharply and then she deflated. 'But now Quin's dead and I don't feel that way. I just feel empty. She was my friend, Tanisha.'

'I know.'

And all the time I'd suffered in my loving and hating of Lance, I had never stopped to imagine how it was for Elayne. How she also had loved and been betrayed by her closest friend. Prison or prism, this river breaks you apart.

'I miss Quin too,' continued Tanisha. 'In fact, I miss all of them, Art and Mordec and Myrtle. It all seems impossible, that they're gone. Every morning when I wake up, I can't believe they're gone.'

If you remember someone they don't really die. That's what Quin had said as we weighted Myrtle's body. And now my name was in Tanisha's mouth. I was glad. I was grateful. Because it's true, if you're remembered, you do not die. You do not die!

Tanisha, who was at heart, a Knight.

'I'd say a prayer,' said Elayne. 'If I believed in God. But I don't. She gestured hopelessly at the Mill and the scrap yard and the canal and the debris in the water. 'How can there be a God of all this?' She kicked a stone, watched it splash into the water.

'We could light a candle,' said Tanisha. 'You don't have to believe to light candles.'

'Yes,' said Elayne, slowly. 'Yes. I'd like that. We could light a candle for Quin. And Art. For all of them, put them on the river.'

'Not the river,' said Tanisha. 'They'd sink, they'd go out!'

'Not if we made them boats,' said Elayne. 'Then we could float them, set them free.'

'Boats?' said Tanisha. 'What with?'

'Stuff.' Elayne gestured again at debris caught in the reeds by the riverbank, a piece of wood, an old Evian water bottle, some polystyrene packing. 'Lots to choose from.'

And that was you, Myrtle, wasn't it? Breathing on Elayne as you used to breathe on me. Showing her you could make something out of rubbish, something out of nothing. Something out of yourself. As if there could be a God – a good – after all.

The girls got to work. They brought candle stubs from the treads of OG's wheel and borrowed knives from the boys.

'What you want with those?' said Garvey. 'Gonna slice some Saxons?'

'No,' said Elayne, 'just some wood, some plastic.'

The boys laughed and the girls went back outside. Shaman followed them. Since my going, he hadn't known where to be, who to be with. He meandered, he looked lost. He watched as the girls fished out the sodden bit of wood.

'Too big,' said Tanisha.

So they split it in two, used the pieces to pull the water bottle and the polystyrene packing ashore.

'Wood for the boys,' said Elayne, 'for Art and Mordec. The water bottle for Quin and polystyrene for Myrtle.'

'I don't think Myrtle would like the polystyrene,' said Tanisha.

The girls giggled. 'No, you're right,' said Elayne. 'But we could decorate it maybe, put some ivy round, she'd like that.'

They set about their tasks. While Tanisha pulled ivy from a wall near the bridge, Elayne poked the point of Pels' knife into the clear plastic. It went through easily. 'Just like into me,' she said, and she lifted up her jumper and looked at the healing wound that snaked across her abdomen.

'Elayne,' said Tanisha.

'I'm blessed,' said Elayne. 'Another half centimetre and

you'd be doing a candle for me.' She let the jumper fall, began to hack her way around the plastic bottle, and soon she had a perfect floating candle holder.

'Quin should have flowers,' she said, 'on her boat.' But there were no flowers by the canal at that time of year, so Elayne used blades of grass and fallen leaves. Golden leaves like an African sun.

They both worked on their different pieces of wood.

'I'll do Art's,' said Elayne. 'You do Mordec's.'

The wood she'd chosen for me was longer and thinner than Mordec's and it seemed to have a natural prow, even before Elayne took a knife to it. As the girls whittled and shaped they also talked, and I remembered the time that the four of us (Quin and me, Lance and Elayne) had lain and talked on that same bank in the high summer and how happy we'd been then.

Tanisha's boat for Mordec ended up as a squat platform but mine, in Elayne's careful hands, was like a real ship, with a square stern and pointed bows, something sturdy and beautiful.

Tanisha lit a match and softened the wax at the bottom of one of the candle stubs, dripped it onto the wood and then tried to make the candle stand there, but it wouldn't because the wood was too wet from the river. Eventually she had to take the knife and carve a tight hollow for the candle and Elayne did that too, for me.

Their work, it was a gift, Myrtle.

Eventually all four boats were ready.

'What about a candle for Lance?' said Elayne suddenly.

'But he's not dead,' said Tanisha.

'He is to me,' said Elayne.

Tanisha was caught off-guard. 'Oh bubz, I'm sorry,' she said.

'Don't be,' said Elayne.

In the silence that followed Tanisha added: 'Four boats. We only have the four.'

'Then I think Lance should go with Quin,' said Elayne.

And I thought her as brave in that moment as she had been when she had gone, without hesitation, to Bladon in search of her beloved, who turned out to be Quin's beloved.

I watched her stick a fifth candle in the water-cup boat, so close to Quin's they were kissing. And when she lit them, they flared and burned together, Lance and Quin, perennial lovers and I, who thought I was past jealousy, was jealous for one last time.

The girls set their little flotilla adrift on the water, pushed the lighted bits of flotsam and jetsam out in to the current of life.

And where were they going, this band of the lost but not forgotten?

To Avalon.

That word, Mama, it came to me from you across the water.

Avalon.

The girls stood and watched the lighted boats float away in the growing dark.

'Perhaps we should have made one for Danny,' said Elayne. 'Danny MacMahon. He was part of this too.'

'Yes,' said Tanisha. 'Maybe.'

And I felt an emotion then that I'd never experienced before. A kind of pride, a filling up, and I wondered whether that's the sort of feeling fathers who really watch over their children get.

The dog came close to the girls, stood with them. And still they watched. Mordec's craft failed first, the candle toppling from its wood holder and snuffing itself out in the water.

Myrtle's burned brightly until the flame caught the polystyrene and the whole fizzed and fused and melted before becoming just an oily puff of grey smoke. Quin's and Lance's boat was a conflagration which roared and burnt itself out very quickly, and my boat, still lit, sailed on and on and on, until it passed the bend in the river and the girls could no longer see it.

But I see it, I see it still, again and again in the mirrors, that gift of remembering and hope.

As for Lance, Elayne's farewell proved premature, because he did come to her one day, waited just the other side of the bridge.

'Elayne,' he said, 'I've come to say goodbye.'

'Goodbye?'

'I'm going north,' he said.

Which she knew.

'I've also come to say I'm sorry.'

Which she did not know.

'Sorry?' she asked.

'For not being what you wanted. Who you wanted.' And then he put his arms about her, held her.

He held Elayne.

And for those few moments she was happy.

But even that wasn't the end of it. The Saxons, emboldened by the clear disarray in our ranks (*our* – you see, Myrtle, I haven't let go even now, have I?), the Saxons had begun a low-level campaign of attrition. They started just by crossing into our territory, lifting the odd push-bike in the roads near Tintagel, then they began penetrating deeper, leaving tags and flags as far south as the ground where we'd had that first running battle. Duane and Borz knew they must do something, but they couldn't agree on what. Donkey eventually persuaded them to sit about the Stone but they only argued. It was about noon on the second day and they were still no nearer to a decision when Pels became aware of someone standing in the shadows.

'Who's dere?' he challenged.

'Least one mans on point,' said a warm, rich, dangerous voice, and a huge figure stepped into the light.

'OG!' cried four or five voices together. 'OG!'

'Bredrin,' said OG, indulgently.

'So they let you go?' said Elayne.

'Looks like it,' said OG. 'No evidence, you see.' He tapped at his nose, grinned widely. 'All the witnesses suddenly off skis.' He laughed. Then he looked at them ranged about the Stone. 'You all turn into gnomes or sumthin?'

Donkey tried to explain.

OG laughed even louder. 'You gone soft, right?' he said and he bounded over towards the great Mill wheel. 'While I was gone, you all turned into pussies?'

The chair that he'd lashed to the apex of the wheel was gone but he ran up the steps and stood in his old place, towering above the Crew. 'OG, respect!' he shouted and balled his hand into the Crew salute.

Thirty fists answered him immediately, the yungas all jumping to their feet and coming to stand below him. Tardis raised his hand too and LameDuck and Lee of course, and Pels and Garvey, instant henchmen.

Tanisha cried, 'OG, OG!'

'Babe,' said OG.

Which left Duane and Borz, Elayne and Donkey isolated at the Stone. Duane and Borz held back, I think, because they had tasted power and couldn't immediately relinquish it, and Donkey and Elayne because, yes, Myrtle, because you had taught them well and they both knew where it might end if OG took the throne again.

'You've been away for time,' said Donkey.

'Wot?' said OG. 'Did dat joey squeak?'

'Donkey's no joey na more,' said Borz. 'He's one of us. A Knight of the Stone.'

'A Knight of the Stone,' jeered OG, just like Mordec used to, only OG was bigger, louder. 'Dat stone's a nada, bruv. It don't mean jack shit. It's a flippin *mill*stone, cuz!'

And I wanted my Knights to stand and defend everything that the Stone stood for: the mercy Lance had shown in the fight with HellRazor; the intimacy we'd shared by the river; the understanding that the Saxons also had faces; that one could love as well as hate; that you could write in the book of the future. But my Knights were silent. They lacked for a leader.

As they dithered, OG drew Lee to him and whispered something in his ear. Lee nodded and left the Mill. OG lit a cigarette. 'Right. Come den Crew, what so we got beef? We jus gonna let flames grill it? Or we gonna arms, munch dem Saxon bois?'

The Crew leapt to their feet.

'Rush em!'

'Jack em!'

'Merk em!'

'Merk! Merk! Merk!'

They were wild with hope and chanting. There was a plan!

And if Donkey tried to say anything – and I think he did – he was drowned out.

'Now,' said OG, 'where's my shank?'

It fell to Duane to try and explain that, about how he might have kept the knife, but Lance had thrown it in the river.

'You let some Milky Bar Kid take my Buck 119? You testin, man? When I was away, you took de piss, bruv?'

'No,' said Duane, 'but –'

'Yeah – and wot? Huh?'

Lee had returned, he was carrying a sledgehammer.

OG came down from the wheel. It must have been November by then and quite cold in the Mill but OG was still wearing one of his baby-blue cut-off tops, and his bare muscles rippled. Whatever he'd been doing in jail he hadn't been skipping his exercise programme. He took the sledge-hammer.

'Move away from dat Stone,' he said. Duane and Borz remained solidly where they were, Elayne and Donkey pulled back, but only a little.

'Let dis,' OG said and hefted the hammer upwards, 'be da sign of my return. Da return of true Crew power!'

The blow he struck was perfect, catching the absolute centre of the Stone, and it simply split in two, cracked apart with the noise of a mountain cleaving. Afterwards I thought there must have been a fault in the Stone for it to fracture so easily and then I thought, that fault was me, or me and Lance perhaps. At the noise the four challengers jumped or maybe fell backwards, and into the sounds of their shock and their fear (and also the ecstatic roars of the yungas) came another noise: Shaman. The dog was howling, yowling, with such ferocity and agony you might have thought OG had put the sledgehammer not to the Stone but to his skull. Even when Borz and Duane and Donkey and Elayne had righted themselves and were clearly unhurt, still the dog howled.

'Hush yur mouth!' yelled OG. 'Respect!' He crashed the stone again. This time small chunks of sandstone ricocheted from the shattered block.

Yet the dog yowled on.

'Shaman,' Elayne called, because she saw the fury in OG's eyes. 'Shaman!' And she tried to make those sounds, those gentle 'tch tch' sounds that you made, Myrtle, and that I made. She tried to quiet Shaman but he was not to be quieted.

So OG picked up one of those shards of sandstone, smashed to the sharpness of a knife, and he hurled it at Shaman, hitting him smack between the eyes.

Shaman did quieten then, fell straight to the floor, his legs just collapsing under him, a spot, just a tiny spot, of blood bubbling on his forehead. And I saw those black eyes that I'd loved so well, fill with astonishment and hurt and – as OG advanced with the sledgehammer – submission. Which was the worst thing of all.

'No,' screamed Elayne, 'no!'

But it was done. The dog was dead.

Yet something still rose. A luminous breath, though not from the dog's jaws, but from his closing eyes. And I knew immediately what it was, that bright smoke rising. I'd seen it before. And I wanted that breath to find its new owner, as I knew it would, as I knew it must. But there was no one waiting. There was no one there that day. So the breath just floated up, floated away.

Then the dog's eyes really closed and something in me closed too, Myrtle. I felt I never wanted to see anything ever again. And that's how I feel today, right now, retelling this final story. That I don't want to look any more. That I've seen enough.

But the looking goes on.

Because it hasn't stopped, the story. And I don't want to talk about how there are gats – guns – as well as knives in the Mill now, and I don't want to tell you what happened to Elayne. Don't want to and can't. Just can't.

Because I need to keep on hoping. And I need to remember that there is no away. That things persist, they remain, the good as well as the bad, like the love that holds you even after death. So that that breath, which was your breath, Myrtle, cannot have floated away completely. It must still be there, somewhere in the world. And there must be someone, even now, waiting.

Some once and future king.

Or, my darling Quin, some once and future queen.

So Myrtle, if you hear me, grant me this one last thing, breathe on that person.

I beg you, Myrtle.

Because someone has to write better than I did in the Book of the Future.

Acknowledgements

I owe a huge debt of gratitude to Jamaal Alfa, who was in a dark place when I met him but who nevertheless held – and holds – within him the brightness of the African sun and the birds of blue and green. Huge thanks also to Ben Robbins, who was generous with his hooded contacts and his personal stories and who taught me – and tirelessly corrected – my street language (any inconsistencies are mine). I thank Matt Calvert of Prospex who helped me find my way about the Bemerton Estate and believes in the kids who live there. I bow to Sensei Lance (yes, he really was called Lance) who took time and demonstrated whirling kicks and defensive blocks and told me about closing your eyes at dawn. And finally, I salute Dr Akin Oyètádé of the School of Oriental and African Studies, who first sang *Blue Toraco* to me and made me realise just how lucky I am to be able to journey and know I have a home to which I can always return.